I0598753

I would like to dedicate this book to those who have helped me most along the way and were always supportive:

Davis Family – Harvey V. Davis Ph.D., Eunice Kirton, Carol, Sheila, Todd, Sasha and Jade.

Extended Family – Michelle Pawula, Rick Denz and Bryan Miller

Brothers Todd & Dean Davis developed their style of storytelling over many years and now they're proud to announce the release of their debut novels - When It Reigns & Shadow Of The Devil, "We greatly appreciate our family, friends and fans for their support. Join us as we delve into the darkest corners of the human psyche."

Senior Editor: Jade Eunice Davis
Editing: By Todd A. Davis
Front and back cover art: By Michelle Pawula

Last Writes Ink

Presents

SHADOW OF THE DEVIL,

The Desecration Of Peter Cameron

By

Dean Julian Davis

And

WHEN IT REIGNS

By

Todd Andrew Davis

When Jesus came into the coasts of Caesarea Philippi, he asked his disciples, saying, Whom do men say that I the Son of man am?
And they said, Some say that thou art John the Baptist: some, Elias; and others, Jeremias, or one of the prophets.
He sayeth unto them, But whom say ye that I am?
And Simon Peter answered and said, Thou art the Christ, the Son of the living God.
And Jesus answered and said unto him, Blessed art thou, Simon Barjona: for flesh and blood hath not revealed it unto thee, but my Father which is in heaven.
And I say also unto thee, That thou art Peter, and upon this rock I will build my church; and the gates of hell shall not prevail against it.
And I will give unto thee the keys of the kingdom of heaven: and whatsoever thou shalt bind on earth shall be bound in heaven: and whatsoever thou shalt loose on earth shall be loosed in heaven.

Matthew
King James Bible

CHAPTER I
THE AWAKENING

Monday 6:57 am
26, August 1978
Vatican City
St. Peter's Basilica

The atmosphere was electric; a vociferous crowd gathered across the depth and breadth of St. Peter's Square as preparations were made for the announcement of the new Pope. Excitement had many of the normally stoic and even tempered bishops nervously pacing through the hallowed hallways. Their thoughts were consumed with the importance of this celebratory day. Young and old, rich and poor, patriot and foreigner gathered in the square; the event was broadcast internationally and the eyes of the world waited eagerly for the election to the papacy.

"Father Layad! Father, may I please speak with you," Father Joseph Principi's voice echoed throughout the elevated ceiling and towering archways of St. Peter's Basilica. He ushered Father Layad into a hall adjacent to the main corridor, "I spoke with the Committee as I said I would. But regrettably, the situation... it's very complicated. It is often difficult in these times to know exactly what the right words are to say, I'm sorry Anton but the answer is still no."

"How could that be? I was promised months ago that I could view the book."

"I know my dear friend and it was a hard decision to make. But after the unfortunate incident with Father Cameron there are those on the Committee that believe it is too dangerous to view such contentious material."

"Too dangerous? We are modern men Father Principi existing in the modern world. We're not living in the dark ages terrified of sailing off the edge of the earth nor are we stationed as the inquisition fighting to rid the world of all heretics. No longer are we compelled to burn books because we fear its wicked effect on the mind and spirit of mankind." Visibly deflated he refused to give up, he pleaded in a softer more measured tone, "I realize that my stance is controversial and that the church deems the book to be blasphemous. But from a scientific view, a historical view, there are many things we could learn from such an ancient writing that predates Aramaic script. Maybe I could speak to the Committee directly…"

"I'm sorry Anton. There's nothing I can do, the verdict has been rendered," Father Principi gripped his shoulder tightly, "the matter has been closed and the Committee will not hold a conference on the subject again."

"Their verdict is incredibly shortsighted, why keep the book if no one is to see it? Please, if I could just …."

"I know how disappointed you are, but the book has been ruled as arrant heterodoxy. The fact you even know such a text exists demonstrates the confidence and trust the Committee has in you. I know your dedication to the church and that you are held in the highest esteem by your parishioners, and for that you have been awarded a post in America. Find comfort in the fact that God has given you the ability to spread his word to the masses," Father Principi smiled, "so many people depend upon you Father Layad and your good deeds." He turned to walk away with his arms outstretched to the heavens, "This is a joyous day. Celebrate with our friends; with the world! And let's have no more needless talk about the book."

Father Layad's heart burned with anger and the utter hatred cut deeply into his normally kind face. He exited St. Peter's Basilica through the door of Good and Evil and pushed his way through the large crowd amassed in the square. He ignored their smiles, cheers and best wishes as he passed them by. He hurried down Via Cola di Rienzo and avoided the gaze of the few tourists that milled in and out of the restaurants and fruit and vegetable markets that lined the sidewalks. A small nondescript brick apartment building melded into its surroundings and stood halfway down the street. He entered through the open corrugated metal garage door. Inside a young Turkish man with wavy shoulder length hair sat at the base of a winding iron staircase. He was clean cut and wore a camel colored leather jacket with dark brown driving gloves. His brown eyes were hidden behind a large pair of designer sunglasses and it gave him the odd appearance of a European cinema actor. He stood, held out his hand and stopped Father Layad in his tracks.

"Emir! Bırak gitsin (Emir! Let him pass)," a deep voice boomed from inside a powder blue Subaru van.

"Benimle gelin (Come with me)," the young man stood exposing the handle of a Russian made PSM pistol tucked neatly beneath his jacket. He saw the confusion on his face then waved for Father Layad to follow him up the iron staircase. Out of breath and still seething with anger, Father Layad climbed the back stairs to apartment 333. Emir knocked on the door twice in rapid succession and waited for a reply.

"Evet, bir dakika lütfen. Kim o? (Yes one minute please. Who is it?)" A voice asked in stern monotone.

"Sizinki bir arkadaşın (A friend of yours)," he turned and smiled at the priest. From within came the sound of the tumbling locks clicking as they opened. The gaunt face of Bishop Atis Martz appeared through the cracked opening, he quickly unlatched the door's chain and ushered Father Layad inside. Two more Turks sat side by side on a fading mustard yellow leather couch. Father Layad had never seen them before but it was obvious to him that they were members of the ultra-nationalist siyah yılan (black serpent). Standing across from the men was his friend and mentor Father Grigory Santeal, casually dressed; next to him was

Cardinal Rudolph Fuerst and Archbishop Alessio Catoia, and behind them near the window was Father Santeal's imposing American 'friend' Robert Stone. He could see the shadow of a mysterious sixth man through the open door of the back bedroom. The young Turkmen was dismissed and he shut the door behind him.

"Anton," Bishop Martz flashed a wide smile, "Is there something wrong? We weren't expecting you until later this afternoon."

"I know, but I needed to speak with Father Santeal as soon as I could."

"Are you crazy? You shouldn't have come here dressed like that," accused the American.

"No one saw me. The streets are empty or have you forgotten today is the conclave." A bay window at the back of the room gave a perfect view of the white dome atop St. Peter's Basilica.

"I'm sure Anton came because he thought it important," Cardinal Fuerst put his hand on Father Layad's shoulder, "we will discuss the matter as soon as we've concluded our business with our friends."

Marko, one of the Turks stood up. He was extremely cocksure and clearly their leader. Like Emir, he looked and dressed very European. "Gentlemen; if we could.... before there are any more interruptions."

"Robert, if you would be so kind," said Father Santeal, "please give our guests their packages."

The American retrieved two large gray stripped duffle bags from the back bedroom and tossed one of them onto the coffee table. A large muscular man seated next to Marko stood up, unzipped the bag and pulled it open. Instantly his eyes lit up with excitement.

"Ten 9mm Stechkin automatic pistols; untraceable. Twelve Browning Hi-Power single-action 9mm semi-automatics; also untraceable," Robert reached inside his jacket and tossed a silver pistol to Marko. "L.E.S. Rogak P-18 holds 18 rounds," he smiled, "this one's extremely traceable." He continued the presentation and dug into the bottom of the duffle bag. "Six M16A2 5.56mm rifles with fully adjustable rear sights. Also very light weight and untraceable."

Marko turned to Father Santeal. "Your friend has a very impressive collection of toys," he examined the Rogak pistol in his hand, "but you know that's not what I came for."

Robert bent down an unzipped the second duffle bag. Inside neatly arranged were a dozen off-white colored blocks. "C4 explosives, primary assemblies, detonator cord... your detonator cord clips," he opened a smaller bag and held it up for Marko to see, "and of course; your detonators."

"Satisfied?" asked Father Santeal.

Marko picked up a green duffle bag lying beside the couch and glanced over at the tiny bedroom near the back. "Tell your friend Mr. Costa; next time I want to meet with Cecellini in person; no more games and no more lackeys." He opened the bag.

"That won't be necessary," said Father Santeal.

"You don't want to count it?"

"We're all friends here. I trust you," Father Santeal extended his hand, a surprised Marko raised his and shook it. "Oh yes, I almost forgot," he retrieved a small black box from the kitchen area and unlatched the hook. Inside were two glass vials held in place by a dark gray fabricated foam molded snugly to their shape; each was filled with a clear and deadly liquid. He took a cloth from the table and carefully removed one of them. "I suggest you use gloves when handling this," he placed one of the vials on the table, shut the box and handed it to Marko. "If you'll excuse us gentlemen."

Marko and the other man left the apartment. Halfway down the staircase Emir offered to carry one of the bags, "Ne yanlış? Sen üzgün görünüyorsun. (What's wrong? You look upset.)"

His face was emotionless and he passed Emir without speaking. The heavy set man sitting in the van opened the rear doors and they tossed the duffle bags inside.

The man who had accompanied Marko to the exchange embraced him and kissed him on both cheeks, "Marko iyi yaptı. Bizim düşman imha edilecek. (Marko has done well. Our enemies will be destroyed)."

Upstairs inside apartment 333, Father Layad ashamedly turned to confront the others in the room, "I'm sorry. I tried my best but they refused to let me see the book."

"Do not worry my friend, all is well," Bishop Martz produced a small black book from inside his coat. The cover was embossed with a circle inside a triangle inside a circle. "You see … fate has willed itself upon us."

"You have the book? Why didn't you tell me?"

"Our enemies blind to our faces are aware that a great storm is coming and a final judgment is at hand. There are those who spoke out against us and spoke of destroying this book. So our mysterious Mr. Costa and the siyah yılan found another who possessed it." Bishop Martz ran his fingers across the ridged cover before handing it to Father Santeal. "I am 80 years old today. It has been my life's work to find the treasure we now have in our hands. I have searched so long for the book; from László to London and to the ends of the earth," he smiled at Cardinal Fuerst. "I've spent decades trying to find the Temple of Metatron and I have waited all my life for his coming. A man must be rewarded for his deeds and he must surround himself with those with like minds for his enemies will be tenfold. I only wish I could be there to see those who stand in our way suffer for their disloyalty and be trampled under our feet. Now…I leave it to you to carry on my work Grigory." Father Santeal gave Bishop Martz the other vial and he tucked it neatly into a plastic lined pocket inside his coat. "One last deed and it shall be done," Bishop Martz grinned as he addressed the rest of his confederates, "I will always be with you. If not in being then in spirit," he turned and left the others.

Cardinal Fuerst slipped away from the others and entered the small bedroom where their guest Mr. Costa sat at the edge of the bed with his head in his hands. He dropped the duffle bag filled with money on the bed, but Costa barely acknowledged his presence. He took one last glance back at the group then quietly shut the bedroom door behind him.

"Gentlemen, a great wheel has been put into motion. We must prepare, for our enemies will hunt and persecute every man in this room. We must prepare for death if need be, for there is no turning back now," Father Santeal was lit with an inner fire, "but I promise you, if you stand by my side, if this circle remains unbroken, you will receive the awesome power and protection of our Lord."

From Sudea in the east I saw the angels falling from heaven with wings torn and bodies charred black. The sky was stained with their blood; the ground did shake beneath them. And the war between heaven and hell begun.

Heironymos
Book of Heironymos

CHAPTER II
THE BEGINNING

Wednesday 9:00 am
20, September 1978
Negev, Israel
Southern Desert Region

The sounds of men toiling in the dry desert heat echoed throughout the span of the archeological dig. The constant clanging of pick ax and chisel filled the dry air with the sounds of an odd rhythmic tune. A young Arab boy raced up the levels of sand tiers stopping only when he reached the mouth of the dig. It was a vast and well organized site that spread out nearly three hundred feet in diameter. The young boy turned to continue his journey and collided with a man draped in a pristine long white tunic.

"Easy my young friend," Father Santeal kneeled and pulled down part of the gutrah that covered his face, "the sun is hot and the day is long, try not to use all your energy running around the pit." He messed the boy's hair, "And just where are you headed in such a hurry?"

"I am to fetch water for the men," he said in his best English.

CHAPTER II: THE BEGINNING

"You look awfully small kid. You sure you can carry all that weight?" Robert Stone stood behind Father Santeal with a large black rucksack slung over his shoulder.

The boy was petrified and stared blankly at Robert's hardened features, nervous he did not answer.

"I'm sure he's plenty strong enough," Father Santeal stood, brushed the sand off his knees and patted the child on the backside, "run along now."

The two men watched the boy run with purpose to the top of the sand piers and away from the dig. "He's going the wrong way," Stone said dryly, "he takes the bus in every day from Beersheba along with some of the diggers and Hafsah's men. That kid's been snooping around here for weeks and asking a lot of questions; even more now that we've located the site of the temple." He glanced up at a ridge not far from the dig site, "We've got company."

"Don't worry Robert," he pressed the book of fallen souls against his chest, "old scores will be settled in due time. Be content in your thoughts, we have found the burial site of the chosen and after tonight no one will dare stand in our way."

The boy was panting heavily as he entered a small campsite above the Negev dig. He rushed towards a dome shaped tent nestled against the mountain side. "Father Rourke! Father Rourke!" he threw the tent flap open. "Fa…." it was empty. The boy was amazed. Hanging from the center post was a large wooden crucifix and laid across an army cot were rosary beads along with some of the Cardinal's personal effects. He walked over to a plastic green card table at the head of the cot. Wide eyed, he sifted through the scattered notes and diagrams and ran his fingers over copies of the King James Bible, Torah and Quran. A few seconds later he found what he was looking for; a silver canteen. In one motion he picked it up and pressed it to his lips. Empty.

"Here, try this one," Cardinal Rourke tossed a canteen to him. "You've forgotten rule number one Basem. Only come at night, when no one can see you."

"Yes I know Father but ..."

"Drink first," he pushed the canteen to the boy's lips.

He eagerly complied and after taking a deep swig he composed himself. "Father why do you have all those different books?" he pointed towards the card table. "Are you searching for God?"

"No," he smiled, "I'm doing very important research."

"Research? Research on what?"

"On what our friends are doing down there in the pit," he picked up the boy under one arm and sat him down next to him on the army cot. "Out with it. Why was it so important that you needed to see me now," he said as he tickled the child.

"Oh yeah," the boy searched his mind temporally forgetting the purpose for his visit. "Today some of the men found the entrance to the temple Metra .... Metra..."

"Metatron," the warmth drained from Cardinal Rourke's face and he eased back on the bed.

"Yes. There was a man with ram horns painted on the door," he made a gesture with his hands to illustrate the immense size of the horns. "When the men saw it they refuse to dig anymore and ran away," he picked up the rosary beads and rolled them through his thumb and fingers. "Father what does it mean?"

"Unfortunately it means the beginning of very bad things," Cardinal Rourke reached into his pocket and pulled out a gold coin. He forced an unconvincing smile, "Also it means the end of our little meetings."

"But Father I'm not afraid," the child's eyes lit up as he held the coin in his hands. "I can go back. I can find out more things if you want," he turned his head towards the direction of the dig.

"No. This is very important," Cardinal Rourke gripped Basem's shoulders tightly. "You must never go back down there. Never!" He eased his hold when he noticed the boy wince. "I need you to promise me Basem."

"I promise."

"Good boy," he produced a second coin from his pocket and held it up, "Now, I need you to be safe and run home as fast as you can and never come back. Is that understood?"

"Yes Father," the boy replied. Head down; he took the coin and started to exit, "but, what about you? What will you do?"

"I'll be fine. Don't worry about me. I'll stay here for a while and when I think it's clear, I'll leave tonight."

CHAPTER II: THE BEGINNING

"Goodbye Father," he smiled and waved.

"Goodbye."

He waited until Basem disappeared down the mountain path then dragged a trunk out from underneath his cot. With a steady hand, he removed a loosely packed pistol and a handful of bullets from inside a green tin box. He loaded the gun and gulped down whiskey from a half full decanter. 'May God give me the strength.' He made a final entry in his journal then opened the Bible, Torah and Quran to pre-marked pages. He carefully spread each across the card table and prepared for nightfall and the battle ahead.

The evening's cool air breeze lessened the morning's stifling heat. The dig site was nearly silent. The rumors about the Satanic relief painted above the temple door had spread throughout the camp. The diggers had abandoned their tools at their stations and left the site in mass. Several lanterns in the east sector illuminated a corner of the site and was the only light visible against the dark blue evening sky. Robert Stone's shirt was soaked with sweat as he repeatedly swung a pick ax into hardened rock in an attempt to clear the entranceway to the Temple of Metatron. Once he had moved aside enough earth, the two men squeezed through the narrow opening. The stench of two thousand years of death and decaying flesh rushed up through the dank corridor. A thin film of blackish slime coated the walls and covered the intricate scripts that were chiseled in the stone. The heavy stale air burned their lungs and they covered their nose and mouths with wet rags.

Millions of fat writhing maggots and worms covered the floor and left only tiny pockets of the beige stone exposed. Father Santeal aimed his flashlight down the slanted walkway and into the heart of the blackness. Robert dragged a rucksack inside, removed a torch, lit it, and left it as a marker 30 feet from the entrance. They descended over 200 feet through a maze of narrow hallways and low hanging ceilings; leaving the lit torches every 30 feet. A wall had been erected as a barrier to the inner sanctum but had crumbled outward centuries ago. On the thick slab was a brightly colored fresco of a crucifix embraced tightly by a menacing horned deity. Stigmata hands gripped its vertical and top section and blood from the open wounds poured down the face of the crucifix cross. They pushed forward through a gaping hole in the barrier wall and on to the other side. Inside the next compartment lay a dozen petrified corpses that had crawled their way up from the temple's depths. Hundreds of fingernail marks were etched in long chalk lines across the wall of the inner chamber of the tomb.

"Slaves offered as a sacrifice," Father Santeal ran the palms of his hands across the partition, "While they were working in the lower cavity the final stones were put in place and the chamber sealed behind them without their knowledge. It is a reminder for those who follow in his footsteps that all great kings require a great tribute."

"Over there," Robert pointed to a circular four foot hole cut into the temple's floor. He knelt down and shone his flashlight inside. "It's pretty deep; about 20 feet." He hammered a piton into the floor then fitted a long nylon rope through the eye, attached a carabineer and tossed the other end of the rope into the pit. "Hold onto it and I'll lower you down."

Father Santeal wiped tiny particles of sand and rock from his eyes as he slowly made his descent into the next chamber then waited for Robert at the bottom. A short narrow hallway led to the inner sanctum of the Metatron Temple. They stepped through the high stone crown of an open archway. The room was circular, nearly 100 feet in diameter. Dozens of ornate stone columns towered 40 feet into the air in support of a large domed ceiling. Robert was fascinated, he lit several torches that adorned the walls while walking the circumference of the temple base.

"Magnificent," said Father Santeal, "this is where the disciples of Thaydien hid the body of the great King. I've waited forty years for this very moment and it is as glorious as I knew it would be."

In the center of the temple lay a limestone sarcophagus atop a circular six step riser. It was broad and impressive and must have required the strength of a hundred men to set it in its place. Among the dark imagery of devils and demons that decorated the lid was a large Thaydien crest of a circle inside a triangle inside a circle. Inscribed in Thaylic script it read, 'Here lies the body of the last ruler of Sudea and Talise and the Kingdome of Thaydien and Kashar; murdered by Sabaoth, Lord of the Armies of Israel and the nations of Syria and Judea. May he seek his vengeance in this world and all worlds beyond.' Robert took a long iron bar from the rucksack and jammed it in-between a half inch gap of the lid and the body of the sarcophagus. He grunted loudly as he put his full weight and muscle into dislodging it. Father Santeal joined the effort, but the two men were unable to move the thick stone top.

"It must weigh a ton," Robert dropped the crowbar and it clanked on the riser's stone surface; exhausted he slumped to the floor. "If you want …. I can get a sledge hammer and break the damn thing open."

Father Santeal placed the book of fallen souls atop the coffin then knelt and placed the tips of his fingers inside the groove between the base and lid. In a barely audible voice he began chanting in Thaylic tongue over and over again. Hot air flooded the chamber from the dozen archways that encircled the temple floor. Robert squinted his eyes as the temperature rose quickly and a haze of heat waves rose from the ground. A tornadic wind shook the temple structure and violently battered the two men. The wind roared like thunder amplified through a giant megaphone as it grew in strength. Robert cupped his ears and placed his head between his knees as he was overcome with a violent surge of nausea. The wind kicked up rock and dust from the floor making Father Santeal barely visible. The torch's flames lapped at the air and were quickly extinguished by the intensity of the unnatural force. Chunks of stone of all sizes fell from the domed ceiling and pelted the temple floor like bullets spat from a machine gun. The incredible sound of the behemoth wind grew louder in decibel until it rattled Robert's teeth; his ears popped and he let out an agonizing scream. Then silence; nothing. The torches were relit one by one by the hand of an invisible firemaker. Robert was dizzy and still held his injured ears as he glanced over at Father Santeal who stood beside the coffin.

"It's done," Father Santeal reached his hand out, "come, we have much work to do. Let us prepare."

Robert staggered to his feet. He lost his equilibrium and steadied himself against the side of the coffin. The enormous slab had been removed and was placed on the floor in one solid piece. Inside lay a giant draped in a wet brown cloth. A portion of his face was covered, but his skin appeared supple and his eyes were clear black pools.

His mouth was agape and his jaw lay at an awkward angle. Perfect ivory teeth stood out against a blackened tongue that had been burnt by fire. His hands and ankles bore evidence of a crucifixion and a heavy chain tightly bound his arms and legs. Father Santeal dug his fingers into the chest of the dead king and a thick green liquid pooled around his hand. He probed with his fingertips and from the open cavity he scooped out a large tooth and placed it on a white cloth. Then his fingers dug deeper and he retrieved the talon and the tip of a horn that belonged to the Red King Sado Satanus. He used a towel to dry the slime from his hands then drew the Thaydien crest in red chalk atop the white stone riser. He read from the book and placed a dozen lit candles around the boundary of the outer circle. Father Santeal fastidiously stuck to the Thaydien rituals and donned a plumb colored robe trimmed with gold leaf. Upon his head he placed a Triregnum that resembled the pope's in size and shape and in its center was the image of a beast with seven heads and ten crowns. He threaded the tooth and talon each with thin gold chains and placed the necklace with the tooth around his neck and the necklace with the talon around Robert's. Robert knelt inside the inner circle and set a six inch Bowie knife by his side. He breathed deeply and desperately tried to settle his nerves. He fastened two six inch iron spikes to a short wooden block base. His hands were shaking and he reached for a small flask of whiskey inside his pants pocket and pressed it to his lips.

"No! Your mind and your thoughts must be clear," admonished Father Santeal. "You are about to do something wonderful and you will be rewarded for your good deeds. I promise you, have no fear."

Robert nodded, tossed the flask on the floor and placed his palms over the spikes. He took a second deep breath, wiped the stream of sweat from his brow and in one quick fluid motion impaled both hands until his palms touched the bottom of the wooden base. The pain was immediate and intense. He quickly put his knee between the makeshift device and pulled his hands free. In near shock, he stared transfixed at the sight of his bloody palms.

"We're almost done Robert," Father Santeal knelt in front of him. He examined his palms and placed a dollop of thick white cream on both sides of his hands then wrapped each hand with a sterile white cloth. "You're so close now. Be strong and the face of our Lord will be revealed unto you."

Reassured, Robert summoned an inner strength. He smiled at Father Santeal, opened his shirt and used the Bowie knife to carve an inverted cross from his chest to his abdomen. He gripped the knife with both hands and plunged it into his stomach up to the handle. His scream echoed off the cavernous walls. His body heaved forward and tears flowed down an ugly twisted face.

"Your body and your soul have been committed to the Lord. This is the sacrifice that must be made; this is the desecration that is required," Father Santeal held him in his arms and gently laid him backward in the center of the circle.

Cardinal Rourke made his way inside the surface entrance to the Temple of Metatron. He leaned against the black slime wall and heaved from the overwhelming stench. Thousands of bugs and maggots caked around his ankles and crawled up the side of his legs. He brushed them off as best he could and followed the lit torches to the lower levels. In the last chamber he found the pit where the two men had descended. He tucked the pistol into his waistband and attempted to uproot the spikes that secured the ropes. After a few minutes with no results, he surrendered the effort. He struggled to pull up the ropes, but neither would budge then he searched the chamber until he found a jagged edged rock. He pressed one of the nylon ropes firmly against the ground and frantically tried to cut it in two but the effort failed. He had run out of ideas and he started to feel the pangs of desperation. Maybe he could go back to the surface and seal the door locking the men inside forever or maybe he could wait until they emerged from the hole and shoot them both. His mind cleared; he knew he had to stop Father Santeal before they completed the unholy ceremony. He steeled his resolve, gripped the rope tightly and lowered himself down. His muscles tightened and burned; his bones creaked loudly evidence of his seventy plus years on earth. Cardinal Rourke lost circulation in his hands, lost his grip and fell the remaining ten feet. He lay on his back dazed and half-conscious. His right ankle was broken and he groaned as he battled to get to his feet. The two ropes dangled loosely and hit him squarely in the chest. He was baffled and stared in amazement; there was nothing at the bottom that secured either.

He entered the final chamber and was astounded by the size and vast expanses of the Temple of Metatron. His gaze moved from the impressive heights of the structure and focused on the prostrate body lying at the temple's center. The body twitched and shook wildly in a fit of epileptic seizures. The man yelped and uttered loudly as if trying desperately to speak as life quickly drained from him. Cardinal Rourke hobbled closer to the platform, his broken ankle sent waves of pain into his spine. Thick red blood dripped down as it coated each step of the riser and beaded on the temple floor. He crawled up the steps on his side and moved closer to the body. The man's eyes were blank; blood spurted out of the corners of his mouth and pumped freely through the gaping wound in his chest. He recognized the face as one of the men he had followed to Israel.

"I've been waiting for you Jeremiah," Father Santeal's voice bounced around the temple walls.

Cardinal Rourke clicked the safety off the gun and eased his way to the far side of the platform. At the base of the steps on the opposite side of the riser, Father Santeal knelt before a small dais with his back to him.

"You're too late. The Lord of the underworld has shown his will and his mighty hand," Father Santeal causally lit several candles, "nothing can save you now my friend." Cardinal Rourke leveled the gun at the back of his head. "It's a shame that you still don't believe," he said confidently.

Cardinal Rourke was overcome with the sense of a dark, unearthly presence that surrounded him. He turned to see the face of Robert Stone who stood directly behind him. His bloody hands reached out and gripped Rourke's throat tightly. Cardinal Rourke struggled violently hitting Robert in the face and chest, but he could not break his hold. Robert lifted his body a foot off the ground and spit in his face. The room began to darken; he desperately tried to aim the gun at Robert's head but fell unconscious and collapsed to the floor.

Friday 10:00 pm
22, September 1978
Small farm
Beersheba, Israel

"Basem! Basem!" a worried mother cried out in the dark. She stood in the doorway of her small stone house, "Basem!" She saw the boy running up the pathway and her nerves began to settle. "Basem, where have you been? Gamal would have paid you well to herd his goats today."

"I'm sorry. But you said it is always proper to help those who need it most."

"You left to help your friend again. The friend I've never met or seen? Or maybe you and Isam were out playing all day."

"No mother. Father Rourke does exist. See," he pulled out two golden coins from his pants pocket, "he gave me these because I helped him."

"Basem! Where did you get this money? Tell me. Now!"

"I told you. Father Rourke gave them to me."

She smacked the boy on the rear and led him out of the tiny house. She bent down and stuck her finger in his face, "Go to the well and get water. When you come back you're going to tell me who you took this from."

"But...." he could tell his mother wasn't interested in hearing his explanation and scampered off towards the well. It was darker than most nights but the moonlight guided his steps. What would he tell his mother if she did not believe him? Maybe he could say Isam had found the coins and gave them to him. He leaned over the well's large opening; the bucket was at the bottom. He dropped a rock down inside and listened for the splash; it was deep. He then used the wooden hand crank to raise a full bucket. Basem stretched his body over the well's mouth, tied off the rope and untied the pail. He caught a glimpse of the moon, his own reflection, and Robert's glowing yellow eyes in the rippling water.

His mother returned to the kitchen and made the sign of the cross as she stared at a crucifixion cross over her sink. She examined the gold coins with wonder then set them on the counter and wiped her hands on her apron. "Father Rourke," she said; the boy was impossible to deal with, "what an imagination."

"But Father Rourke does exist."

She spun around. A man was sitting at her kitchen table, "Who are you? Are you … Father Rourke?"

Father Santeal laughed, "No. I'm something… much… worse."

"Why are you here? What do you want?" she tried desperately to hide the fear rising inside her.

"I want your son."

"My son. Why?" she asked. The man said nothing. "Here," she picked up the coins, "if he took these from you please take them back." She pressed the coins into his palm. "Please," she said her voice trembling.

"I didn't come for useless tokens," Father Santeal's gaze never left her eyes; he opened his hand and the coins rattled as they hit the floor. "I came for a sacrament, a holy offertory; I came for your son's life."

She turned a pale white and ran to the front door. "Basem! Basem! Pleeease!" she sobbed uncontrollably. The boy was nowhere in sight. "Basem! No... no no. What have you done with my son!" Father Santeal stood behind Basem's mother. He reached around her with his right arm firmly secured under her chin and in one quick twist and loud pop her lifeless body fell to the ground.

The great beast, the deceiver had transformed himself into the form of man and ruled the lands beyond Israel with much terror as the Red King Sado Satanus, the Antichrist on earth.

Heironymos
Book of Heironymos

CHAPTER III
BURNT OFFERINGS

Monday 11:42 am
25, September 1978
Public Park (Villa Doria Pamphili)
Rome, Italy

Agent Michael Cavilary, SISDE (Italian Secret Service) sat on a wooden bench alone and agitated. Unable to admire the sprawling green Renaissance gardens he fidgeted anxiously and constantly checked his watch. He unpacked the brown paper bag that lay next to him on the pine slats. In an attempt to blend in with the hundreds of tourists he began devouring a spicy homemade cudighi. Cavilary heard the dull thuds of footsteps on the path behind him; a long thin shadow was cast across the tips of his shoes.

"You're late," he said without looking up.

"You forget I know longer work on company time my friend," a sharply dressed middle aged Vincent Gallo looked in amazement at the massive seventeenth century Villa. He placed his hand on Cavilary's shoulder. "Besides, all things considered it's a beautiful day. Instead of stuffing your belly with that crap, you should walk the grounds with me."

"You forget. I am on company time," he continued eating.

"You sure, looks like you put on a few pounds since I last saw you," Gallo's attention was focused on scanning the groups of nearby faces gathering in the park.

"As much as I wish I had contacted you to reminisce about the good old days like old friends.... I called you here strictly for business." He observed Gallo's demeanor and could tell he was uncomfortable. He opened his jacket. "You can search me if you want. I'm not wearing a wire."

"You'll never make Director if anyone sees you with me," Gallo laughed. "Knowing you as I do, I should probably be afraid of what you're going to ask me next?"

"Sit," Cavilary cleared off a space on the bench and pulled out a black flower sealed in a plastic evidence bag from his briefcase. "What do you make of this?"

"I don't know Michael; I've never been much of a horticulturist," he examined the bag, "although I'm pretty sure you'll need a permit if you want to plant those here."

"Black Orchid. It's a hybrid between foxglove, wisteria and a few other poisonous plants. The sap from this little flower can cause nausea, serious heart problems and enough of it in the right dose... death. Every part of this plant is poisonous. It's also a symbol of siyah yılan or black serpent a group of anti-Catholic Turkish nationalists. A few months ago I was contacted by Cardinal Jeremiah Rourke and Father Joseph Principi concerning the existence of this group, and the possible existence of another that was more ominous."

"What do you mean more ominous? Another terrorist group?"

"Something darker, some sort of Luciferian cult. They believed this second group was trying to infiltrate the Catholic Church all the way to the papacy. Some of my underground sources told me they knew of a buyer willing to pay any price for a certain book scholars thought was only held in the vault of the Vatican's secret library. The book is libri of cado animus and was considered by the Pope's council to be corrupting to the soul of man and so dangerous that it had to be destroyed." Cavilary tempered his voice and spoke in a more guarded tone, "The death of the Patriarch, Boris Georgievich Rotov while attending last month's conclave is still officially categorized as natural causes by the police and Swiss Guard. One of these black orchids was found near where he fell ill. At the time we didn't attach any significance to it because St. Peter's Square was overflowing with well wishers with handfuls of wreaths and flowers. When Pope John Paul was found dead ten days ago the official word coming out of the Vatican was that it was a heart attack. We found a second black orchid inside the Basilica of Saint John Lateran."

"The Pope's church, the mother church of the whole world," Gallo said with disbelief, "not exactly sending a subtle message are they."

"This note was found with it," he handed him the letter to read.

"Cessante ratione legis cessat ipsa lex--When the reason for the law ceases, the law itself ceases. Condemnant quod non intellegunt--They condemn what they do not understand," he handed the note back to Cavilary.

"I think the law refers to faith. When the reason for faith ceases then faith itself ceases," Cavilary then tucked the orchid and letter back into his briefcase. "They condemn what they do not understand probably refers to the libri of cado animus."

"The book of fallen souls. I've never heard of it, have you?"

"No. But it appears it may have been important enough to kill for, at least that's what Cardinal Rourke believed. He also thought Bishop Atis Martz was a member of the secretive sect that infiltrated the church."

"Really?" Gallo raised an eyebrow, "Bishop Martz is one of the most popular and well respected figures around the world. I remember meeting him when I was a kid and even back then it was obvious that he was completely devoted to the church and its teachings. It's hard to believe a man like that could belong to any cult."

"I have confirmation. Two weeks ago the state police arrested a young man in the Bari Province, named Emir Saldalha. Apparently he was feeling very tormented that night. He almost drank himself into a coma and crashed a stolen car into several parked vehicles. A group of nuns found him inside the courtyard of the Hospes of St. Cecilia kneeling at her sculpture, sobbing and begging for forgiveness."

"St. Cecilia the incorruptible," muttered Gallo.

"When they arrested him he had a loaded pistol tucked in his waistband. We were able to trace it back to a crime involving the shooting death of a Naples Banker. It seems he was desperate and had already made up his mind that he wanted to talk. After a few hours of rather intensive interrogation, he confessed to being a member of siyah yılan. And, that he and other members of the group had come here to purchase guns and explosives. He named a fellow Turk he would only refer to as Marko as their leader. Emir said that on the day of August 26, they had met with a group of Catholic priests and an American in an apartment somewhere in Rome."

"You sure that information's legit? I know how ruff your interrogations go Michael. Besides, he could have been scared of facing a long prison sentence and confessed to anything. You thoroughly check his story out?"

"Thank you Vincent," Cavilary said acerbically, "I know how to do my job. Of course I checked it out. At least... the parts of the story I could. He was reluctant to give up the names of the priests, but eventually he named Bishop Martz as one of them."

"You think he's stalling for a deal?"

"No. More like scared out of his mind. He doesn't fear Marko as much as he does the priests. He claims he didn't recognize the others and he couldn't identify any of them from photographs. That's not all, after the death of the Pope; I went to question Bishop Martz. He was staying at Villa di Sangiamo, the personal guest of Chief Magistrate Sangiamo."

"You must be looking for early retirement if you raided Sangiamo's estate."

"I found him outside the guest house sitting, legs crossed; he had doused his clothes with petrol and set himself on fire." Cavilary tossed the rest of the uneaten sandwich back into the bag, "I can still see him staring at me with that wicked grin on his face. We searched the guest room and found this letter tucked inside a bible lying on the nightstand."

Gallo read it, 'Kill them all. For the Lord knows those who are his.'

"The Catholic Church launched a crusade against the Thaydien capital where over 20,000 men, women and children were killed and their city burnt to the ground."

"You really believe this is the hand of revenge being dealt out after a few thousand years?"

"You have a better theory? I arrested Sangiamo, but he wouldn't talk and soon after I was ordered to release him. I got taken off the case and the investigation into siyah yılan, Emir Saldalha and Bishop Martz was officially closed. We're talking police, SISDE, military intelligence, judges, politicians and God knows who else maybe involved. We may be looking at a second coup d'état to take down the government." Cavilary let out a deep breath, "I haven't been able to contact Cardinal Rourke for weeks. I don't know who to trust anymore Vincent, so I came to you because I know you have contacts on both sides of the law and you know how to operate discretely."

"And because I'm your friend," Gallo said sarcastically.

"And because you're my friend."

"If I take the case and that's if, I can't have you or anyone else from SISDE shadowing my every move."

"SISDE doesn't know I'm here. No one knows I'm here. I told you, officially on or off the books this case is closed."

"I wouldn't have to get your approval on my methods?"

"You never did."

"I do this my way, no questions?"

"Are you done or should I write this down?"

"I'm done."

"Sooo that means you'll take the case, right?"

"Yes."

"Also there's something else you may find interesting. Emir said Marko was particularly upset because he was expecting Cecellini to be at their meeting in Rome and he wasn't."

"I spent too much time chasing after rebel conspirators like Cecellini, Chiaie and Borghese just to see them escape justice. Besides, Alberto Cecellini is a phantom. Everyone wants to believe that there's someone out there to blame for all the corrupt judges and politicians; someone who has power and control over the most significant to most mundane part of their life. Fact is no one's ever seen him or heard his voice and no government has come close to tracking him down. Face it Michael, he doesn't exist."

CHAPTER III: BURNT OFFERINGS

"I don't know," he gave Gallo the briefcase, "if the priests and siyah yılan did meet in Rome without anyone in the services knowing about it; I can't think of anyone other than Cecellini that could have made it happen."

"I'm only agreeing to take the siyah yılan case and find your missing priest ... nothing else," Gallo started up the footpath towards the villa. "Do yourself a favor Michael, let Cecellini stay a ghost and concentrate on the mortals that you can capture. Otherwise you'll drive yourself insane. Trust me."

"Goodbye my friend," Cavilary snickered.

"Goodbye."

The morning sky had turned a deep blue; the two men left the park in opposite directions. Gallo stopped on top of the hill at the end of the stone pathway. He was overcome with the restless feeling of being watched. He scanned the faces of the young couples, children, old men and women as they strolled passed him. Get it together, he thought to himself. You took precautions... extra precautions. There's no way anyone could have followed you; you know how to lose even the best tail. Relax. Unable to shake the sense of unease, he hastened his pace until he was out of the park.

Monday 9:45 pm
25, September 1978
Beersheba, Israel

Cardinal Rourke opened his eyes. His head, hands and feet were throbbing. It took him a second to realize he was hanging upside down with his palms and ankles crucified.

CHAPTER III: BURNT OFFERINGS

They had moved him to a strange new location away from the Temple of Metatron. Below, his stare locked onto the terrified face of a young teenage girl with her arms and legs bound to a stone altar. She shook her head slightly; with her eyes she tried to signal Cardinal Rourke to remain still.

"Ahhh. Finally you're awake. I was afraid you hadn't survived the journey," Father Santeal gently slapped Rourke's cheek, "After all this time it would have been a shame to have lost our only pious sacrifice and replace you with another less deserving."

Cardinal Rourke had trouble focusing, but he could see the girl's cherub face more clearly. A cloaked and hooded Robert Stone stood behind Basem with his hands on his shoulders. The boy was shaking and visibly weeping. Was this the man he had trailed to Israel? Was this the man whom he had seen lay dying? Was he the man who attacked him at the Temple of Metatron? Was this a man at all? He could feel the evil seeping from Robert's soul and infecting the entire room.

"That's right Jeremiah," Father Santeal enjoyed the moment, "the child has been very very bad... spying on us as he did and he will atone for the offense against me. Really, it was your hand that chose him to be a part of our glorious day and now, I choose him as the innocence offering to our Lord. And as for the girl," he put his hand between her legs and glided his fingers to her crotch, "so sweet; so untouched, she will make the perfect virgin sacrifice."

"You should never have come to Israel," Cardinal Rudolph Fuerst stood in the shadows, "There is no way to stop the coming of the Lord. If only you had decided to join us and had been Bishop Martz's apprentice years ago, today would be so very different."

"You wish me to worship the blasphemer," Cardinal Rourke voice was strained, "you seek to raise the abomination. Do you really think you can control him?"

"The powers of the great beast were divided among three," said Cardinal Fuerst, "Mr. Stone is becoming the fallen Angel Qeynan even as we speak. His powers are growing ever stronger, in time he will visit upon the world a great plague and only those who stand with us will survive his wrath. Father Santeal has within him the power of the Angel Thaydien and he will lead the army of Satanus," his breath shown in the cold air. "And as for the abomination... Sado Satanus the Anti Christ on earth; a child sharing the bloodline of Thaydien's disciple Kyameron has already been found. Unfortunately for you, you won't be alive to see it."

"And condemning your souls for all eternity is worth having the ultimate dark power?"

"A thousand year rule over every nation before the rise of Satan and the return of his power is worth giving up everything," Father Santeal interrupted, "I shall bear witness to a millennia of suffering and the torment of those of your faith and every other. The world will be remade in his image and we shall be there by his side."

"Let him down! Please," Basem ran to the altar. "Let us go!"

"I need you to be strong Basem," Cardinal Rourke said in a soothing voice, "remember, the Lord is my shepherd, I shall not want; He makes me lie down in green pastures. He leads me besides green waters; He restores my soul. He leads me in paths of righteousness for his name sake…" Robert stepped forward an intense heat emitted from his skin; his beastly face and hollow eyes were inches away from Cardinal Rourke's, "though I walk through the valley of the shadow of death, I fear no ev…"

Robert placed both of his hands inside Cardinal Rourke's mouth; with a simple twist he effortlessly snapped his jaw. The dirty rags that wrapped his hands and were stained with his own blood were coated with a steady stream of the Cardinal's fresh blood. His fingers pried the jaws apart at an abnormal angle and he gripped his tongue and tore it out. Cardinal Rourke grimaced in pain and spat globs of blood profusely from his mouth. The agony was unbearable but he had to focus, he had to save Basem and the girl. They had chosen their dark paths long ago and he knew what these men would do to them. Barbed wire securely wrapped his entire body, iron spikes went deep through his palms and into the wooden cross and another had shattered both his ankles. There was no way to save the children or himself, yet he refused to stop believing that he could.

"You see how useless it is to fight us; you can't stop what's inevitable," Father Santeal knelt and looked the boy in the face. There was a cruel darkness in his eyes and he whispered in his ear, "Centuries ago men of his faith destroyed a great city built to worship our's, those who survived hid in this very cave. They were betrayed by one of their own and were discovered. Every man, woman and child in their mother's arms were put to the sword. On that day all but a tiny handful of our nation was wiped from the face of the earth. It's only fitting that the rise of a new world begins here. Take heart young man you are about to give your life for something… wonderful."

The girl began to hyperventilate, her heartbeat raced and she struggled to free herself. She breathed heavily and loudly; her eyes were frozen in fear as Robert approached the altar. He removed the hood and his face slowly transformed from barely-human to something ungodly and blasphemous. The girl's screams were deafening and fueled with agony that pierced the stillness of the night.

And I saw the great beast lay dying upon the shore and unto him came the Angels that had been cast out of heaven for their treachery. He called them forth for he knew them by their names Qeynan, Thaydien and Hector.

Philetos
libri of cado animus

CHAPTER IV
THE UNSEEN

Wednesday 1:35 pm
9, October 1978
Hospes of St. Cecilia
City of Madonnella
Bari Province, Italy

A chiming of the bells rang out and children gathered in from the yard and headed towards the school. The grounds were divided into two distinct and contrasting parts. On the east lot stood the Hospes of St. Cecilia, a depressing three story Romanesque red brick hospital marked by its imposing dark windows and sterile façade and to the west a modern well kempt white stone elementary school. The buildings were connected by a courtyard that was enclosed by eight foot walls decorated with numerous statuettes of lion heads and Roman warriors. In the center was an impressive white stone statue of the martyred St. Cecilia lying on her side with her face turned downward. The hospital and school itself were tucked in between a long row of gray uniform apartment buildings that lined the main street. From street side a brick wall entranceway pushed back against the fastly encroaching modern world. A simple black iron archway adorned the entry and on it read: ad vitam aeternam (to life everlasting). The City of Madonnella was a city in name only. It lacked the beauty of Venice, the style of Milan, the significance of Rome and the importance of Bari the capital city of the Bari province. It was an odd mixture of a small but fashionable cosmopolitan class surrounded by old world farms and vineyards. Green valleys and rolling hills dominated the landscape making the landlocked Madonnella an island within an island. A single endless two lane highway connected her to the outer world, but few buses rode out and even fewer buses came into the heart of the city. Father Neil Story walked the gated grounds of St. Cecilia with a visibly anxious Isabella Stone. Her eyes scanned the many faces of the young children playing, shouting and singing loudly until their voices were a cacophonous wall of sound. Then her gaze fell upon her 10 year old daughter Emily standing alone oblivious to the chorus of the other children.

"Thank you for seeing me today Father."

"Of course, I am always happy to see the faces of the children's parents and dispel any concerns they may have," he said in a distinct British accent.

"Has Emily seemed any different to you, acted any differently?" It had been a year since her father Robert had left the family and six months since she cut her wrists in an attempted suicide.

"Oh. No," Father Story was caught off guard, "unfortunately when a child's parents separate, they often internalize a lot of their pain and become withdrawn and introverted. But, I wouldn't worry too much. The Sisters are very good at drawing the children out of their shells."

"It's just.... a few days ago Emily told me a strange story. She said she saw her father... he was floating like a spirit outside her bedroom window. She said his face had changed, his eyes were different but she knew it was him and she was so happy to see him Father. I told her.... I told her it was nothing but a silly dream and that she should forget it."

"No doubt she misses her father dearly," Father Story tried to mask his discomfort. "She is a very bright child. I'm sure in her mind she's blaming herself for the separation. These dreams are her way of connecting with her father," he smiled warmly. "If you want I'll make sure we keep an extra eye on her."

"Yes. Thank you Father," she took a deep breath, "It's only that I've had dreams too; only Robert isn't Robert in my dreams. His face is distorted; he's something wicked-- something unspeakably evil. I can tell in the way he looks at me that he wants to hurt me; hurt Emily."

"You've been under a lot of pressure raising a child by yourself. It's only natural that your stress would manifest itself in a dream. Why the unconscious mind can conjure up the worst and most terrifying images that mean absolutely nothing. Just remember dreams are just that... dreams, they're not real," he held her hand tightly. "Don't worry my child; we will see that happy joyous face return to her soon. I promise."

Emily knew her father would be coming home; even if she couldn't explain how she knew, even if the very thought terrified her mother. He would be home and soon. The color of her skin had turned a pale alabaster white and like her soul it was slowly being drained from her body. There was something insider her now, something unknown to others and unseen to all, but she welcomed it all the more if it meant she could have her father back in her life. At first Emily thought her mother might be right, that it was only fantasy that kept the thin thread connection between her and her father. He had always made promises to her; a promise to always love her, a promise to send for her, a promise to come back one day... but in the end, they all seemed to be promises unkept. Now she took a leap of faith, one in which the direction of her life would radically change and it was still unclear just where her journey would end. She could feel the transformation within her blaze like an inferno and believed with all her being that her father would be at her side in the end. Her mother, her friends, the priests and nuns could never understand or comprehend the reasons for her choices, but she believed and that was all that mattered. She stood alone at the back gate with her fingers tightly gripping the metal mesh fence. Her face was cold and void of feelings. A black cloud swirled around the speckle blue of her iris and began to pool into the depths of her pupils. She was happy now; she would wait for him. Emily smiled as she stared out over Madonnella's rolling hills and sparse landscape and off into the orange horizon.

Friday 3:30 am
13, October 1978
Manna Book Store
City of Madonnella
Bari Province, Italy

It was dark, a thick gray fog emanated from the soft earth of the green valley. It was dark. Low but audible breathing came from the blackness that was more animal than human.

Stepping into the moonlight appeared the form of the great beast, the Red King Sado Satanus, the Anti Christ on earth. An uncontrollable fire spread over the horizon heaping destruction throughout the terrain. The beast's skin was scaled and colored deep crimson from head to hoofs, black horns spiraled from its skull and black wings blotted out the sky. Sado Satanus stood a menacing 20 feet tall with total annihilation burning in his malignant heart. His rotted fingernails dug into the flesh of an ill-fated victim and his razor blade teeth eagerly devoured the man's living head. The earth was made repulsive and the tormented cried out from Madonnella and the world beyond. The Red King had risen from the depths of hell and Peter Cameron knew he alone was responsible. As though sensing his presence, the eyes of the demon locked onto his. Peter awoke to the sound of a blaring alarm clock; his nightshirt drenched in sweat. The room was dark... too dark. For months he had been terrorized by some iteration of the dream; but now the images were clearer, the danger clearer and so was the fear that his life would soon come to an end. He clicked on the lamp next to the bedpost then grabbed a handful of downers off the bedside table and set his alarm clock for another 30 minutes. In the weakness of the morning light he could see the outline of the sparse furniture in his room and the cross that hung from the wall. He said a quick prayer for his soul and drifted back to sleep.

Upstairs in a small one bedroom apartment of the Manna Book Store, Eddie Bertucci lit a joint, leaned against a post and stared out the skylight that ran the length and height of the apartment. The building was at the heart of the town surrounded by Madonnella's meager cityscape and sat at the top of a steep incline. From his perch he could easily see over the rooftops of most of the buildings in the business district and down into the prevailing countryside.

"Come back to bed Eddie," his girlfriend Angela mumbled from underneath a pillow.

"In a minute."

"You always wake in the middle of the night and stare out that window," she said, "there's nothing out there. There's nothing in this entire town."

He knew she was right. With the exception of a few downtown buildings erected nearly ten years ago, Madonnella had barely changed in centuries. There were fewer and fewer of the younger generation that had decided to stay and make this city their home. He also knew that like all of them she desperately wanted out.

"We grew up here all our lives. Our fathers and fathers' fathers made this land. This city is our city," he looked back towards the bed, "your father would whip your hide raw if he heard you talking like that."

"I can't stay here. I won't stay here," said Angela now fully awake. "I think if I live here one more day I'll go insane. Then what would you do?"

"Then you wouldn't care where you lived," with his fingers he spun imaginary circles around his head, "you'd of lost your mind you poor soul."

"That's not funny Eddie," she threw a pillow at him, "this place drains every bit of life out of you. It's stale; boring. When I lived in Milan…"

"You lived in Milan for a summer... half-a-summer," Eddie laughed, "That doesn't exactly make you a vaunted world traveler."

"I don't care. Anywhere is better than here."

"Even if I'm here?"

Angela got out of bed, walked over to where Eddie was standing and wrapped her arms around his waist. "Have you told Peter about the job offer?" she rested her head on his shoulder.

"Not yet."

"Why not?"

"There's something going on with him; he won't talk about but it's something heavy."

The pipes of the old building led directly from the attic apartment to the cellar, and for weeks Eddie would stir at the sound of Peter screaming wildly in the middle of the night.

"It's just like you Eddie; you're not going to take the job are you?"

"I will. It'll just be a little bit later than we planned," he didn't relish taking the dockworker's job in Bari, but that was the plan. Work there a year and save up enough money to start over in England or France or anywhere but here. Angela was more than Eddie could ever want, she was beautiful, young and exciting and also impatient. He stared out at the old church that was being rebuilt a mile away and at the old white barns and silos that lay far off in the distance. He stared at the highway that appeared and disappeared from beneath the blossoming green trees and further away at the red rooftop of the barely visible Hospes of St. Cecila where he had gone to school as a child. A thick white mist rolled in from the Mediterranean Sea and covered much of the lush emerald valley. There was something different, something that electrified the early morning air, something in the mist itself that was foreboding and stood as a warning and an omen of bad things to come.

"You're freezing," Angela felt the sudden drop of body heat from him. She grabbed his hand and led him back towards the bed.

Finally morning came and with it light. Peter showered, shaved and donned a freshly ironed shirt and slacks. The basement apartment was depressingly meager and held one small bed, a display case and a tiny bathroom that was located in front of the boiler room. A small wood frame window was his only access to the outside world. He made his way upstairs into the heart of the bookstore. There were several aisles of new books and carbon copies of old text stacked neatly upon the shelves and rows of cabinets containing magazines and newspapers dating as far back as 1703. He had Eddie paint the slight dome in the ceiling in vibrant colors that resembled the designs in the Vatican Library. It comforted him to be reminded of the place he had once worked and spent most of his early years as an archivist. His title may have changed but his life bore great similarity to that of the former priest he had once been. On the balcony that led up to the attic apartment was a large glass pantry that proudly displayed religious artifacts.

There were many stone figurines from Rome, an ivy tusk from India and an antique soapstone Leviathan from Israel.

"You're up early" Eddie said as he descended the stairs.

Peter picked up a life sized cardboard cutout of author Mario Pascale with a green banner across the waist that read, 'The Human Mind - possibly his best book ever.'

"Possibly the biggest ego ever," Eddie said, "he writes like shit."

"Watch your language please Eddie," sneered Peter.

"Forgive me padre," Eddie made the sign of the cross and held his hands in prayer, "for unlike others I cannot worship false idols. Not even cardboard ones." He grabbed the cut out and examined it closely, "How many of these did you order?"

"Just one. But there is a banner I need you to put up over the entrance."

"Greatest book ever huh; he writes about your ability to remember every paragraph, every line from the thousands of books you've read and then barely credits you in his book," Eddie raised his eyebrows. "If you want I can paste your picture over his face... although, I'll have to blow it up a couple of times to cover such a huge head."

"Mario's our friend, he's an acclaimed author, an international celebrity and he's generously agreed to hold a book signing party at our store. We should be thankful."

CHAPTER IV: THE UNSEEN

"First, Mario the Pretentious is your friend, not mine and if you think hosting a single party instead of paying you what you're actually worth…"

"I have all that I need and my heart is content. Besides, the more people that come, the more eyes there will be to see your beautiful paintings." He patted Eddie on the back.

"I'd rather sell my soul to the Devil than be beholden to Mario. I can see it now. You're welcome Eddie, without me your paintings wouldn't be hanging in the private galleries of the world's most influential and famous. Why if it wasn't for me your art would be consigned to the barns of Mondonnella's pig farmers. Thanks but no thanks."

"Come on, Mario's not that bad. Besides …"

"Breakfast is ready," Angela came out of the kitchen wearing only a flannel shirt. "Sorry," she said shyly, "I didn't think you were up. It's no big deal…"

"Go get dressed," Eddie said sternly.

She exited quickly and ran up the staircase. It was all part of an unspoken game they played. Angela would spend the night and be gone before morning and Peter would pretend to be ignorant of the arrangement.

"You two getting married?"

"Not on what you pay me Peter."

"I realize you must be anxious to get out and see the world. I was like that at your age."

"At my age you were studying language and theology and a hundred other things. Who knows, you could have become the next Pope," he leaned against the kitchen doorway, "besides, I'm not the one who's so anxious to leave this place."

"Ahh, of course. You know you're really lucky she hasn't left without you."

"There's been something I've been meaning to talk to you about Pete...."

"See, all dressed," Angela stood at the balcony; painfully aware of the awkwardness of the statement. She pretended to fix her hair as she walked the stairs, "Breakfast is ready; we'd better eat before it gets cold." She led them into the kitchen.

"You wanted to tell me something Eddie," Peter sat down at the small round table.

"I'm going to take a job in Bari," he looked sheepish and ashamed, but Angela couldn't contain her growing excitement.

"How long do I have before you leave?"

"You see, I have a friend who already works at the docks. He says he can get me a job in November... or any time later if you need my help around here," Eddie was losing his nerve and Peter sensed the disappointment in Angela's face.

"Don't be ridiculous. I'll be fine," Peter dug into the eggs on his plate. "Bari's a great place you'll love living there."

"Bari's only temporary. We want to live in America," Angela's eyes lit up with the anticipation of leaving Madonnella for good.

"What exactly do you know about America?" Peter asked.

"Nothing," Eddie wasn't happy, he hadn't been consulted with the new change of plan. "You're the only American we know."

Peter looked towards Angela, "Then you'd better work on your English, lest you be cast out as an ignorant foreigner."

"My English is fine enough," she refused to let Peter spoil her moment of victory.

"Where in America?" asked Peter.

It was clear she hadn't thought it through and was left with a quizzical expression on her face. She settled on a suitable answer, "Anywhere."

"Well there's New York--New York; that might suit you... very fast paced. Los Angeles, California; great weather. Albuquerque, New Mexico..."

"Alberkergi? Is there such a place?" she asked as Peter laughed.

"Al-bu-quer-que," Peter said in his clearest enunciation.

Angela mouthed the word to herself repeatedly. Frustrated she left the kitchen.

"I'd better make sure she doesn't break anything," Eddie trailed out after her. He turned in the doorway, "Again, thanks for understanding Peter."

"Ablekergi!" Angela's proud face appeared in the doorway.

Peter smiled. He was well known in Madonnella but he had few friends that were close to him. Eddie Bertucci and Mario Pascale were the only one's he really trusted and felt comfortable around. With the nightmarish visions he was having lately, he didn't relish the thought of being left alone. Peter opened the store and welcomed the meager flow of customers inside. The telephone rang and he hurried around the cashier's counter to pick it up.

"Hello," he cradled the receiver between his head and shoulder, "Manna Book Store, can I help you? Mario! Hey we were just talking about you. How's your tour of London going?"

Eddie and Angela sat in the middle of the store and were busy unpacking the shipment of Mario's new book, he rolled his eyes at the mere mention of his name.

"Eddie says hi," Peter grinned.

Eddie tilted his head, stuck his tongue out and pretended to hang himself, then he and Angela headed out the front door.

"When's your flight back?" he grabbed a piece of paper and pen, "You sure. It's no problem I can pick you up from the airport. Alright. Then I guess... I'll see you on Sunday. Talk to you later. Ok. Take care. Bye," he hung up the receiver and the phone immediately rang again. "What happen, change your mind?"

Silence.

"Hello."

"Eh eh eh eh eh eh eh eh eh eh eh eh."

"Hello."

A high pitch wine emanated from the ear piece. Peter listened intently as dozens of disjointed voices spoke out of tune. The voices of men and women were intricately layered over each other. The speech was low and indecipherable at first but grew in intensity and sped up in an unnatural manner. Again silence.

"Hello. Who is this?" Peter held the phone close to his ear; his hand began to tremble.

"The end is only the beginning," a man's voice spoke in a whisper before the line went dead.

Then the LORD saw that the wickedness of man was great in the earth, and that every intent of the thoughts of his heart was only evil continually. And the LORD was sorry that He had made man on the earth, and He was grieved in His heart."

Genesis
King James Bible

CHAPTER V
THE DARK HEART

Monday 9:43am
16, November 1978
Ben Gurion International Airport

Vincent Gallo grabbed his worn carry-on from the overhead compartment and debarked Alitalia Airways. Two Israeli soldiers examined him and his passport thoroughly before letting him pass customs. He retrieved his luggage from the Terminal One baggage carousel and glanced briefly at the female officer who had followed his every movement. He scanned the terminal for a janitor's door or employee only sign in case he needed to run, but not surprisingly they were well guarded. A short stocky man wearing a dark blue chauffeur's cap and dark glasses stood at the exitway and held up a sign for Dante Costa. It was the name he had used to purchase the ticket and book his hotel, but he hadn't ordered the driver. He almost lost his nerve until he recognized the man holding the sign as François Minot. Minot was an old friend and a former Israeli spy who had won the Medal of Valor during the Yom Kippur war.

"Mr. Costa," he had a thick French accent, "your limousine awaits." An eyebrow sheepishly rose from beneath the rim of the glasses.

"You have room for two?" asked Gallo.

Minot eyed the young female soldier and smiled, "More like room for fifty," he took Gallo's bag. "Using an old Cecellini alias is almost good enough to get you shot on sight."

The two men walked through the airport terminals under the blaring sound of the public address system announcing the inbound/outbound flights and under the watchful glare of the authorities. Gallo made a mental count of the number of security trailing their movement. Two soldiers with automatic weapons slung over their shoulders stood at the ticket counter, two more near the level 2 escalators, a woman rubbing the back of her ear signaled another who took up the task of shadowing their next steps. Outside near the outgoing airline transport buses were three men seated across the street in a light blue BMW E9.

"Nice car," Gallo threw his baggage in the back seat of a 1975 mustard yellow Lincoln Town car with white wall tires. "It might be harder for them to follow us if you set it on fire first."

"It was the best I could do on short notice, besides the first rule in trying not to look inconspicuous is to not look inconspicuous." Minot turned the key and the engine rattled to life. He pulled away from the curb and the BMW followed suit.

CHAPTER V: THE DARK HEART

"The deal I made was with Hafsah and we weren't supposed to meet until later tonight. I assume he filled you in on the details," Gallo sorted through his carry-on and opened a secret compartment, "I had a Plan A on getting out of the airport you know." He leaned forward and tossed an envelope filled with cash onto the passenger's seat.

"Step one go to jail. Step two call François," he laughed.
"You're lucky I showed; the Mossad is convinced Hafsah is doing business with Arafat and they're looking for any excuse to arrest him these days. They've already bugged your hotel room and placed a man at the concierge desk." He looked in the rearview and eyed the BMW trailing six cars behind, "So I say to myself, my old friend must have a good reason for drawing all this attention by using a known Cecellini alias. You do have good reason right?"

"I'm looking for someone who's not too keen on being found. Someone who's really eager to contact our friend Alberto Cecellini. So I figured I'd save myself the trouble and have him find me," he removed an envelope containing a 3" x 5" pencil sketch from the inside lining of his blazer. "His name is Marko; he's a Turk with a group called siyah yılan and he's probably traveling with this man; Emir Saldalha," he handed Minot Saldalha's arrest photo.

"Obviously you haven't been back to Israel in the last 2 years if you don't fully appreciate the danger in messing with a member of the Saldalha family."

"Relax François, I don't need you to ask anyone questions on their whereabouts," he patted Minot on the shoulder. "Like I said, they'll come looking for me. All you have to do is wait till they show up and follow them back to where ever it is they're hiding. Simple enough, you can handle that. Right?"

"Just follow?"

"Just follow."

"It's never that easy with you Vincent."

"You're getting soft François; nothing like the fierce warrior I use to know," he eased back in his seat. "I can always find someone else if you think it's too dangerous a job for you."

"There's a streetlight in front of the American Restaurant," he ignored Gallo's childish attempt at an insult, "It's nine minutes walking distance from your hotel; if there's an 'X' taped to the bottom of the streetlight you will find directions to their location inside the restaurant." There was a certain confidence in his voice as he held out a folded newspaper, "Hafsah said he has information for you and will meet you here, tomorrow. "

Gallo unfolded the newspaper and scanned the many appliance advertisements and the black and white travel adverts beckoning young Israelis to visit the Great Pyramids of Giza and the tomb of the Pharos in Egypt. His eyes fell upon an advertisement for a noon tour of the Elazar Lighthouse, Haifa; on it one of the bricks of the lighthouse had been colored in by pen.

Minot stopped outside the Hotel Efron and opened the rear door for Gallo, "Do you remember Saul Aronoff?"

"Tipy?"

CHAPTER V: THE DARK HEART

"He has a jewelry store two blocks away, I'll leave you a package in the alleyway," Minot held out his hand for a tip, "just make sure you get there before the garbage man does."

Gallo dropped a lira in Minot's hand, "Don't forget, I've put on a few pounds... and don't get anything to flashy, okay?"

"I have done this before," Minot cynically eyed the lira then pocketed it. "Good luck my friend."

Gallo swung the bag over his shoulder and headed up the staircase of the hotel. He made his way through the lobby and up to the concierge desk, asked for his room and showed his passport.

"Here you go Mr. Costa," the female clerk was visibly nervous, "forth floor room 412. If you need anything just ring the desk. The bellhop will help you with your bags."

"That won't be necessary, it's just the one bag," said Gallo. The bellhop/agent was an obvious plant.

Gallo exited the elevator glancing only slightly at the hidden overhead camera. He tossed his bag on the bed and locked the door behind him. He put a wooden chair under the door handle, entered the bathroom and lifted the tank lid. He tapped the flush handle, waited for the water to drain and picked up a plastic package taped to the bottom of the tank. He opened the bag and pulled out a Berretta 93R machine pistol with silencer, a flat bottle of Jack Daniels and a letter from Minot that read, 'Remember Lebanon.' He closed the curtains in the bedroom and pushed a cushioned chair against the wall opposite the door then turned on a free standing lamp. He made sure the gun was loaded then attached the silencer and placed it atop a small round coffee table. He leaned back in the chair and took a deep swig of the whisky. It was a risky gamble to pose so publicly as a Cecellini alias but, he was sure it would pay off in the end. 'Remember Lebanon'; the 1973 raid into Lebanon where Israeli commandos killed several PLO and Black September leaders. Minot had always been allusive about his military background but Gallo was convinced that he had taken some part in the attack.

9:50 am
Manna Book Store
City of Madonnella
Bari Province, Italy

Peter waded through the books stacked high in the storage room. He had no specific book in mind, still he felt compelled to search. There was something important there; something hidden among the giant piles of stacked text. If he concentrated he could find it instantly; but he was afraid that if he did, he would find the answers that would confirm the growing terror rising within. He clouded his mind, satisfying the urge to postpone the inevitable then to get the answers and face down that fear.

"Peter," Angela stood at the edge of the doorway. "Eddie wanted you to come look at the sign."

"Of course," he was relieved; he was too close to stumbling on the truth. "He hasn't done anything to it has he?"

She smiled, "As much as he pretends to hate Mario, he really would do anything for him. Anyway, he knows how much it would help your bookstore and what it means to you; personally I mean."

"That would be a change, I usually have to play referee whenever they get together."

"I'm sorry about this morning. It won't happen again. Eddie says…"

"Don't worry," Peter locked the storage room behind them, "it's already forgotten."

"Eddie said you'd say that," she grabbed his arm and whispered, "Please don't tell him I brought it up, I promised him I wouldn't."

Outside at the entrance Eddie stood near the top of a ten foot ladder and had hung part of the banner across the doorway. He was busy adjusting it when he noticed Peter standing below.

"Long live Caesar," Eddie stared at the green banner, "Mario Aurelius Antoninus Augustus Pascale."

"That's enough Eddie," sneered Peter.

"Fine. I'm just not sure the streets are wide enough for the hundred or so horse drawn chariots that will accompany his return," he pointed to the center of the city square, "right over there we could erect the most magnificent statue to his greatness."

Peter turned his head to where Eddie had pointed. He was about to reply, when he glanced over at a small boy standing across the street. The child was Arab and dressed in a dirty white thobe. The boy took a step off the curb oblivious to the oncoming traffic. Peter's heart raced, the child's image flickered through the passing cars and still the boy kept walking forward while a large truck barreled down on him. Peter stepped away from the ladder and toward the traffic. Like the low rumbling of a freight train far in the distance, the ghostly voices that tormented him over the phone grew louder and rattled in his head. He wanted to scream out to the boy, but couldn't make a sound.

"How's this look Peter?" Eddie adjusted the banner, "Peter?"

Peter stepped off the curb and ran into traffic towards the boy's direction. The driver of a black sedan blew his horn and slammed on the brakes. He turned as the car hit him mid waist and threw him to the ground.

"Are you fucking crazy?" The driver leapt out of his car.

"Jesus Pete," Eddie knelt over him. "Are you alright?"

"I'm fine." Peter sat up, "there was a boy…"

"Father Cameron," the driver of the sedan had a horrified look on his face. "I … I'm sorry Father I didn't see you…"

"There was a young boy… he was over there," he pointed to a spot where he had last seen the child, the sidewalk was empty and the traffic had continued without stop.

"I never saw any boy," Eddie said.

CHAPTER V: THE DARK HEART

Peter looked at the driver for a sympathetic conformation, but he shook his head. The cars behind the sedan honked their horns as all traffic behind them had come to a halt.

"We'd better get you off the street before we start a riot," Eddie helped Peter to his feet and walked him to the sidewalk. "Are you sure you're ok?"

"Yes, I'm fine," Peter rubbed the back of his head and pointed to the banner, "you'd better fix that before it blows away."

12:03 pm
Isabella Stone's Farmhouse
City of Madonnella
Bari Province, Italy

The lavish three story mansion sprawled across acres of immaculate farmland. Plantation trees imported from America had been planted on either side of the long drive that led up to the house. Fourteen months had passed since the stables for the Arabian horses had been converted to a storage garage for Robert's large industrial equipment. The dozens of tractors and trucks parked side by side and end to end inside the structure now sat unused and abandoned. An enormous shed held the souvenirs from Robert's shipping business; a giant propeller from a Wolfe and Stone cargo ship, an anchor from a decommissioned barge, and a gold stripped smoke stack from a cruise ship he had once owned. And on the far plot of the land was Robert's private sanctuary where Isabella avoided at all cost. Although the land still maintained its air of opulence, the once vibrant and down home feel seemed lifeless and isolated from the warmth of everyday life in Madonnella.

It had been ten years since her affair with Peter Cameron; ten years since that affair had produced her only child. Her marriage with Robert had slowly disintegrated after she confessed of the infidelity. He was always distant but became more so as Emily grew and looked less and less like him and a lot like Peter. He had spent most of those turbulent years on the east lot far away from the main house where he had built his refuge, a giant domed structure which he had named Morgenstern. She had always been concerned about the late night visits from the many faceless strangers that passed the farmhouse only to leave in the dim light of early mornings. But, it was typical of Robert to seclude himself with close compatriots and handle things on his own time-in his own way. She never questioned it; in the months leading up to his disappearance his feelings for her were warmer and they had seemed to grow closer to each other as husband and wife. She had rarely been out there while Robert had lived at home and only once since her terrible visions had started. It was a cold place that looked as if the thick concrete and ridged stone had erupted from the depths of the soft earth. No longer were there any visitors and no longer was there life within its inner sanctum. The hired men kept the grass and field around the farmhouse immaculate, but they were always too afraid to enter the deep woods to Morgenstern; nothing grew there and they kept their distance. The building lay adjacent to her distant neighbor's farm, an elderly couple Serge D'Alisa and his wife who periodically kept watch over her and Emily. Isabella had thought about tearing it down, but it was the only thing that truly remained of Robert. She had decided to sell the property and move far away from Madonnella, but the decision had done nothing to shake the fear she had for herself and for her daughter. Moving boxes had been piled up in each of the many rooms and the antiques were covered by vanilla colored sheets and moved off to the corners.

The driver and the house staff had all been let go; Isabella, her daughter and a single housemaid were all that remained. Her decision to leave was only reinforced by her vivid nightmares; she knew she had to find a place far away, somewhere Robert would never find them. The maid was busy in the backyard collecting the hanging clothes and stacking them neatly in a laundry basket. Isabella had searched the house for Emily, she had promised to go to her bedroom but wasn't there.

"Have you seen Emily?" Isabella stepped off the back porch.

"Isn't she in her room?" asked the Spanish maid Rosa.

Isabella headed towards the rows of vineyards, the leaves bristled in the slight breeze. Each row was marked with circular white signs; in the center red numbers designated the rows 1 thru 15 and beyond them lay an ocean of dark green corn stalks. She stood nervously at the edge of the field, her heart raced and she yelled out for her daughter but heard no answer. She took a deep breath then disappeared beneath the tall waving corn.

"Emily!" it was difficult to see through the dense stalk, "Emily! Emily!" her voice began to tremble.

Isabella heard Emily's soft voice speaking in a low whisper. She headed deeper into the field toward the sound of her daughter; her hands shook uncontrollably. She saw Emily kneeling on the ground with her back to her. She had pressed down the stalks around her feet in a perfect circle that stretched six feet in diameter and sat in the center.

"Emily?" she said with anxious relief. "Who are you talking too honey?"

The child stopped her chanting; she slowly looked over her shoulder and shouted happily, "Daddy!"

The green leaves shuddered slightly as though someone or something was approaching. Terrified, Isabella scooped up her daughter; pressed her to her chest then ran back the way she had come. Emily complained as the leaves scraped across her backside; she covered the child's face with her hand and tried to comfort her.

"But mommy, I want to see daddy."

"Emily please!" tears streamed down Isabella's face. She was lost in the field. She stopped and started and turned in a new direction. Isabella stood in an open part of the crops where another larger circle of downed corn had been carefully arranged. The loud rustling of the leaves encircled her then stopped silent; she listened intently. Through the green she saw a pair of glowing yellow eyes but neither face nor body was visible. Isabella slowly backed away and waited; she took a step forward. Nearby she heard a faint noise rising from the ground, "Eh eh eh eh eh eh eh eh eh eh."

"It's ok mommy, don't be scared," smiled Emily.

Isabella was horrified; her daughters blue eyes had changed to black and she hugged her in a close tearful embrace. Isabella stretched out her arm, with her hand she carefully pulled back the leaves of the stalk. Suddenly there was a loud high pitched screech; she fell to her knees as a flock of black crows flew overhead. Behind her, the husks bent slightly leaving a path that beckoned back to the inner part of the field. The wind circled wildly around them and the edge of the stems cut the air sharply; the field was alive and dangerous. Dozens of nearby ears of corn emitted an audible thump-thump of a heartbeat, and inside bellowed the muffled moaning of a thousand tortured souls. A sick sense of hatred and vengeance was directed at her and her alone. It was as though the field had ensnared them in its trap and refused to let them go. The faint breathing of a wild beast from a hidden place deep within the maze terrified her like nothing ever had. Isabella leapt to her feet; through the tassels of stalk she briefly glimpsed the roof of the white farmhouse. Her legs were numb from carrying the weight of Emily in her arms but she summoned the courage to move. Each stalk was like a pricker bush that clung to their clothing and painfully scraped and sliced at their skin. Isabella swatted the branches away with her hand and as she touched them they withered, turned black and died. Those that fell and were trampled on spurted their thick red blood onto her legs. She raced to the edge of the field, stumbled and fell on top of the child cradled in her arms. The startled maid dropped the laundry basket and immediately ran to their aid.

"No comeback daddy!" Emily's tearful voice beckoned towards the waves of green. "Come back please!"

Isabella found the nerve and turned her head; the corn stalks shook violently, there was something very close, something large that gradually moved away from the farmhouse and deeper into the heart of the field.

The fallen Angel Qeynan was made to stand before the great beast. From his foot he tore a mighty talon and said; Takith of me and you shall have the power of the sword to craft war, to bring forth plague and disease and to hasten the coming of the apocalypse. And Qeynan was turned into wind so that no nation could bar him from its border.

Philetos
libri of cado animus

CHAPTER VI
THE LORD AND THE LAMB

Wednesday 10:10 am
18, October 1978
The Hotel Efron
Jerusalem, Israel

Two men sat in a gray car and waited across the street from the Hotel Efron. A silver haired man elbowed the other younger agent who had been sleeping for the last thirty minutes.

"This is post 33," the silver haired spoke into a walkie-talkie,

"The tourist has left the hotel."

"You have authorization to follow," replied an authoritative voice on the other end.

The Tourist, Vincent Gallo walked slowly but deliberately down the sidewalk, stopping only briefly to peer inside the many restaurants and shops that filled the old city.

"What the fuck is he doing?" asked the younger man.

"I don't know and I don't care, just keep your eyes open for anyone he might be trying to contact."

Gallo had quickened his steps and the men trailing took great effort to keep pace without giving away their positions. He darted through the crowds of native and tourists alike and vanished within the ancient city walls. He cautiously stepped into the alley behind Tipy Aronoff's store and quickly scanned the turf for possible occupants. He knelt behind a large industrial trash container and removed a brown shirt, black cap and dark khaki shorts from inside his jacket. His fingers desperately searched for the package that Minot had stashed and dragged it out from underneath the large garbage bin. Wrapped tightly in clear plastic was an expensive looking brown traveler's bag. Inside were four white tee shirts, four pairs of underwear, two dress shirts (one black, one red), a toothbrush, toothpaste and a hair brush. He unzipped an inner pouch and found a billfold filled with traveler's checks and his picture on a fake passport with the name Stefano Fabiano scribbled underneath. He tossed his former outer clothing into the bag, slung the strap over his shoulder and causally headed out of the alley. On a side street he found an Alfa Romeo Spider convertible with the top down parked in front of a brown brick apartment building. Gallo scanned the street in both directions, threw the traveler's bag in the back seat then hopped in and promptly hotwired the vehicle. He placed his gun on the passenger seat and concealed it with his cap. He adjusted the rearview searching for any signs of the trailing agents then pulled the roof up while he sped away from the curb.

"This is Post 33," the silver haired agent said, "Post 15, has Tourist come your way?"

"Negative."

"Post 5?"

"Negative."

"Alright, listen up," he gripped the walkie-talkie tightly and held it close to his face, "we're gonna do a quick perimeter search, if we don't find him we'll start back at the hotel and see if we can't find any clues he might of left behind and track him down from there."

12:10 pm
Elazar Lighthouse
Haifa, Israel

Gallo parked the stolen car a block from the Elazar Lighthouse; he retrieved the gun and the rest of his belongings and walked up the precipice towards the lighthouse. He was received at the gate by one of Hafsah's large barrel chested bodyguards with an automatic weapon strapped over his shoulder. Hafsah was an old friend, part time architect, part time construction contractor, and full time criminal. The grounds were thoroughly deserted; it was odd for a man of his stature not to have thirty or forty armed men guarding him at all times. The place felt jarringly ghostly and abandoned. The museum connected to the lighthouse had ceased in the middle of construction and the outbuildings on the property looked as though they were in the process of being torn down. They walked through the museum's vast hall with its decorated marble checkerboard floor; each step echoed through the infinite emptiness. They made their way to the red and white striped lighthouse that stood at the back of the property and overlooked the edge of a steep cliff. Without saying a word, his broad shouldered companion showed him the entrance door and walked back the way they had come. Gallo climbed the winding stairs all the way up to the outside observation deck. On the floor above he could see that the large reflecting lens had been disassembled and most of its parts removed from the Lantern Room. Sitting alone in a lawn chair was a very thin, very frail looking Hafsah dressed in a white robe. Gallo was shocked by the extreme change in his appearance. It had only been a few months since he had last seen him face to face and even at the age of seventy Hafsah had always been a hulk of a man.

"Vincent," said the skeleton, "beautiful isn't it." His gaze was squarely focused on the vast blue-green water of the Mediterranean Sea and the magnificent Port of Haifa.

Gallo walked the outer edge of the deck eyeing Hafsah as he went. It was always hard to get a good read on the man, but he did his best to size him up. He was heavily perfumed with scented oils and the sweet smell of burning incense coated the air.

"It is," Gallo peered through the mounted telescope that was fixed towards the direction of the bay, "or it was. What happened out front?"

"Those Jewish bastards revoked my permits and are forcing me to tear everything down," Hafsah took a long sip of tea from a silver cup that sat next to him. "They think I'm a terrorist, ridiculous isn't it? They accuse and insinuate with their slanderous words, but they have no evidence to charge me... so instead they're trying to make my life a living hell."

"Or maybe it's because of your new friends and the company you keep."

"New friends?"

"Arafat," Gallo sat down in the chair next to him, "You're pressing your luck doing business with someone like that."

"I see François has been busy filling your head with wicked ideas," he laughed, turned his face and coughed blood into a handkerchief, "Israel is changing rapidly my friend; it's always good to know who the top players are."

"Sure seems like an awfully dangerous game you're playing."

"It certainly is an awfully dangerous game you're playing Vincent or should I say Cecellini. You're lucky you weren't shot before you took one step off the plane."

"Harkir Saldalha?"

"He's one of many."

"Who is he?"

"A murderous thug trying to make a name for himself. He rose through the ranks of the Hherev syndicate," Hafsah took another sip of black tea, "two years ago he took charge after the former leader Yoseph Ham was murdered outside a casino in Monaco."

"And they let an outsider like Saldalha take control."

"Things don't work they way they used to in the old days Vincent; assassination and mindless brutality are his signature and he does it well. He's not crazy, just ruthless and everybody who knows of his reputation is rightly afraid of him. Saldalha the Turk owns casinos, hotels, politicians and large swaths of Beersheba."

"A man after your own heart, sounds like you know him well."

"He asked me for the use of my equipment for an excavation at Negev and I gave it to him."

"When did you become interested in ancient civilizations?"

"When a man like Saldalha asks you, it's better if you don't turn him down. I even had my son work as the Second Shift Forman," Hafsah cleared his throat. "I also found out that the man you're searching for; Cardinal Rourke had gone to Negev."

"Did you talk to him?" Gallo leaned forward now more engrossed, "Cardinal Rourke I mean."

"No. But I know thirty of Saldalha's men were hired to work for a man named Grigory Santeal, or should I say Father Grigory Santeal."

"Do you know what they were searching for?"

"They unearthed a great evil at Negev," Hafsah sounded more reflective, "my son was one of those who exhumed the ancient Temple of Metatron. He told me that he had stared down the doorway to hell; he was so ashamed and so distraught at what he had done. He changed; he wouldn't talk to anyone not even to his wife. I brought him into my home to settle his troubled mind. I tried to comfort him, but nothing I could do helped. One night he smashed the window of his bedroom and with the broken shards of glass he tore himself to pieces. To the best of my knowledge none of the men who saw the entrance to the temple are alive today."

"I'm sorry for your loss," said Gallo. It was the first time he noticed Hafsah's eyes were covered with a thick blue haze.

"I went there, to Negev. I had to see it for myself; I wanted to make sense of it all. That's when I found Cardinal Rourke's camp; he had kept a safe distance hidden on a mountainside overlooking the dig site. Among the many books I found this, his private journal," Hafsah handed the book to Gallo, "he wanted to stop Father Santeal; he planned to kill him and I think he tried, but I don't think he survived. I spent a horrible night at that campsite. I felt the evil that surrounded that place rush through every part of my body and it changed me. In the early daylight I watched the dust storm barrel down from the east and the earth swallow up the temple and send it back to its grave. There's no trace of it now; absolutely none."

Gallo skimmed through the journal trying not to look at Hafsah's face, "What happen to you?"

"I was made to bear witness with the death of my son and with the destruction of the temple. I've seen what no sane man should see Vincent. I know I sound crazy, but I was given a dire vision of the future triumphed by the rise of men dedicated to an unholy purpose. I was left afflicted and cursed with the eyes of the damned; I know of the resurrection and the coming of the unspeakable."

"Is there anything I can do for you, I mean I could talk to Cavilary and have him fix things with the Israelis," Gallo knew if Hafsah was sent back to Egypt he was as good as dead.

"Don't worry about me; I am at peace with the choices I've made. My father used to tell me the story of the Lord and the Lamb when I was a young boy. He told me... he whoever comes into the land and worships the Lord shall be shown favor before the Lord, and he who does not cherish him and commits desecrations against him shall be slaughtered like the lamb. I assure you Vincent, I am no lamb," Hafsah flashed an unconvincing smile. "Everything will be made right in due time."

"I'm sorry my friend," Gallo stood, "but I have to go." He walked over to the entrance of the stairwell.

"Vincent," Hafsah's voice strained, "I know there's nothing I could say to dissuade you from your journey and the choice you will make, so I won't waste time. Just remember, don't be fooled by his words; he will tempt you. Read the journal--all of it; make sure you are prepared when the time comes. If afterwards you are still determined to continue your quest I can tell you now... you won't like what you find."

Gallo nodded his head, said his goodbyes and left. Hafsah's bodyguard had gone and the grounds were empty. He wandered through the museum and let himself out the front gate. When he got to the street he walked in the opposite direction from which he had arrived and caught the bus headed to Tel Aviv.

Hafsah wanted to enjoy this day of all days but the pain was too severe. "Eh eh eh eh eh eh eh eh," the sound from inside the lighthouse bounced off the walls with increasing ferocity. Hafsah agonizingly rose to his feet; his bones creaked badly from the strain. His robe fell open and revealed the thousands of bugs and maggots that clung to his belly. The flies had already laid their eggs inside his stomach and the larva had hatched in his intestines. They voraciously ate away at the raw red skin from his midsection to underneath his breastbone. Hundreds of the bug and beetle infestation fell off in piles of thick clumps of decomposing flesh and chunks of putrefied organ as he stumbled towards the railing. "Eh eh eh eh eh eh eh eh," it made its way up through the lighthouse and edged nearer to the observation deck. His hands gripped the cold metal railing as his atrophied legs desperately needed the support. Even through the near blindness he could tell that today was a beautiful day; he remembered with clarity how beautiful his adopted country really was. He smiled thinking of his only son who had once been his biggest source of pride and the wife he had loved a lifetime. He rocked back and forth then with the last of his strength heaved himself over the guardrail. His diseased body fell a hundred and ninety feet and crashed upon the serrated rocks below. His thin frail form instantly shattered into a thousand pieces and was quickly washed out to sea.

Gallo sat by himself on the long ride to Tel Aviv. He opened Cardinal Rourke's journal, there were some words written in English, some in Latin and some in a language he had never seen. There was a telephone number scribbled on one of the pages and beneath it Rourke had written several reminders:

'ask Peter about Metatron.'
'ask Peter about the circle of life.'
'what is the Trilogy?'
'what are the desecrations?'

On the next page was a sketch of a demonic creature with large ram horns bursting from the sides of its head. In its palms he held the earth, and on the earth was drawn a circle inside a triangle inside a circle. Underneath the picture was scribed the name of the Angel Hector.

Around 3:00 pm Gallo entered the Ra'anan Hotel and gave his name to the woman at the front desk.

"Mr. DiMartino," she said, "your room is still being prepared, we weren't expecting you till later tonight."

"That's all right," Gallo placed the traveler's bag on the counter. "Can I leave this here with you?"

"Of course," she nodded.

"I have some business to take care of and then I'll be back say... around five."

"That'll be fine," she handed over the room keys, "I hope you enjoy your stay with us."

Gallo stepped back onto the street; he kept the journal, forged passport and checks with him and slipped them inside his jacket. The street was fairly crowded but he felt sure he hadn't been followed. He lit a cigarette to calm his nerves; the sight of Hafsah in his weakened condition and the reading of only a few pages of Rourke's journal had made him feel uneasy. He turned down a street crowded with restaurants and markets that lined each side and enjoyed the aroma of grilled hamburgers that wafted out of the American Restaurant. He chose to be seated at an outside table and disinterestedly thumbed through the colorful menu. His eyes methodically searched until they found Minot's 'X' taped across the base of a gray light post.

The fallen Angel Thaydien was made to stand before the great beast. From his mouth he tore a jagged tooth and said; Takith of me and you shall have the power to judge and condemn mankind, the power to rule over living earth and the power to resurrect the dead. And Thaydien was made mortal and given the libri of cado animus so that he may rule over the lands of Sudea and Talise and the Kingdome of Thaydien and Kashar and lands beyond.

Philetos
libri of cado animus

CHAPTER VII
THE EYE OF THE STORM

Friday 11:49 am
20, October 1978
Hospes of St. Cecilia
City of Madonnella
Bari Province, Italy

Isabella's eyes were heavy and bloodshot. She spent the night beside her daughter's hospital bed dutifully watching over her. Her daughter kicked and thrashed so violently that she destroyed two of the standard wooden beds and forced the orderlies to bring a heavy reinforced iron frame from storage. Her feet and hands were then strapped to each of the thick posts. Emily's condition had steadily worsened since Isabella had pulled her from the depths of the cornfield. Her skin showed no trace of color and had scabbed horribly around her face and neck. There were dark circles underneath her eyes; the doctor's had heavily sedated her and her breathing was leaden and congested. There were no private rooms in St. Cecilia sixth floor Children's Ward; instead a thin curtain encircled the small space around her bedside. Father Story led Isabella out of the ward and into the hallway to where several nuns had gathered for their daily afternoon shift changes.

"What is it? What's wrong with my child?" Isabella wanted Father Story to tell her the answer she already knew.

"We have the best doctors in the world and they will do everything they can to help Emily through this."

"You saw her face; you saw her eyes," her voice was shaky; "the doctors can't treat the sickness she's suffering from, you know that. I brought her here because I need your help Father. I need you to save Emily."

"Your daughter is very sick and because of that she will need you to be strong; if not for her than for yourself."

"Why aren't you listening to me?" Isabella leaned back against the cold gray wall for support. "I thought it was just a horrible nightmare but it isn't, it's all real and it's only getting worse. You can't tell me that you don't know what's happening to her?"

"If you and I are to be of any help to Emily now, I insist you go home and get some rest," Father Story put his arm around Isabella to comfort her. "I will contact you if her condition changes in any way. I promise you."

Isabella gathered herself together, her resolve had collapsed. She knew Father Story was desperate to avoid any use of the word possession; to even think that it could be was madness. Maybe the doctors could diagnose her illness, maybe there was a cure but it all seemed like nothing more than empty comfort and wishful thinking. She tried to explain away her daughter's condition with reason and logic, but she knew the truth; her daughter's soul was dying and she was helpless to stop it. Isabella turned to face Father Story, "I know only you can save her now."

The young Sister Marian doted over Emily as she lay comatose. She held a string of rosary beads in her hand and knelt beside her bed and prayed. Sister Marian had been present when the mysterious child was brought to the hospital screaming and thrashing in the grips of agonizing pain. She had never seen a child so sick before and had brought with her a six inch wooden crucifix with the delicate image of Christ carved on its face. With the tips of her fingers she searched for a small hook that protruded from the cement wall above the headboard. She stood on a chair next to the bed and hung the crucifix above Emily's head. "Rest peacefully my child," Sister Marian enclosed the curtain around her bed, "God is with you now."

Friday 1:09 pm
Manna Book Store
City of Madonnella
Bari Province, Italy

Peter had fallen asleep at a desk in his basement bedroom. He hadn't slept through the night in months and it began to manifest physically. He was sure he had heard the strange voices on the telephone and seen the young Arab boy walking into traffic, but now he questioned everything. Was he just hallucinating? Was it the drugs he took? His mind drifted back to his childhood, back to Portland, Oregon where he was born and spent the first eight years of his life before he had moved to Madonnella. It was strange, in the past he had few memories of his father or growing up in America, but his feelings about that time were clear even if the images weren't. They raced through his mind in an odd and fairly disjointed manner. He was five years old playing in the living room with his best friend Billy; then it jumped to the sorrow of Billy's family after they found his body at the bottom of their well. Flashes of being baptized in the icy Cowlitz River; the priest gently holding his head underwater and seeing the ghostly figures of the congregation and his father's images distorted by the flow of the current. These dreams must hold some truth within them, undoubtedly they served a purpose, but to his conscious mind they were absolutely meaningless. The visions kept repeating themselves over and over as though they were being shown on an endless film loop. It was subtle, but in each dream he heard something faint in the background, something he knew had not been there at the time. "Eh eh eh eh eh eh eh," the sound was a loose wire that interconnected each of the visions from his past. In this new version of his dream after hearing the eerie noise, Billy's flesh instantly rotted to the bone and turned to dust. The faces of Billy's weeping family standing near the well melted like hot wax, and with his own eyes he witnessed the baptismal water above his face churn thick with blood. The fear jolted him awake and he pushed himself away from his desk. He heard voices and a commotion at the front of the store where the hometown celebrity Mario Pascale had entered and was greeting a few of the stunned customers. He washed his face, quickly dressed and headed up the stairs.

"Peter!" Mario's voice was filled with excitement, "At last the prodigal son has returned and I've come bearing gifts."

"Runaway Peter he's trying to buy our love," Eddie held up an expensive set of paint brushes and a finely handcrafted wooden easel, "sadly it's working."

"I love it, "Angela had a handmade French scarf slung around her neck; she kissed Mario several times on the cheek, "It's perfect thank you-thank-you-thank you."

"I didn't forget you Peter," Mario held out a large rectangular frame wrapped in plain brown paper. "I was in Spain for the last week of the tour and I thought of you; I don't know it just spoke to me."

Angela and Eddie excitedly gathered around Peter. He tore away the paper revealing an old oil painting of the biblical Leviathan, and in the distance shrouded in early morning mist was a large white monastery. The hands of the creature tightly gripped the body of a man; it had already consumed the head and hungrily ripped away at the flesh on his chest. The image was like the beast that had haunted his nightmares for months; Sado Satanus the Antichrist on earth.

"It's beautiful," Eddie instantly recognized it, "Marino's The Devil of László. He painted this and several others like it on the walls inside the Abbey of László called the dark paintings."

"A portrait of his long descent into madness," Peter was mesmerized, instantly he found himself sharing a kinship with the troubled artist.

"I'm impressed, it looks authentic," Eddie held the frame and closely examined the canvas. "Where did you find this?"

"I told you--Spain," Mario grinned, "and I paid through the nose to get it so it better be real."

"I think it's dreadful," Angela averted her eyes, "he must have been really sick to have painted something so evil."

"Nonsense, Eddie's right it's beautiful; I couldn't have asked for a better present," Peter looked for a suitable place to hang the picture. "So, what was it that made you think of me when you bought this?"

"It's old and unapologetically religious... just like you. According to ancient mythology, the Devil was defeated on the field of battle as he took the form of the Red King and was trapped inside the Abbey of László," Mario placed his hands on Eddie and Angela's shoulders. "They say there's a pit in the abbey where mummified corpses stand guard; twelve priests staged around the gate of hell under the watchful gaze of King Sabaoth, Lord of the Armies of Israel."

"I remember the Village of László from my youth; it's only a few hours' drive from here. When I was a child my father sent me away to study at the oldest school in the province. You'd love it," Peter turned to Angela, "It's like the town's been permanently frozen in the middle ages. I still have a few odd memories of that time; the one that stands out the most is of Father Fuerst, the Chancellor of my school. The stern look from his cold blue eyes always terrified me down to the core."

"Peter you're not really going to hang that up here? Are you?" asked Angela.

"Of course I am," he found a place above the entrance to his basement apartment. "All who see it shall beware the gates of hell."

"I also found this," Mario removed a plastic cylinder from his bag; inside was a worn and tattered scroll, "an original page from The Book of Heironymos; in Latin."

A cold chill ran through Peter's body; instantly he knew it was the book he had been searching for, the book that would force him to confront his fears. He had worked as a researcher and librarian for the Vatican, read and translated thousands of books on nature, theology, history and more and could recite every page, every paragraph, every line and every word. He knew the Book of Heironymos was only a small part of a greater picture--a picture when fully developed would lead his memories back to the libri of cado animus, and through the pages that would foretell of obscene horrors to come.

Saturday 2:00 pm
21, October 1978
Kadira Apartments
Beersheba, Israel

Gallo walked through the rundown courtyard near the Kadira Apartments. There were dozens of Arab and immigrant African children playing soccer on a dilapidated pitch that was more rock than grass. He strolled along a four foot high chain link fence listening to their raucous noise. He passed several of the six-story Kadira apartments that sat only a few hundred yards from each other on the sprawling dirt lot. Gallo took another look at the map Minot had hidden in the bathroom ceiling of the American

Restaurant. He was beginning to wonder if he had actually tracked Marko and the siyah yılan back to this slum or if he had gotten bored and picked the first name that came to him. Then he spotted a powder blue Subaru van parked on the grass in back of building 6 and began his slow approach. He could see the belly of a fat man seated behind the wheel and a broad shouldered man loading bags in the back. Both men were Turkish and very well dressed; they easily stood out in the poor mainly Arab neighborhood.

"Merhaba beyler, bir dakika var? (Hello gentlemen, you have a minute?)" Gallo approached the man loading the van first, but was ignored. "Avete un minute?" Nothing; the man kept loading the van. "Look, we need to talk."

"Fuck off!" replied the Turk.

"So you do speak English. Great." Gallo glimpsed inside the van, "I'm looking for a couple of guys you might know…"

"I said fuck off!"

"It's important I speak with Marko or Emir. Are they here?"

"Perhaps my English is not so good, I don't know any Marko or Emir," he jumped inside the van, tossed a large gray striped duffle bag onto the passenger seat and began stacking cement bags behind the driver's side seat.

"We can play this game all day or you can tell me where I can find the leaders of siyah yılan," he could see the man had a reaction to the name, "let me guess, you're gonna tell me that you've never heard of them either?"

"No, I heard of them."

The man slowly reached inside his jacket for his gun. He spun around quickly, but before he could aim Gallo squeezed off a single shot from his silencer. The man was thrown back against the side door; a thick spray of blood burst from the back of his head and coated the inside walls. The Turk slumped to the floor with a dime sized hole in the center of his forehead. In one fluid motion Gallo leapt inside the back of the van and closed the distance to the front seats. In a panic the driver lunged for the glove compartment, his lower half lodged between the seat and steering wheel while his left arm was trapped underneath him.

"Don't kill me! Don't kill me!" The fat man begged. "I'm just the driver."

Gallo used his elbow to break the man's nose then struck him several more times; the van shook wildly, the glove compartment dropped open and a handgun fell to the floor.

"Just the driver," Gallo picked up the gun, "And what were you planning on doing with this?"

"I have a family, four kids ..."

"I just want a few answers then I'll be on my way." Gallo handcuffed the man's free hand to the steering wheel. "Where's Marko?"

"I don't know," his answer was met with another elbow to the face. "I swear I don't know. He told us to stay here and he and the priest went to find someone named Dante Costa."

"And?"

"Costa's hotel was overrun with Israeli ajanlar (agents) so they took off. Marko told us to wait here and he would contact us later; I swear that's the truth."

"Who was the priest?"

"Father Lanyard or Lynward. I'm not sure." The man struggled to clear his thoughts.

"You need to do better than that." Gallo raised his fist.

"Layad!" the man blurted out, "Father Anton Layad."

He hadn't heard the name before, it wasn't in Cavilary's report or Rourke's journal and he was skeptical of the new information. "What about Emir Saldalha?"

"He's here, room 9."

"Anymore siyah yılan with him?"

"No. It was just us."

"Good," Gallo threw the key for the handcuffs on the floor."

"Thank you. I just want to go home; I swear I won't say a word to anyone."

"I know." Gallo fired two shots into the back of his head then slipped on a pair of black gloves. He stepped over the dead Turk lying in back and slowly exited the van closing the doors behind him. He entered building 6 from the front and made his way to the downstairs apartments. At the end of the long badly lit hallway was room 9. He carefully traversed the corridor with his hand tucked inside his jacket gripping the handle of the silencer. The door to room 9 opened; Gallo pretended to unlock the door to room 7. A Ghanaian prostitute exited Emir's room and smiled as she passed him by. He waited for her to leave, drew his gun then swung the door open. Bob Marley's Ambush in the Night spun on the record player and he could hear the shower running from the next room. On the bed was an open backpack and in it were several light blue uniforms with James Wolfe and Robert Stone Shipping and Freight embroidered on the back. He walked into the small kitchen area; on the stove was a pan of leftover sini kebabı and on the front burner was an open pot of boiling water. Gallo holstered his gun; turned up the heat on the water and ate a slice of the kebabı. The music stopped and he reset the record:

> *"...Ambush in the night,*
> *All guns aiming at me;*
> *Ambush in the night,*
> *They opened fire on me now.*
> *Ambush in the night,*
> *Protected by His Majesty..."*

"Bu seni Jorin? (That you Jorin?)" Emir shouted from the shower as he washed the soap from his face. "Van yükleme bitirdin mi? (Finish loading the van)" There was no answer. He stepped out of the shower but kept the water running and slipped on a pair of jeans. Emir picked up his gun from atop the toilet tank and slowly clicked the safety off. The music from the living room was louder now as he crept towards the door. "Is that you my little flower?" he slowly twisted the doorknob, stepped into the short hallway and scanned the living room. "Come back for more?"

"Not exactly," Gallo threw the boiling water in his face.

Emir cried out, dropped the gun and instinctively raised his hands to his eyes. Gallo hit him across the back of the neck and he fell to the floor. He kicked him hard in the side of the head and his body fell limp. After twenty minutes Emir awoke after receiving a firm slap to his face. The room was darkly lit. His eyes were swollen shut and his face was bright red and covered with blisters. He found himself tied to a chair with his hands handcuffed behind his back.

"We need to talk," Gallo's voice was like a siren from the abyss.

"Fuck you," Emir choked on blood from his battered jaw and broken nose.

"I need to know where Marko is," Gallo set a chair in front of him and sat down, "and I need you to tell me who Father Layad is."

"Fuck you. You're going to kill me anyway so why should I tell you shit."

"That's just it; there are quick'n easy ways to die, and there are slow and hard ways to die. I found this in the boiler room, it might help you think about which path you're willing to take," Gallo held a blowtorch in his hand and ignited it with his pocket lighter.

"FUCK YOU!" He spit a glob of blood in Gallo's face.

"Great! The hard way it is," he adjusted the valve until a long orange flame streamed out the end of the burner.

Saturday 7:09 pm
The Old City (near the Temple Mount)
Jerusalem, Israel

Cardinal Rudolph Fuerst, accompanied by a heavy set innkeeper descended the lengthy stone stairway far beneath The Old City. The innkeeper's hotel was a popular tourist destination and sat directly above the entrance to the primeval catacombs.

"Brother Fuerst, it's obvious to me that the deal I made with you and Brother Santeal has put me in an untenable position. It's bad enough I had to lend rooms to the siyah yılan, but your Mr. Stone is reckless."

"You've been paid quite handsomely for your inconvenience Brother," Cardinal Fuerst was visibly annoyed by the innkeeper's constant complaints. "If you want to change the terms of our agreement you'll have to talk to Brother Santeal."

"You think I want more money?" laughed the innkeeper. "What good will money do me if I'm hanging from the end of a rope?"

"Then what do you want, Brother?"

"My hotel has a reputation for being friendly and safe," the innkeeper unlocked the door to a mile long maze that led beneath the Temple Mount, "Two days ago a woman from Romania disappeared, and today two young women from England went missing after that; all three were guests at my hotel. They have friends and families, and I'm sure their schedules were well known to both."

"And why should any of these missing women be of interest to me?"

"I saw these women with Mr. Stone, no doubt others did too," he held the oil lamp in front of his face. "People have seen me holding private conversations with you, Brother Santeal and Stone; it won't be long till the police come around and start asking questions and connecting us together."

"You're beginning to bore me Brother, just tell me what you want," Cardinal Fuerst adjusted the flame in his lantern.

"I want you to leave; tonight."

"We will leave once Father Santeal has completed his work."

"Father Santeal! Father Santeal!" cackled the innkeeper, "your position in the Catholic Church means nothing to me and as far as I'm concerned BROTHER Santeal and I are equal in the eyes of the Council."

"Of course, I meant Brother Santeal."

"That brings me to another matter, one that I find very interesting. I contacted the Council today and they didn't even know you were here in Israel," the innkeeper stopped walking. "Just what are you up to Brother Fuerst?"

There was a sound of heavy sobbing coming from a hundred feet away; the two men ventured off the safe marked trail and entered a catacomb that lay near the bottom of the unearthed maze. Inside the two English women lay chained to the far wall; one still had the gag tightly wrapped around her mouth. It was her cries that the men had heard; the other voiceless victim sat against the wall with her eyes staring blankly into the darkness. She was in shock, her legs and forearms had been chewed to the bone. The deep animalistic breathing and yellow eyes of Robert Stone filled the room with horror. The innkeeper held out his lantern; Stone's face was much more demonic than man. Gray skin covered the ten foot behemoth; his skull was large and wide and white tusks protruded from his jowls. He sat hunched over in the corner opposite his prey. His powerful hands gripped the girl's severed femur and his sharp teeth gnawed away at the specks of remaining muscle. In a haphazard pile at his feet were a collection of bleached white bones and large fragments of broken skull.

"It can't be, this is impossible," the innkeeper turned to leave as quickly as he could, but Father Santeal blocked the entrance.

"He wanted to know what we were doing down here," Cardinal Fuerst felt the presence of Father Santeal, but never averted his gaze from the feeding. "He also told me something very interesting; it turns out our friend contacted the Council today."

"You should never question my word... Brother," Father Santeal stepped towards the frightened man pushing him backwards into the room.

"What... is... he?" his voice was shaking.

"He is part of the resurrection and the coming of a new age," Father Santeal put his hands on the innkeeper's shoulders and pressed him against the wall, "You however are an annoyance, a mindless and feckless creature who can no longer be tolerated," he raised his right hand and put his palm flat against the innkeeper's forehead, "And you shall live the rest of your life down here in the darkness feasting off the insects and rodents to survive."

The innkeeper felt his skull vibrate, his forehead burned and blistered from where Santeal's palm made contact with his skin. He wanted to raise his arms and swat the hand away, but his mind was paralyzed. The cerebrospinal fluid in his head boiled then quickly thickened into a toxic green slime that seeped into his brain. He saw flashes of bright white light, then his eyes rolled up into his head and in an instant all intelligent thought was gone. Father Santeal released his grip, ushered him away and left him to haunt the depths of the catacombs for all eternity.

"If he's made contact with the Council, they will certainly send someone to Jerusalem; it may not be the wisest of ideas to try your little trick with all of them," said Cardinal Fuerst.

"I have found what I needed," Father Santeal knelt in front of the dead girl, fascinated by her cold stare. He handed a heavy object wrapped in purple cloth to Cardinal Fuerst.

"The sword of Sabaoth, Lord of the Armies of Israel," Fuerst unraveled the cloth to reveal the long straight blade of a giant Claymore. It's shine was dull and had shown the wear of being encased in earth and rock for centuries far below the Temple Mount Mosque. "The sword that killed the great beast, the Antichrist on Earth."

Father Santeal closed his eyes and placed his hand on the dead girl's forehead. Her body twitched, air rushed through her lungs and she took a deep breath. Her eyes opened, she raised her severed limbs and screamed from the depths of unimaginable hurting. Father Santeal gripped her by the neck and effortlessly tossed her across the room to the beast Robert had become. Like a wild dog he viciously tore into her and devoured her remains. Father Santeal moved on to the second girl; her body was shaking and her eyes were tightly shut. He gently brushed the hair away from her face and wiped away her tears.

"We're leaving now Robert," Father Santeal said over his shoulder, "finish your meal and get dressed."

Robert had transformed back to his human form and from a large metal bucket he washed the blood and various bits of chewed guts and tissue from his face and body. His handsome face and dirty blonde hair had returned but his eyes stayed a permanent glowing yellow. The inverted cross scar from his desecration remained on his body and was imbedded in his skin like a permanent tattoo.

"You should really find your own kills," Robert quipped.

"You'll be alright... for now," Father Santeal turned his attention back to the frightened face of the young English girl.

"Well gentleman, how do I look?" Robert blurted out as he donned a pair of pressed slacks and dress shirt. "You boys have fun now; I'm off to conquer the world." He slipped a pair of dark glasses over his eyes, flashed a bright white toothy grin then vanished from the room with inhuman speed.

"He has a keen habit of disappearing," said a concerned Cardinal Fuerst. "I hate to admit it but the innkeeper was right, he should never have chosen women he was seen with."

"Until the circle is complete we won't be able to take full advantage of our powers," Father Santeal held the girls trembling hands. "The feedings are necessary; they help replenish us every time we use them."

"Please, don't' kill me," the girl managed to spit out her gag, her eyes teared and her nose ran as she snorted the words, "I promise not to tell anyone."

"Shhhh," Father Santeal leaned toward her, "you know I can't do that." His eyes burned red, he dislodged his lower jawbone and revealed a set of long sharp fangs. He sank his upper teeth in just above her hairline and his lower incisors into her jawbone. She began to kick and claw her nails across his face, but it only heightened his sense of enjoyment. With the sickening sound of crushed aluminum, he bit her face off and sucked her brain out leaving only the empty cavity behind. He put his hand on her shoulder and her body burned, broke apart and floated through the room like tiny fragments of tissue paper placed on an open fire.

The fallen Angel Hector was made to stand before the great beast. With his dying breath he gave him his greatest power. He tore the tip of a ram's horn from his head and said; Takith of me so that you may have dominion over all mankind, living and dead, and rule Tartarus the land below hell for a thousand years until my return. And Hector was made deity, the Red King Sado Satanus and sent to reign in Hades and on earth for a thousand years.

Philetos
libri of cado animus

CHAPTER VIII
THE POSSESSION

Sunday 7:00 pm
22, October 1978
Hospes of St. Cecilia
City of Madonnella
Bari Province, Italy

Sister Marian walked the sixth floor children's ward, her attention only diverted slightly by the laughing of her closest friend Sister Boyett and the Nigerian maintenance man standing near the elevator. The two women were French; the only twenty-one year olds that staffed the Hospes and the generational difference made it difficult to relate to the older and more stately nuns. She sat at her station behind the cluttered counter just outside the Children's Ward room. She took notice of a strange sound. It was faint at first, but she definitely heard the sound of metal screeching across the cement floor. Again, in a short burst but this time much louder. Sister Boyett and the maintenance man were still engaged in conversation and unaware of the odd noise that bellowed from within the children's quarter. She had a sudden overwhelming fear for the little girl Father Story had brought into the Hospes. Slowly she walked into the darkness of the open doorway and disappeared into the black.

A long ear piercing screech startled Sister Boyett and she looked over toward the empty counter where Sister Marian had sat moments earlier. She heard the repeated thumping of metal hitting the cold cement floor, then a loud boom and glass shattering into pieces. The sixth floor shook, instantly the cries and screams of the terrified children poured out of the ward. She and the maintenance man ran to their aid and found Sister Marian on the floor seated in the broken glass. Her eyes were wide with disbelief. She was oblivious to the others around her and the expression on her face was locked in a vacant stare.

"Are you alright?" Sister Boyett knelt next to her friend and held her hand; she didn't respond. She examined her arms and legs but there were no cuts.

"I saw it. I saw it," Sister Marian shook her head in bewilderment as tears streamed down her face.

"What did you see?" the Nigerian tried to help her to her feet, but she refused to budge.

He and Sister Boyett turned in the direction of her gaze. Emily Stone's heavy metal frame bed was five feet off the floor and the thick legs were imbedded in the cement wall. The soiled mattress and tattered bedding lay overturned on the floor. Hundreds of fat meal worms crawled through a large pile of human excrement. The crucifixion cross above Emily's bed lay on the floor broken in two and a trickle of blood flowed from the palms and ankles of the Jesus carving.

"I saw it," Sister Marian cried as she looked into the face of her friend. "I saw the face of the Devil," she sank her head in her hands and sobbed hysterically, "It was horrible. So evil, so…"

The maintenance man inched towards the broken window; in the moonlight he saw the silhouette of a child in a hospital gown running east into the valley. They were six stories up in a building with no trellis or fire escape. He shook his head knowingly, "Within that child I see the end of the world."

Father Story and the maintenance man trekked deep into the forest until they came upon a small clearing at the edge of an old graveyard. The Nigerian shined his flashlight on the soft ground, tiny footprints were rooted in the thick mud. A six foot fence surrounded the perimeter of the cemetery and a corner of the steel mesh had been torn and pulled back.

"The child is here," Father Story pulled the mesh wire up and the two men entered.

The cemetery was an enormous collection of marble and stone mausoleums, crypts and gravestones. They traced the footprints until they abruptly stopped and the two men separated to continue the search for Emily. Father Story made his way up towards a ranch house that sat at the top of a hill. The door was open; a wide trail of blood led from the stoop into the interior. Father Story slowed his pace and cautiously moved closer. His weight creaked the planks of the old oak steps and the sound stirred motion within the house. He stopped in his tracks and listened for an instant then took another step. A dog's low growl and nails scraping on the wood floor warned of imminent danger. A large brown Rottweiler barreled through the doorway knocking Father Story to the ground and took off towards the graveyard's inner sanctuary.

The maintenance man walked pass a dozen well kept mausoleums and ornate tombstones until he finally saw her. She knelt under the shelter of a tall elm tree with her back to him.

"Hey little girl, everyone's been looking for you," he tried to hide the fear in his voice as he bent over and reached out to her. She abruptly turned and her face sent chills down his spine. The whites of her eyeballs were turned into pools of lifeless black. Her neck and gown were covered in dried blood and a fresh stream of crimson poured from the corners of her lips and coated her chin. Her tiny fingers picked at the bones of a half eaten forearm and hand. The Nigerian backed away in horror as the grave keeper's dog emerged from behind the trunk of the elm tree. The corners of the dog's mouth tensed and it bared its teeth. The man ran blindly into the heart of the graveyard with the dog closing the distance in pursuit. He saw the light of the grave keeper's house and changed his direction. The dog leapt into the air, its jaws sank into his shoulder and the sudden force knocked him to the ground. He hit the Rottweiler with his flashlight and staggered to his feet. The dog grabbed hold of his arm, flailed its head back and forth and burrowed its canines down to the bone. The Rott temporarily released its grip only to barrel into him and hurl the two combatants into the mouth of an open grave.

The Nigerian was rapidly losing blood and he knew he was close to passing out. His shaking hands clawed at the roots and tumbling dirt as he tried to pull himself up and out. He heard the deep guttural growl of the dog below and desperately tried to hoist the lower half of his body out of peril. In the moonlight he could see the deep tear in his flesh that ran from his wrist bone to the middle of his bicep. He managed to fold both arms underneath his chin and slowly raise himself up. He glanced upward towards the sky; Emily stood above him with hatred in her face. She struck him across the cheek with the pointed edge of a shovel and he lost his hold and fell back into the grave. She was content, she couldn't see him but she heard his mournful cries as the dog destroyed his body.

"Emily!" Father Story stood only a few feet away. He extended his arm and held a small silver cross in front of her face. "My poor child, your soul is impure, contaminated by the seed of the Devil but you must fight it. You must stand against the evil coursing through your being and God will see it in his heart to save you." He stepped forward, his voice tempered, "From the snares of the Devil, deliver us O' Lord. That thy church may serve thee in peace and liberty; we beseech thee to hear us. That thou may crush down all enemies of thy church; we beseech thee to hear us."

Emily's legs weakened, her world spun at a dizzying pace and she fell to the ground unconscious. Father Story cradled her in his arms and brushed the strands of hair from her face. He pulled her close and stared at her ashen features; he could see the contours of her skull had physically warped in its shape.

Father Story whispered in her ear, "The Devil roams around like a roaring lion, looking for someone to devour. Be firm in your faith and resist him." He kissed her on the forehead and carried her out of the desolation of the graveyard.

Sunday 7:26 pm
Manna Book Store

Mario leaned against the kitchen doorjamb and watched his friends Peter, Eddie and Angela set up for the night's gala honoring him. He stared at Peter; he had lost a lot of weight and physically looked to have aged quite dramatically.

"You look like shit," Mario put his hand against Peter's face and examined the dark circles underneath his eyes.

"Office hours are closed doctor," Peter smiled and carried off empty boxes to the storage room.

"So what'd you give him?" Mario found it hard to control his anger.

"You mean me? What did I give him?" Eddie was surprised.

"Cut the shit Eddie, I can tell he's on something and you're the only resident addict here," Mario grabbed him by the wrist. "Jesus I can smell the weed all over your clothes."

"I didn't give him anything," he yanked his hand from Mario's grip. "He wanted something to help him sleep but I told him I only smoked joints. Look he was in desperate shape so I gave him the number of a guy I know."

"So you don't give a shit if he gets screwed up and becomes a junkie?"

"Fuck you! You weren't here for him Mario; you haven't heard the way he screams through the night. You were off living your life and traveling the world." Eddie stormed off, "Sorry if I was the only one left in his life who gave a damn."

Peter moved the rolling ladder down the isle of cluttered shelves in the back storage room. He climbed to the top of the ladder and searched through the boxes of Christmas ornaments and holiday decorations until he found a small carton of green and blue ribbon. He looked up as the fluorescent ceiling lights flickered then went out. He knew the sound was coming even before he heard its unnatural tune, 'eh eh eh eh eh eh eh eh eh'. His heartbeat quickened and he gripped the arms of the ladder tightly. Countless seconds passed as the room was bathed in total darkness. The lights flickered on and the room was brought back to life. At the bottom rung stood the small Arab boy he had seen walking precariously through the oncoming traffic. Peter's body started to shake; consciously he slowly moved down the ladder. He knew the boy wasn't real--he couldn't be real, but there he stood at his side with eyes cold and empty. The boy held out his arms and in his hands held a large brown book.

"Who are you?" Peter reached out to touch the child.

"Save me," the boy said in a ghostly whisper.

"Peter," Angela stood at the end of the row of shelves. "I think you'd better get out there before World War III erupts between the boys."

"I was just on my way out," he held up the box of green ribbon. He kept his eyes towards her direction and dare not look behind him to where the boy stood for fear that his ghost might still be there.

"You all right?" she was startled by the pale and frightened look on his face.

"Yes of course. I'd better get out there," he gulped as he past her by. "Turn off the lights when you leave."

Angela made a half turn when she noticed a large book lying on the floor next to the ladder. She was about to call out to Peter when curiosity got the better of her. She knelt down and opened the large leather bound text. Inscribed on the first page were the words Liber Heironymos' (The Book of Heironymos), fascinated she began flipping through the pages.

Sunday 7:55pm
Isabella Stone's Farmhouse

Father Story had brought Emily home; it was far too precarious to leave her at the Hospes of St. Cecilia. He had made an anonymous phone call to the police telling them where to find the bodies of the maintenance man and the grave keeper knowing that it would be impossible to explain that the child had been responsible for both their deaths. She lay in her room on her bed with the belt of her mother's robe binding her hands to the posts. The room was ice cold. Candles were placed on the nightstands on either side of the bed and atop the windowsill. Emily's eyes slowly opened and an unnatural grown surged from her mouth. Father Story steadied himself; he had performed three exorcisms in his past with other priests present, but now he found himself by himself and trembling.

The child looked at her restraints; she laughed and sat up, "You think these are the chains that can bind me?" Emily's spoke with two voices; one in the gravelly pitch of an elderly woman and the other in the soft tenor of a much younger female.

"In the Name of the Father and of the Son and of the Holy Spirit, Amen. Let God arise and let his enemies be scattered: and let them that hate Him flee from before his face!" Father Story stood by the side of her bed. "As smoke vanisheth, so let them vanish away: as wax melteth before the fire, so let the wicked perish at the presence of God. Judge Thou, O' Lord, them that wrong me: overthrow them that fight against me."

An insipid laugh penetrated Emily's lips, "Your simple Christian ways can't save me Father."

"Let them be confounded and ashamed that seek after my soul," he breathed deeply. "Let them be turned back and be confounded that devise evil against me."

Emily's face was contorted with anger and she repeated his words in a backwards tongue, "Demahsa dna dednuofnoc eb meht tel!"

"Who are you that mocks the word of God?" asked Father Story. "What is your name?"

"I am Whore, birthed by Whore." Emily stared at her mother standing in the doorway. "I know of your broken vows mother and of your betrayal before Christ!"

"My God," Isabella wept and covered her mouth.

"Don't say anything. Don't engage her; she is not your daughter," Father Story shouted over his shoulder.

The bed rose inches off the floor; boom-boom-boom-boom it slammed into the wall repeatedly. Emily locked her gaze with Father Story, "Do you want to know what hell is really like Father?"

"What is your name immoral beast?"

"Immoral? You forget I know your secret too. Have you told mother yet? Have you told her how you let Cardinal Rourke go to Israel by himself because you were too afraid to follow? You knew how dangerous it was for him, yet you hid away at the Hospes." She spat out blood and it trailed down her chin and covered the front of her nightgown. "Do you know what happened to him Father?" She had a wicked smile on her face and laughed hysterically.

As Emily broke free of her restraints Father Story sat on the bed and wrestled her arms down. She grabbed Father Story by the wrist and began squeezing like a vice. The skin on his hand sizzled as though it had been branded by a red hot cattle prod.

"My bag... hurry!" the pain bled from his voice.

Isabella removed a syringe from the black bag on Emily's dresser. She ran to his side and rolled up the sleeve of Emily's gown.

"Mommy no! Please!" she begged in her natural voice.

CHAPTER VIII: THE POSSESSION

She dug the needle into her daughter's arm and emptied the injection. Emily's eyes rolled back into her head, her eyelids closed and the bed quietly came to rest on the floor. Isabella helped Father Story to a chair in the hallway outside Emily's bedroom. She liberally applied ointment to his burnt wrist and wrapped his hand in cheesecloth.

"Oh please Father tell me what to do."

"She will sleep through the night," Father Story's was out of breath and his voice was labored, "I have to leave for the Hospes for more supplies, but I'll be back in the morning before she wakes." He held her face gently and handed her his black bag, "Her demons are strong and her body is weak, watch over her and make sure she remains bedridden until I return."

Sunday 8:50 pm
Ra'anan Hotel
Tel Aviv, Israel

Gallo was physically exhausted and hadn't slept since arriving back at the hotel. He lay on his stomach and fumbled around for the nightstand then reached for the lamp and pulled the chain.

"Evening Mr. Costa, welcome to Israel," said a strange foreign voice.

The light illuminated the intruder's legs and hid his upper body in darkness. Gallo struck out breaking the lamp as he knocked it off the table. A man jumped on his back and held him down, while another pressed a handkerchief doused in chloroform over his nose and mouth and did not release the hold until he stopped fighting. Gallo had streaks of lucidity; faint visions of the hood placed over his head, the laundry cart that he had been dumped into and the motion of being pushed down the hallway of the hotel. Then unconsciousness and nothing but black until he heard the metal wheels scrape against the cement of the hotel's cavernous underground garage; then black. He felt the sensation of being placed in the trunk of a car; then black. When the hood was finally ripped off his head; he sat tied to a chair in a cold shadowy room. There was a hot light pointed at his face and a spotlight dangled from directly above. He squinted from the brightness but could make out the figures of two men sitting behind a gray steel table.

"Good you're awake… so let's begin," said a silver haired man, "It should be easy for you, I only have two questions I need answered. Who are you and why are you here?"

"I'm a businessman here on business," Gallo's mind was slowly clearing; he could feel the wires attached to his head, chest and fingers. He focused on a second man who sat dispassionately with large headphones draped over his ears and a large black box set in front of him.

"We ran your fingerprints and found something interesting. It seems that you are Mr. Dante Costa… or should I say Mr. Angelo Agucci, Commercial Pilot or maybe Luigi Bartoli, International Exporter. On the eleventh you checked into the Hotel Efron for a three day stay as Mr. Dante Costa. You stayed one night and never returned then you checked into the Ra'anan Hotel in Tel Aviv at 3:00 pm as Mr. DiMartino." The man threw pages of names at Gallo's feet, "So I'll ask you again, who are you?"

Gallo leaned forward in the chair; he pointed his toe to a random name on the third page, "I'da know, that one will work."

"This is the man who picked you up at the airport," the man held up a grainy black and white picture, "his name is François Minot, he is a gun runner and mercenary." He picked up a second picture of a healthy looking Hafsah dressed in a white robe standing at the observation deck of his beloved lighthouse, "This man's name is Hafsah Halawani and he is the millionaire whose money and interests have filtered down to various groups that are hostile to our government."

Gallo showed no emotion, he kept steady with his breathing exercises to slow his heart rate, once he had seen Hafsah's picture he knew had been trailed from the lighthouse to the hotel in Tel Aviv. How could he be so stupid? He knew agents had been watching Hafsah but he was sloppy and careless, too sure of his ability to shake any tale. He was almost surprised they hadn't asked him about the killings of Emir Saldalha and the two men at the Kadira Apartments.

"This man is Yasser Arafat," the man held out a third picture of Arafat with a short black beard and dark sunglasses surrounded by men with guns, "he is the leader of the PLO, the Palestine Liberation Organization and we hold him solely responsible for the killings back in March. The name you provided on your passport... Dante Costa is a known alias of Alberto Cecellini, a man who attempted to overthrow the Italian government ten years ago. You can see why we would be so concerned with your presence here in Israel. Once again, who are you and why are you here?"

"I told you I'm a businessman; the people I work for are very discreet, they needed Mr. Halawani's contacts in Egypt and throughout the Middle East."

"Contacts for what?"

"My clientele are Americans and Europeans who have heavily invested with Mr. Halawani's lighthouse project and your government shut it down. They were afraid Mr. Halawani might decide to disappear with their substantial contributions and they would be out of millions of dollars. As for the other men... I don't know who they are."

The man operating the black box studied the paper readout and shook his head, the results were inconclusive. The silver haired man was visibly frustrated; he gestured to two men that stood behind Gallo and they gripped him under the arms and dragged him to a freestanding bathtub filled with dirty green algaefied water. One of the men grabbed him by the hair and dunked his head under. Thirty seconds under, then they brought him up for air, one minute under then air, one minute forty seconds under and he heard their voices arguing before his head broke the surface.

"You really want us to believe that your association with all those dangerous men was just coincidence?" The silver haired man grasped Gallo's chin, "In Israel, there is no such thing as coincidence Mr. Costa; C'mon you'll have to do better than that."

"Fuck you," Gallo frantically gasped for air.

The men picked him up roughly and sank his upper body into the tub. He took a deep breath a second before his face hit the cold water. One minute thirty seconds and he began to struggle, two minutes and his lungs were aching, two minutes twenty seconds under he gave in and gulped the water in his mouth and inhaled it through his nose. They released him and his body collapsed on the floor at the base of the tub. The inside of his nose and chest stung and he coughed up the slimy water as he lay on his side on top the cold tiles. The men righted the chair and placed him back under the hot bright lights. The silver haired man took a syringe off the metal table, knelt down next to Gallo and injected sodium pentothal into his arm. The door opened and a fifth man was in deep consultation with his captors, after several bouts of shouting they untied him and released him from the room. The man escorted a wobbling Gallo out the front of the Civil Defense Building. At the bottom of a million stone steps was a young, well dressed blond haired man leaning against a light blue BMW E9 with his arms folded. He recognized it as the car that had trailed him from the airport to the hotel in Jerusalem.

"Hope your stay wasn't too unpleasant Mr. Gallo, get in." He opened the passenger door and made his way to the driver side, but Gallo didn't move. "Please, we have much to talk about."

Gallo walked down the steps and reluctantly sat in the passenger seat; in the rearview mirror he noticed two men in a black sedan parked behind them.

"My name is Elon Gutman, I'm with the IFA," Gutman leaned over and smiled, "you're a very lucky man the Mossad could have killed you if they wanted to."

"It wasn't that long a drive; I knew I was still somewhere within the city. I could tell they took me to a place with an underground garage and elevators. If they wanted to kill me they would have done it someplace far more deserted."

"I know why you're here Mr. Gallo," Gutman kept his eyes on the road as they drove through heavy traffic.

"I already told the Massad why I 'm here," he could feel the sodium pentothal coursing through his veins and the blunt effect made him woozy. "Unless you have a better technique, I'm sure you can ask them for a transcript."

"Defiant to the end," Gutman managed a smile. "Aren't you even curious to find out how I know who you are?"

Gallo didn't react; instead he kept eyeing the black sedan in the rearview. The lights from the oncoming traffic blurred into long streaks of red and yellow. He was slipping under into a hallucinogenic haze, but he was determined to fight all the way. "I saw you--you were there in Rome... at the park," Gallo blurted out in a emotionless manner. "You monitored my conversation with Agent Cavilary. I remember, I passed you by when I left Villa Doria. And you weren't alone; you were with an attractive female agent."

"Very good Mr. Gallo; I applaud your powers of observation," Gutman glanced over but Gallo's face was still a blank slate. "We were having trouble with siyah yılan gaining a foothold here in Israel and tracked Marko and Emir Saldalha back to Turkey and then to Italy. About a month ago I was contacted by a friend of Cardinal Rourke's; a man named Father Joseph Principi. Father Principi was worried about the safety of his old friend and wanted me to find him. The Cardinal vanished soon after he arrived in Israel and it had been weeks since they last spoke. Cardinal Rourke had deliberately kept him in the dark and warned him not to come; warned him there was a danger here that he could not imagine. Father Principi also told me that he had uncovered the identity of another conspirator, Archbishop Alessio Catoia. Unfortunately Archbishop Catoia was tipped off that he was a person of interest to the authorities and hung himself from the King Hussein Bridge before we could discover any other details."

"Then your agents uncovered Cavilary's investigation into Saldalha"

"That's right Mr. Gallo. We put pressure on Saldalha and were attempting to turn him," Gutman squeezed the steering wheel, "he might have been our best chance to break siyah yılan for good."

"Did he mention any other group that was working with them?"

"You mean the more ominous secret society attacking the Catholic Church? We haven't found any evidence of their existence," Gutman checked his rearview mirror while waiting at a stoplight. "What puzzles me is why you chose a Cecellini alias?"

"I knew Marko was eager to meet Cecellini. I thought why go looking for him when he'll come looking for me."

"I get it; find Marko, find his conspirators and find where they held Cardinal Rourke."

"That's right, accept your agents scared them off. They were so eager to bust Cecellini that they made themselves to visible at the hotel."

"Well then, I guess you're out of luck. We found Emir and a few of his friends shot dead at the Khadir Apartments a few hours ago; looked like a professional hit too. Two men were found dead in a locked van with bullets in their brains and Emir was left tied to a chair with definite signs of torture on his body. What's funny is we have an eyewitness, a prostitute who gave us a full description of the man who entered Emir's apartment and it matches yours perfectly."

"Emir was a possible informer for the SISDE, ask Cavilary yourself if you don't believe me," Gallo rolled down the window; the nauseating effects of the drug were enhanced by his intense feeling of motion sickness, "and he was my best lead to finding Cardinal Rourke."

"You mean other than Hafsah."

Gallo leaned his head out the window and threw up, then eased himself back into the seat. His muscles tightened, he felt a heavy pressure on his face that pushed down on his entire body. His eyelids fluttered shut and he drifted off into oblivion.

"Wake up," Gutman shook him by the shoulder; he stood by the open window on the passenger side door.

Gallo, barely awake glanced over at the dashboard clock that read three fifteen. The early morning darkness was pierced by the flashing blue lights of a dozen police cars and vans parked in the sand at the base of a hill. The Vice

Inspector General met Gutman near one of the morgue vans and was clearly surprised to see Gallo staggering from the car. He walked close behind the two men as they made their way up the hillside. The narrow path rose from the desert floor and cut a crevasse into the high stone walls of the mountain range. They entered a cavern that was strewn with bright area lights and secured with police tape. Inside, the cave opened up into several chambers that extended out into every direction. A heavy object had been dragged into the cavern and left deep grooves in the earth for several feet then suddenly stopped.

"You'll need these," the Vice Inspector General tossed the both of them two plastic packages; inside were charcoal lined cloth surgical masks. "It'll keep the awful smell from burning your lungs and keep you from passing out."

They followed a marker post tied off with braided rope that led down into the heart of the cave. The descent was steep and the air warm and stagnant. There was a buzz in his ears as his head was slowly clearing. He had been an experienced agent and seen his share of brutal crime scenes, but the horrific site of the atrocities profoundly shocked him. The body of an old man was hung upside down and crucified from the ceiling of the cave like a perverted stalactite.

"About three weeks ago a couple of teenagers found the bodies," the Vice Inspector said nonchalantly, "They come up here all the time and smoke dope and do... whatever it is teenager's do. A few of the boys were bragging and brought more friends here to come see the bodies. It wasn't until dayss later that one of their girlfriends made them call the police."

CHAPTER VIII: THE POSSESSION

"We'll have to run some test, but I believe we found are missing Cardinal," Gutman beamed his penlight at the mutilated body hanging in the center of the room.

Cardinal Rourke's lower jaw was missing and a big gap in the back of his skull had stained his gray hair dark red. The rib cage had been pried apart and the internal organs removed. Below his body; a teenage girl lay nude and chained atop a decoratively painted altar that held testament to the end of her life. A large hole ran from her breastbone to her abdomen and its contents meticulously hollowed out. On the floor lay the decapitated head of a young boy that had been cleanly sliced from the bridge of the nose to the back of the head. The cut line was so straight that the halved head sat perfectly on the dirt floor.

"Each victim suffered the same fate," the Vice Inspector pointed to several jars that encircled the bodies, "three of the jars contain their brains, three their hearts and three their intestines and genitals. Only the boy's body was burned and the ashes spread around the base of the stone."

Men in hazards suits and masks methodically collected evidence and took pictures of the corpses and surrounding crime scene area. Gallo moved closer and when one of the detectives stopped to change film he picked his pocket and slid the roll inside his shirt.

"Well?" asked Gutman.

"Well what?" Gallo was startled.

"Does that look like the man you were looking for?"

"Yeah, that's him," sighed Gallo. "If those boys found their bodies weeks ago then how come there are no flies or maggots around any of them?"

"Well… it might be the desert heat and dry air." The Vice Inspector was caught off guard. "We still find mummies from time to time that are remarkably preserved."

"No he's right," Gutman knelt near the altar; it was caked with dried blood and guts, "there's enough raw meat here to attract every wild animal for miles." He patted his hand on the top of the stone altar, "And this rock isn't native to this area either, someone must have moved it here."

"It was dragged in; there are grooves cut into the dirt by the entrance of the cave," answered Gallo.

"That's impossible; it must weigh over a ton," the Vice Inspector chimed. "The walls of the hillside are too narrow for a crane to bring it up and even if you had a hundred men the sand is too soft; it would have gotten stuck."

"I'm not looking for a hundred men," Gallo's eyes stayed fixed on Rourke's body, "just one."

At five o'clock the morning showed greater signs of life as the sun cast a faint orange hue across the sky. Gutman dropped Gallo off in front of the Ra'anan Hotel.

"Unfortunately your search has ended Mr. Gallo, with Rourke dead that makes it murder and it's my investigation now. I expect you'll be leaving Israel later tonight." Gutman didn't wait for a reply; he donned his shades and sped away from the curb.

He was dead tired and his body was physically drained as he made the long walk down the hallway. Two of Gutman's agents were posted outside his room. One leaned against the wall and the other sat on the floor cross legged eating a breakfast of toast and orange juice off a brown hotel tray.

"You guys need a key, or are you waiting for me to open it," Gallo said dryly.

"We're here to make sure you don't get lost again Mr. Gallo, our boss wouldn't like that very much," the tall man standing flashed a faint smile, but the second didn't bother looking up from his tray.

Gallo opened the door; the room had been ransacked. The mattress, sheets and couch cushions had been haphazardly tossed in a pile in the middle of the room; the chairs were overturned and all the drawers opened and emptied of their contents.

"Horrible crime wave we have in Tel Aviv, you should make sure you lock your door next time." The agent folded his arms and raised his eyebrows while the second officer half-snorted-half-laughed as he peered up from his food and into the room.

Gallo locked the door behind him then searched the inside for hidden cameras and audio devices but found nothing. He went into the bathroom and turned on the tub faucet until the cascade of water echoed off the ceramic tiles. He balanced himself on the toilet seat and carefully removed a grooved square from the ceiling. Rourke's' journal, the travelers checks and passport were still taped to the other side but there was something new; a foreign piece of white paper floated to the sink. Gallo left the items in their stead and pushed the square back into place. He climbed down, fetched the paper and sat on the closed toilet lid. It was a letter written in shorthand from Minot:

Found Marko
Left due to uninvited guests
Tailed to warehouse, Doc 9, Port of Haifa
Harkir Saldalha lost mind, trashed place
Must be something you did
Marko leaving country today 5 or 6:00 pm
Couldn't access port Haifa office
May need Hafsah's help
Tried to contact him
No answer
Will try again

It seemed to confirm the information he was able to obtain from Emir before he died. At 9:00 am Gallo emerged from the room; he left it trashed. His two escorts stood outside; the taller one nudged his compatriot awake.

"I'm starving," Gallo yawned, "I'm goin' out. I can't stand eating shitty hotel food; don't worry I won't be long." He casually walked down the hall.

"Where the fuck do you think he's going?" asked the short agent.

"Haven't got a clue," answered the second.

They walked with him to the elevator and out the front lobby. Gallo nodded to the bellhop and he whistled for a cab. Immediately a yellow Haifa All Service Taxi stopped near the curb and he reached for the door handle.

"Uh-uh," The tall man grabbed his arm and pushed it away from the door handle then signaled the cabbie to drive on.

"You gotta be kidding?" Gallo fumed, "I have until tonight to leave or didn't your boss fill you in on that little detail?"

"Wherever you go--we go," the second agent pulled up in a black Citroen DS and he opened the rear door. "Get in."

Gallo made them drive to a seafood restaurant near the port of Haifa. They sat amongst the tourist at an outside café facing the street. What had once been a colorful crisp morning sky quickly turned dull and gray; faint raindrops splattered on top of the patio deck. The lights from the restaurant and all the surrounding buildings in the area were turned on and most of the other patrons had decided to seek shelter indoors. Gallo checked his watch; twelve o'clock. The blue sea stretched across the horizon like a perfect scene from a picture postcard. The deep sound of ships' horns resonated in the air as they trafficked in and out of the harbor, and were accompanied by the squawks of a dozen seagulls gliding in the cool sea breeze. Far off in the distance he could make out the contours of Hafsah's lighthouse that appeared like a child's small toy against the big sky.

"I'm assuming this has something to do with the case?" Gutman walked up the slight incline and sat next to Gallo under a hastily erected blue and gold awning.

"Your friends don't eat much, but you're welcome to join me Agent Gutman." Gallo sipped his coffee.

"You know I had the feeling you weren't telling me everything you knew."

"Well I'm sorry," Gallo pushed away his plate of half eaten crab and shrimp cocktail, "I have a real aversion to needles and I hate being shot up with a concoction of black market drugs administered by an amateur pharmacist. It kinda gave me a bad headache."

"Maybe you can discuss it with the Massad Mr. Gallo; I can arrange that for you if you'd like," Gutman put his hand up and waved the waitress away before she made her approach, then leaned forward in his chair. "I think I can safely assume you never left the hotel without my men becoming aware of your absence."

"That's a major leap of faith you have in your men," Gallo smiled, "but no, I didn't leave the hotel."

"Did you miraculously discover a new lead since we last met or were you simply holding out on me."

"Let's just say that before I was seized by the Massad I was able to obtain some very important information regarding the investigation."

"Are you planning at any point in this conversation to divulge this information?"

"Well that really depends on you."

"Very well, we can have this little tête-à-tête downtown if you want," Gutman folded his arms, "we have very nice jail cells there."

"Ahhhnt wrong answer," Gallo took a full sip of ice water. "I'm not going to tell you anything unless you agree to take me with you."

"You're in no position…"

"But I am."

"You're bluffing Mr. Gallo," Gutman said confidently, "you don't have anything new to offer me."

"Let's see, what's the tally? Oh yeah, a mysterious two ton altar stone placed in a cave that you can't explain how it got there, a horrific crime scene that has ritual killings written all over it and you're left with an unsolved case with no idea of what to do next."

"For all I know you're a part of this. Maybe you're stalling in order to give your associates enough time to leave the country."

"Maybe, but can you really afford to be wrong? The clock's ticking Agent Gutman and time is running out; without my help this case is going nowhere."

Gutman slumped back in his chair; he couldn't hide the tense look on his face. He rubbed his chin and nodded his head to acknowledge his concession to Gallo's terms, "Why are we here Mr. Gallo?"

"We found the bodies early this morning but we haven't found the killers," with his head Gallo motion toward the Port of Haifa. "We're here because they're--there."

The great beast was swallowed by the tides and sent to Tartarus, the world below hell to slumber for a thousand years. He had divined his powers separately to the fallen Angels Qeynan, Thaydien and Hector so that no one angel could claim dominion over him. And the great beast kept the power of deceit for himself so that he might regain his power and his throne.

Serafeim
libri of cado animus

CHAPTER IX
THE HELLMEN COMETH

Monday 6:00 pm
23, October 1978
Manna Book Store
City of Madonnella, Italy

The yellow and white lights lit up the main avenue while dozens of cars lined the promenade. The Manna Book Store was overflowing with well wishers and celebrity gawkers as they filed in to meet the acclaimed author Mario Pascale. Even Eddie dropped his disdain for Mario and fake pageantry and was swept up in the excitement of the night. He stood guard at the front entrance and checked a clipboard for the names of the invited guests. Peter stood on the second floor landing that overlooked the entire room engaged in conversation with several couples, nervous that the festivities go off without a hitch.

"I can assure you there are many things in nature in which the untrained mind cannot comprehend," Mario held court with a dozen people surrounding him. "Take for instance the ability of a child with no formal training who plays

Beethoven's 5th on the violin, or a man who can bend metal with his mind..." There was snickering from many in his company. "Ladies and gentlemen, I can assure you these things and so much more are possible." He scanned the crowd, "Peter... Peter!"

She appeared like a faint whisper and was just as beautiful as the last time he saw her ten years ago. Peter's heartbeat quickened as Isabella Stone entered through the glass door. He was about to make his way down the stairs when a large hand grabbed him by the shoulder.

"Your father was a great man," said Serge D'Alisa, a 65 year old farmer whose 6'5" frame was still imposing even at his age, "we miss him very much." His eyes searched Peter's for understanding, but he only nodded uncomfortably.

"The boy doesn't want to talk about the past," Serge's diminutive wife seized her husband's hand, "You're always welcome to stop by the house for a good home cooked meal Father Cameron."

"Peter," he said, "I haven't been a priest for years, although everyone seems to forget that." He smiled and only politely half listened to the elder woman drone on about her pride in her acres of cornstalks, wheat fields and prized pigs. He searched the crowd for Isabella's face once again, but she had melted into the throngs of half drunken party goers.

"Peter!" Mario's deep voice cut through the raucous chatter, "Come down here please," he waved his arm above his head and welcomed any excuse to leave the couple's presence.

Peter made his way downstairs and cut a path through the crowd that encircled Mario's perch. They were all well dressed in pressed tux and formal gown and had the air of big money oozing from their pores. Mario put his arm around his shoulder, a few of the faces he didn't recognize and it made him slightly uncomfortable.

Mario had a cat's grin on his lips and held up Charles Dickens leather bound book, David Copperfield. "Chapter ten, first sentence, third paragraph," he stated confidently.

Peter said the words with automatic precision, "There was one change in my condition, which, while it relieved me of a great deal of present uneasiness, might have made me, if I had been capable of considering it closely, yet more uncomfortable about the future."

There were confused yet amazed faces of the small group that was in earshot of their conversation. There were also the disbelievers which he had been accustomed to and he responded without hesitation. He did the same thing for The Old Farmer's Almanac 1952, The Great Gatsby and two other obscure books offered by the stunned guests.

"Peter can recite chapter and verse from cover to cover," Mario proudly announced, "and he can do the same for every book in the store." He continued speaking loudly over their applause. "His mind is able to capture each passage as though it was as clear as a photograph, isn't that right?"

"Something like that."

"Do Mario's book!" A voice shouted from the gallery.

"I can't," Peter placed his hand on Mario's shoulder and grinned, "I haven't read it yet." They laughed, cheered and raised their glasses to toast him.

"I have a book," a familiar voice caught him off guard, "page two hundred ten, paragraph one." Angela held out his tattered copy of the Book of Heironymos.

"Where did you..." the color drained from Peter's face and he snatched the book from her hands.

"What about it Peter," a well dressed man said, "someone finally got the better of you?"

"Not everything's a game."

"Not everyone keeps secrets," Angela stood her ground.

"Very well," Peter gave the book to the stranger, "page two hundred ten, paragraph one: Kyameron said unto God, not all good was truly good and not all evil truly evil. And God saw that evil ruled the land of Thaydien and marked the impious and sinful with scales on their skin and eyes of blackened coal so that all may see the wickedness of man."

"Very good," the stranger smiled as he ran his hands over the cover. "How much do you want for the book?"

"It isn't for sale," said Peter.

"C'mon, you haven't even heard my price. I'm willing to pay top dollar," the stranger was befuddled. "This is a book store isn't it? You're in the business of selling books aren't you?"

He stared at the man intently and wrenched the book from his hands, "Like I said; it's not for sale."

"I need to see you Pete," Eddie tugged at his shoulder, "in the kitchen."

The intensity on Peter's face subsided and he politely excused himself from the group. Eddie grabbed Angela by the arm and led her to a secluded corner near the kitchen door.

"You wanna tell me what the fuck you were doing back there?"

"There's something wrong with Peter," she pleaded to deaf ears. "You can't see it or don't want to see it, but he's changed. I saw him in the storage room the other day as though he was staring at someone who wasn't there and when he saw me he tried to hide that book."

"It's his store, his storage room; he can do whatever he wants. Okay?"

"Have you looked at his eyes? His eyes were blue and now they're black," she exclaimed.

"Black as coal?" Eddie rubbed his forehead in frustration, "For God's sakes, what are you trying to say Angela?"

"I don't... I don't know," she held her head down.

"Whatever's going on between you and Peter, you gotta let it go," he pushed the kitchen door open and was quickly followed in by Mario.

Isabella Stone sat at the kitchen table and was visibly nervous and fidgeting. Peter hadn't seen her for close to a decade, but she appeared just as youthful as the day he fell in love with her.

"I shouldn't have come," she stood up, "I have no right to drag you into this."

"Please, sit," Peter held her hand, "you know I'd do anything for you if you need my help."

She hadn't really thought about him in their time apart, but there was something different about his face, his eyes and it was a little offsetting, "Something's happened to Emily." Tears fell from her eyes and she placed a hand over her mouth, "I know it will sound crazy, but she isn't my daughter; she's sick in her soul. God help me she's possessed."

Peter knelt in front of her, "Isabella I…"

"I know what you're going to say Peter, but Father Story has witnessed for himself, he's with her now."

"Father Story believes its possession?" Peter relaxed a little, "Did he…"

"I didn't think the church acknowledged possession or exorcism," said Mario.

"They don't," Peter answered before he turned his attention back to Isabella, "Did he send for me?"

"No, he doesn't even know I'm here," she sighed, "I think he's afraid to tell me he can't help her, that the beast will take her away from me."

"You know, there are many documented cases of possession," Mario chimed in once again, "Giuliana Abruzzi, Eliodoro Urso, Anneliese Michel; they've tried to explain it away as epileptic seizures or mental disorders, but the Devil is real. Matter-of-fact, once when I was in Turkey…

"Oh give it a break Mario," Eddie leaned against the sink, still unnerved from his encounter with Angela, "just admit it; you're only interested in a subject for your next book." He crossed his arms and said mockingly, "Life and death as Mario Pascale sees it."

"I'm sorry, this was a mistake I shouldn't have come," Isabella seemed lost as she stood up, "I have to go…"

"Isabella wait…" Peter chased after her; the door swung wildly and Angela's stoic face peered through the opening. He pressed into the crowd and out onto the street, but she was gone.

The lights from Nonna's Grocery Store across the street flickered then succumbed to blackness. Several street lights lining the avenue popped and rained bright sparks onto the curbside below. A full moon cast a silver hue and intensified the eerie feeling building in Peter's psyche. He deeply inhaled the crisp night air and tried to regain his right mind. A florescent light from Nonna's strobed and illuminated the silhouette of a young boy standing inside. The child pressed his face and hands against the glass leaving streaks of smeared blood and torn flesh. His eye sockets had been hollowed out and a wicked cut ran underneath his nose and across his face from ear to ear. "Eh eh eh eh eh eh," the sound reverberated from somewhere within the store. A neon green mist enveloped the boy's body and he struggled to hold his ground. His hands loudly thumped against the window and threatened to shatter the glass. He cried out as the fog grew heavier and his head shook violently side to side blurring his features. A veil of green mist poured from the ceiling and seconds later the apparition vanished into the ether.

"Basem..." Peter whispered. He stepped off the curb and as the heal of his shoe touched the pavement the streetlights and the light from Nonna's Grocery store reanimated into a bright white radiance.

"You alright Pete?" Eddie stood at the opening of the front door.

"Yeah, yeah I'm fine," his hands were sweating and his hair was matted to his head. He shook off the night's cold embrace and headed back to the party.

Monday 6:00 pm
Port of Haifa, Israel

The tiny Citron passed the very bureaucratic looking Haifa Port of Shipment and Customs Office building. They drove pass the burned out dockside warehouses 8 and 9 that belonged to the Wolfe and Stone Import/Export company. At the security gate Gutman flashed his badge and the group was allowed to continue on their way. They traveled along the transport road where the vehicle dodged dozens of forklifts, straddle carriers and lorries that moved with great precision. In the harbor lying at a 40 degree angle was the 1,122 ft Eelyeese, a behemoth Wolfe and Stone cargo ship. An explosion had ripped away most of the bow and left her lying on her starboard side. A second blast left a 20 foot gap that exposed her portside bulkheads and girders just above the waterline. The air was basted with the heavy stench of burning oil and burnt mechanical equipment. Thick black crude continued to pour out of her wounds and cast a sheen on the water as waves from the Mediterranean threatened to pull her to the bottom. Three tugboats dwarfed by the size of the ship hovered around her like hummingbirds and sprayed arcs of seawater across her burning surface. Several 20 foot cargo containers crashed into each other then slid into the blue water and were submerged beneath the sea.

"Wonder how many millions that's costing them?" Gallo sat in the back seat between the two agents and leaned forward to view the sinking ship. The moniker of Wolfe and Stone was barely visible beneath the heavy layers of soot and grime.

The tall agent rested his hand on a holstered gun and with his left arm gently pushed Gallo back in his seat. They stopped the car just outside the open doors of the gigantic Wolfe and Stone warehouse. It was filled with powder blue Subaru vans with the company logo emblazoned on the side panels in black lettering. A hundred worker ants labored in unison on assembly lines, forklifts and various cherry pickers. Gutman quickly flashed his badge as the foreman approached the group of unwelcomed outsiders.

"You gotta be fucking kidding me," the large bellied Turk looked on incredulously, "we already paid you fuckers yesterday."

"We're not inspectors," said Gutman, "take another look at the badge asshole." He raised his eyebrow, "You just tried to bribe a..."

"Okay, okay, before you give me a speech about shutting the whole place down and forcing me out of the country, you mind telling me what this is about?"

"Where's Mr. Stone?"

"I don't know," he could see Gutman wasn't sympathetic, "honestly I haven't seen him for weeks; I'm telling you guys the truth."

"How many ships you got going out in the next couple of hours?"

"Including freighters, barges, transports and the overflow we're handling from Mega Shipping... 32."

"Fine, Main Office; I want to see shipping logs, manifests, estimated times of departures," Gutman registered the foreman's resistance, "unless you want me to..."

"Shut the place down, yeah-yeah-yeah," he walked them to the metal stairway leading up to the Main Office. "In fifteen minutes my shift ends and I never saw you--I never met you, after that you can deal with Mr. Carson, Mr. Wolfe's right hand man."

"Keys?" asked Gutman.

"It's open," snarled the foreman, "fifteen minutes."

At the top of the twenty four steps was a 16'x 20' dull gray corrugated shack that was the office. The three men shuffled inside, unaware of where they would begin or what they were looking for. Gutman sat Gallo down in a thick brown leather captain's chair as he and his men rifled through the desk drawers, filing cabinets, totes, loose papers on desktops and garbage bins; nothing.

"Is this just another goose chase Mr. Gallo?" Gutman leaned against the foreman's desk, "Are you stalling for time?"

Gallo leaned back in the chair and eyed the large white magnetic grid board hanging on the wood paneled wall. "Pier Sixteen in about twenty minutes," he said coolly.

Gutman stared at the board filled with black magnets that were in the shape of the many different types of ships. "How can you be sure?" his eyes rested on the cargo ship next to Pier Sixteen.

"Oriens Astrum is Latin for Morning Star," he saw the others were unable to make the connection, "Morning Star is the name for Lucifer." He stood, but Gutman pushed him back in the chair.

"You're staying here," he eyed the short agent, "keep him company. No one enters till I return."

"You're not serious; we had a deal," protested Gallo, "this is still my case."

"You forget you're in Israel Mr. Gallo and unless I say otherwise you have no case."

Eight agonizing minutes ticked by as Gallo gazed at the round black faced clock hanging on the wall. "Great, your boss goes off to claim all the glory and leaves me with a hired gorilla trapped inside a sardine can."

"I'm already tired of being around you Mr. Gallo so shut up and quit your complaining," the short agent leaned against the wall.

"Is this all your boss lets you do: wait in the car, wait at the hotel, wait in a tiny office with me. Say, aren't you curious to see what actual investigative work is really like?"

"Shut up Gallo or I'm gonna come over there and shut you up."

A short stocky man entered the room dressed in a light blue construction hat with a Wolfe and Stone jumpsuit. He held a clipboard in his hand and kept his face down, "I need someone to sign off on this paperwork," he said.

"Do I look like the fucking foreman?" snarled the agent, "Go away."

"I'm just doing my job."

"I said go away," the anger rose in his voice, "beat it!"

François Minot raised his head and revealed a snub-nose .38 Special from beneath the clipboard and stuck it in the agent's ribs, "Like I said, I'm just doing my job." He handcuffed him, then struck the back of his head with the gun and locked him in a small bathroom in the corner of the office. "I followed you from the hotel... you know there was a time when a guy like that couldn't get the drop on you." He took the man's gun from his shoulder holster.

Gallo held his hand out, "Gimmie his gun."

"Sorry," Minot smiled sheepishly as he tucked the agent's .38 into his waistband, "I only had enough cash on me to bribe the guard for his pistol; no bullets."

"Remind me to thank you later."

"It's beginning to be a habit," Minot tossed him an extra uniform, "me saving you at the last moment. You know, you should really have a better Plan B."

"I would have figured something out," Gallo adjusted the blue helmet, "besides it helps keep you sharp and puts some excitement in your life."

"Excitement," he laughed, "this kind of excitement I don't need."

Sunday 6:15 pm
Pier Sixteen, Oriens Astrum
Port of Haifa

Three men stood in the open air on the deck above the Bridge Room of the superstructure. It was the highest point aboard the massive cargo ship Oriens Astrum. Two of them stood at the metal railing while the third paced nervously. A low rumbling thunder crackled in the distance and the evening sky turned a deep gray. The loading dock was covered with 20ft and 40ft containers with a phalanx of straddle carriers headed for the giant dockside crane looming over the Oriens Astrum's massive deck.

"Are either of you listening to me?" asked Marko, "Have you heard anything I've said?"

"Of course we have Marko, I'm in exactly the same place you are; on the outside," Father Layad lit a Davidoff cigarette then took a deep drag. "I don't like being kept out of the loop anymore than you do."

"They killed Emir and two of my best men," Marko said unapologetically, "if I don't do something soon they'll kill me next."

"We're all expendable. You brought them the book and siyah yılan served out its purpose," Father Layad closed his eyes and breathed in the electric air. "More to the point, do you really think they would have used a bullet to the head to kill your friends? He would have sent Robert and he would have simply cut them to pieces."

Marko seemed to regain a slight sense of prospective, "How 'bout you, what do you think? You're different from them... I mean your eyes..."

"Robert didn't kill your men," said the third man. He leaned over the railing; his eyes were fixed on Gallo and Minot as they jumped aboard the giant heavy lift loader while it was slowly driven into the cargo bay. Cardinal Rudolph Fuerst smiled then turned to face Marko, "Your men were sloppy and undisciplined and anyone who had a score to settle with siyah yılan, say for instance the Council or even Arafat could have easily tracked them down."

"What were you planning to do anyway, threaten Father Santeal and Robert with a gun?" Father Layad laughed and shook his head, "Face it Marko, you're the very last of a dying breed."

"I told them I'd do anything; I just want my fair share of the power and not to be treated like a child," he couldn't shake the feeling of impending doom. "They've got no reason to kill me, I've been loyal... they have no right." He leaned against the ship's stack and began to confess, "I told Emir's uncle..."

"Speak of the Devil," Father Layad flicked his cigarette and watched Harkir Saldalha and twenty of his men with Kalashnikov rifles slung around their shoulders storm up onto Oriens Astrum.

"Men like Father Santeal and Robert have tasted only a small bit of what it truly means to be all-powerful, once they have more they won't feel the need to share it or worship like we worship," he closed his eyes. "Did you mean what you said, that you would do anything for a share of the power?" Cardinal Fuerst's cold blue eyes stared through Marko like an x-ray.

"Yes."

"And you?" he asked Father Layad.

"Sure, why the hell not," another cigarette dangled from Father Layad's lips, he withdrew a lighter from his pocket and cupped his hands around his mouth.

"Good. Marko, you take the first plane back to Rome; to the apartment where we met and wait there until I contact you," he turned to Father Layad, "You're going back to America in a few days aren't you?"

"Yeah," he said dryly.

"I need you to find someone for me. When you arrive in Seattle, I will contact you with further details." Cardinal Fuerst walked away then stopped with his back to his co-conspirators, "I needn't remind either of you that you are to talk to no one about our meeting tonight."

"And what about you?" Father Layad asked.

"Me? I'm on my way to meet our new guests."

Three levels down towards the midship section and on the car deck was a makeshift office and back bedrooms. Father Santeal sat with a map of the Mediterranean laid across his desk and updated the captain with the new change in course. The door flew open startling both men.
In the doorway stood the six foot five, three hundred pound Harkir Saldalha. He walked into the room with five of his bodyguards; his eyes never left Father Santeal's.

"I knew I'd find you on one of your boats," Harkir's deep voice boomed throughout the cabin. "I was prepared to destroy every ship in your fleet until I found you."

"So, you're responsible for sinking the Elysees."

"And you're responsible for a missing innkeeper that was under my employ," Harkir's tone was unsympathetic, "and you're responsible for the death of my nephew Emir." The expression on Father Santeal's face changed. "Don't look so surprised, I have witnesses that describe hearing the voice of a man who spoke to my nephew in English like an American. I gave you thirty men and to the last they're either dead, insane or have walked off into the desert with neither water nor provisions. Can you tell me what would make a man do such a thing?"

"You and Hafsah were duly compensated for your men while they worked for me," Father Santeal handed the course chart to the Captain, "What they did on their own time is none of my concern."

"It seems your little desert dig was nothing more than a mirage. I went out there to see it for myself and it's vanished from the face of the earth," he put his hands on his hips and his open jacket revealed the handle of a gun. "My men tell me Cecellini has also arrived in Israel, perhaps you've decided to do business with him or Arafat instead. A man in my position can't afford to be made fool of Mr. Santeal; all the little rats would eat me alive."

"I'm not interested in any ridiculous civil war you might have with Arafat or the Israelis, and as for Cecellini, I've never met him."

Gallo and Minot cautiously maneuvered through rows of sixty vehicles parked side to side and bumper to bumper on the ship's car deck. Minot had spotted Harkir and the two men had followed him down to the third level. They stopped; a ten foot gap divided the last row of cars from a long hallway that led deeper into the ship's interior. They knelt behind a green Range Rover and listened intently as Harkir and Father Santeal's voices resonated off the metal walls.

"Tell me you have a Plan B for this," whispered Minot.

Gallo held a finger to his lips signaling Minot to be quiet when he felt the cold muzzle of a Berretta against his ear and heard the safety as it clicked off. He slowly turned his head to see Gutman standing above him.

"I'm not even gonna ask how you got in here, just tell me my man is still alive." Gutman's face was stone cold as he squatted opposite the two men.

"He's alive," Gallo raised his hands, "he's just got one hell of an awful headache."

"I know you, right?" Gutman crooked his head to get a better look at Minot's face.

Minot lowered his helmet, raised his shirt collar and shook his head, "No, no I don't think so."

"Enough talk Mr. Santeal, I'm losing patients. Tell me where I can find Mr. Stone." Harkir tossed his jacket onto Father Santeal's desk.

Cardinal Fuerst appeared in the doorway and two of Harkir's men pointed their Kalashnikov's at his head. "I wouldn't do that if I were you," his stare reinforced his warning and the men lowered their sights.

"Oh good you're here," said Father Santeal, "I need you to go over the course changes with the captain."

Surprised and somewhat annoyed, Cardinal Fuerst nodded in compliance and he and the captain left the cabin for the bridge; Harkir signaled one of his men to follow. A man standing next to Harkir handed him a blue backpack and he placed it on a chair in front of Father Santeal.

"Last chance Mr. Santeal," Harkir pulled a brick of C-4 explosive from the bag and held it in his hand. "Where is Robert Stone?"

"If you insist," Father Santeal leaned back in his chair, "Robert would you come out here please!"

The lights flickered; the men flinched and held their weapons at the ready. It was an odd and out of place sound at first, but a low murmur manifested into loud laughter that whipped around the room. Harkir tossed the backpack to a man standing at the doorway.

"Blow up the goddamn ship," said Harkir. "I gave you more than a fair chance Father Santeal, and now you'll learn what happens to people who cross me. I've had enough of your silly games." He unholstered his Browning pistol, leveled it at his head and pulled the trigger.

The bullet struck Father Santeal in the left temple, his head snapped backward and he lay motionless in the chair. The lights went out for several seconds then began to strobe; there was something else in the cabin. The men squinted their eyes in a futile effort to fix upon a black wisp of smoke that circled around the ceiling. The laughter returned, but this time it emanated from the center of the room. A creature manifested itself in the flickering light and its black wings sliced the necks of two of Harkir's men. Their throats were brutally slashed as their heads flopped back to their shoulder blades. Nearly decapitated, they were dead before they hit the floor. The other two men panicked and shot wildly until Harkir gave them the order to cease fire. He turned quickly at the sound of a squeaky chair and stared into the red eyes of Father Santeal who spat the bullet out onto the floor. The hole in his forehead sealed and he smiled wickedly as the blood trickled from the corners of his mouth. The black smoke engulfed Harkir; his body was lifted up and pinned against the ceiling. His arms and legs were spread by an unseen force and a thick red incision line formed from his neck to his abdomen. He began to scream loudly as his flesh was torn wide open. His rib cage was wrenched apart and vital organs were emptied and splattered like thick tomato soup onto the floor. The two men sprayed suppression fire into the cabin while backing out towards the exit.

Minot dashed towards the sound of the gunfire as Gallo yelled after him to stop. Gunfire erupted from topside as well as the two sides fully engaged in the battle. Minot reached the open door of Father Santeal's cabin; with his gun drawn he held his breath and peered inside. He was knocked to the ground as one of the bodyguard's corpse was hurled towards him and slammed against the wall of the outer corridor. The man had been twisted like a wet towel from head to toe and ivory bones jutted out through the skin. He heard the laughter from inside and braced himself to face the dead man's attacker. The silhouette of a seven foot creature stepped out into the hallway. Minot scooted backwards then rose to his feet; his heart raced as a set of glowing yellow eyes locked onto his. He raised his shaking hand and fired two shots into the beastly form. The hanging light bulb above the creature exploded, then another and another, casting the length of the hallway behind it in total darkness. He turned and ran towards Gallo standing twenty feet away at the open entrance of the hallway. One by one the overhead lights behind Minot burst in electric sparks until he too was enveloped in the darkness.

"François!" Gallo's voice bounced off the walls. He peered into the black, but saw nothing. He heard dull wet thuds and Minot's tortured cries as his body was violently hacked and dismembered. A river of blood pooled around his feet and a pair of ghostly yellow eyes floated in the abyss. He stood frozen in place, Gutman was yelling at him, but it barely registered over the sound of his pounding heart.

"Move it! Now!" Gutman shouted as he stood half way up the emergency stairwell.

The topside hatch opened and one of Harkir's men stumbled down the stairs with a gaping bullet wound in his left shoulder. He tried to focus and point his Kalashnikov at Gutman, but the blue backpack hanging loosely over his shoulder impeded his ability to aim. Gutman shot him twice; he fell over the railing and his body slammed on the floor below. The C-4 in his backpack exploded and the shock waves sent Gutman flying backward twenty feet until he crashed onto the car deck floor. Blood trickled from his ears and nose, a loud ringing blared in his head and his body ached all over. He lay on the floor unable to move when Gallo picked him up, slung him over his shoulder and ran down the aisle of cars. He could hear Robert's heavy footsteps behind him as he effortlessly tossed several trucks and cars across the wide berth of the deck. He neared the end of the line when a black Range Rover tumbling roof over underbelly flew above his head and sprayed him with a deluge of gasoline. It landed on a gold Mercedes and crushed its roof sending tiny shards of glass projectiles through the air. The foul odor of twisted burning metal and the stench of bursting petrol tanks mixed with the oxygen and salty sea air. Out of breath and out of energy, he pushed himself up the stairwell and out onto the peril of the cargo deck. The Oriens Astrum had left the dock and began its long exit from Haifa harbor. There were sporadic sounds of gunfire and men shouting at each other. Gallo dumped Gutman on the deck and sat next to him as he leaned against the stack of twenty foot cargo containers.

"What the fuck was that?" Gutman tried hard to focus.

"You might find out soon enough," Gallo gasped and tried hard to get his breath, "we're not safe yet."

"You know if the situation was reversed, I probably would have left you."

"Trust me," Gallo sneered, "I thought about it."

Their laughter stopped abruptly as Gallo spotted the glowing orbs at the entrance way of the stairwell. He scooped up Gutman and ran as a heavy hail of bullets rained down around them from the top deck of the superstructure. He didn't stop until he reached the foredeck at the front of the ship. He leaned Gutman up against the white railing opposite the winches and fairleads.

"Wait here," Gallo winked then disappeared amongst the cargo containers.

Gutman gripped the handrail and listened; the gunfire had ceased and the only sound came from the hum of the floodlights on the mass platform. He had a concussion from the explosion; it was entirely possible that he had imagined the beast that hunted them now. In fact, it made more sense that the creature really didn't exist, but was conjured from the imagination of an injured mind. Hell it was possible that he was at home and asleep in his bed, he didn't know for sure. A wide beam of light from the bridge scanned the deck and shook him from his stupor. Gallo returned rolling a tire from a diesel truck; he slipped it over Gutman's head down to his waist then propped him up against the rail. White water broke around the side of the ship and the wake spread out across the bay.

"You gotta be kidding me," Gutman said petrified.

"Sorry, but we're out of options," Gallo lifted him up in his arms and held him over the side.

He could see something leaping from container to container as it hurriedly made its way toward their position. He dropped Gutman overboard and promptly leapt over the handrail. The surface of the Mediterranean was hard and the cold stung his exposed flesh. The water filled his nose and burned his eyes. He swam to the empty tire then dove under until he snagged Gutman's limp body. He pulled him close and swam away from the Oriens Astrum's giant propeller blades as it chopped the sea and raced overhead. An unseen force made impact with the water and pushed them slightly downward. The outline of a head twenty feet wide with a hideous face formed from the tiny white bubbles. The nose was broad and lips barely covered a set of serrated fangs. There were horns on the forehead and he could clearly make out the eyes that stared at him intensely. The disembodied head turned back towards the ship as if being summoned by some higher being. Once more it looked upon the men, with a roar it opened its jaws and snared them in its mouth. Gallo's ears popped as he and Gutman were sent on a high speed ride to the bottom of the bay. Then suddenly, without warning their attacker slowed, faded, and dissipated into the current of the sea; their descent was over. He furiously swam upwards with the last bit of air remaining in his lungs. He broke the surface and he and Gutman coughed and spat out copious amounts of salt water. He saw Cardinal Fuerst and the human form of Robert Stone standing at the rails on the back of the ship. Their eyes were trained on the two men, Stone's face was dejected and he turned and walked out of view. The mighty Oriens Astrum had opened up full engines and was quickly disappearing from sight. Gallo clung to the tire with one arm and seized Gutman around the neck with the other as they bobbed up and down in the waves more than a mile off shore. The distant oasis of Haifa's city lights lit up the night sky and spread across the horizon. It would have been difficult enough to swim the distance by himself, but carrying Gutman's dead weight made the task impossible. The water was calm and the reflection of a full moon rippled off its solid blackness. Gallo closed his eyes and desperately hoped the current wouldn't take them out to sea.

And a child was born of great evil, henceforth great evil was set upon the land... be wary of he that bears the marks of Satan for he shall make your lands barren, your rivers dry and your nation his legion.

Iaeiros
Book of Heironymos

CHAPTER X
A WHISPER IN THE DARK

Tuesday 9:00 am
24, October 1978
Morgenstern (Morning Star)
Isabella Stone's Farmhouse
City of Madonnella
Bari Province, Italy

The Spanish maid opened the double doors of the farmhouse and entered the kitchen. Her arms were loaded down with bags of groceries and Isabella rushed to her aid before their contents spilled out onto the floor.

"Thank you, for everything you've done to help us," her voice was burdened with sorrow. Isabella fished inside her pockets for the maid's payment, "95,057 Lira?"

"Yes ma'am..." her eyes stared at the ceiling as she heard Emily's bed slide across the floor. "Dovessi tornare domani, se avete bisogno, (I return tomorrow if you need,)" she said in her best Italian.

"Yes--yes please," Isabella ushered the woman out the door.

Father Story held the banister with his full weight as he staggered down the staircase. His face was drained of its healthy color and his shoulders slumped with exhaustion. Isabella seized his hand and helped him sit down on the steps.

"Emily is strong and the beast inside is unwilling to release her, but she will win," his leg throbbed from nerve damage he had suffered during Hitler's war.

"You need to rest Father," she put her hand on his back, "please you have to let me help you."

He pointed to a medical bag and she retrieved it from a side chair set near the entrance way. He pulled out the last vial of haloperidol then stuck a hypodermic needle in the top and filled the tube with 6mg of the fluid.

"Give her the full injection in her hip. I'll prepare another dose and in five hours give her another," Father Story rose to his feet. "I have to review the new patient charts with the Mother Superior, but I'll be back later tonight."

Isabella took a deep breath and ascended the staircase; she was used to the strange coldness that clung to the walls. She walked to the end of the hallway and gently squeaked Emily's bedroom door open. Emily lay still with her breathing labored and congested. Her hands and feet were tightly bound to the bed and her chin rested on her chest. Her eyes were closed and there was no detectable movement of her arms or legs. She had physically deteriorated from the beautiful girl she had once been and appeared somewhat gaunt and disturbingly anorexic. She had torn out large clumps of her hair and ugly red scars covered her scalp. The skin on her face was so thin that it had the translucent appearance of wet tissue paper laid over her skull. Dry skin flaked from her lips and pus seeped from purple bruises painted underneath her eyes. As she neared the bed, Emily's eyes opened and she forced herself to brave the terror building within.

"It's good to see you mother," the voices of a middle aged woman and a young girl simultaneously resonated from her lips.

She ignored the child, weary of her ability to inflict emotional and physical harm to those who would display weakness in her presence. The thought of being alone in the house with her daughter hadn't seemed like a daunting proposition before, but now she wondered if Emily did attack her whether or not she was strong enough to defend herself. How long could she hold out until Father Story returned? She pushed away the fear from her mind and the endless scenarios of doom and death, after all Emily was still her daughter. There was an unbreakable bond between mother and child no matter what demons clawed away at her spirit. She was her daughter and they couldn't have her. She steadied her hand, removed the covers and lifted Emily's nightgown. The girl's eyes were probing her mother's face looking for any signs of discouragement. Isabella kept her movements calm and deliberate. She remained affectless showing no cracks in her veneer; in response the child defecated on the bed and laughed hysterically as she screamed out a tirade of expletives.

"Putain de cunt, la mort sera ta recompense," growled Emily through clenched teeth. "He's trying to kill me and you're helping him mother. Don't let him kill me. Please… pleeease!"

A tear ran down Isabella's cheek, "Father Story is trying to help you… and so am I." She swabbed alcohol on the girl's hip and injected her with the drug.

"We will never release the child," a man's harsh voice taunted. Emily's mind had deteriorated and her reason conjured up mostly random and distorted utterances, "Is father coming too… Peeeter…" She reached out for her mother and her eyelids tremble then closed.

How could Emily have known she had sought Peter's help? She hadn't discussed it with Father Story or told the maid she had gone into town to see him. Was it possible that the child had gotten into her head and read her thoughts? She wanted to wake her daughter and question her, but knew the demons would only lie and torment her. She knew Emily desperately wanted nothing more than to return to the field and find Robert. Was he somewhere out there hiding beneath the long green stalks, waiting for her, waiting to take his revenge? Those disturbing yellow eyes and the sense of overwhelming hatred she felt while in the fields made her wonder if Robert was still alive, or had he devolved into something evil that would haunt her the rest of her life. She cleaned the bedding and her daughter, then covered her with a linen sheet and stayed by her bedside. She opened the King James Bible that Father Story had left and eased back in her rocking chair. She thought about the words Peter had spoken and his promise to help. She had been wrong and regretted forcing him out of her life, out of Emily's life and prayed that he could find it in his heart to forgive her; they both needed him now more than ever.

CHAPTER X: A WHISPER IN THE DARK

Monday 11:45 am
Manna Book Store
City of Madonnella
Bari Province, Italy

"You intend to be silent the whole day?" Eddie tossed Mario's decorations into a box he carried underneath his arm. "Or are you thinking of a clever excuse to drop by Isabella's house?"

Peter wasn't in the mood to talk, "You heard the lady, she wants me to stay away. My hands are tied, there's nothing I can do."

"I get it, you want to pretend you're just some poor helpless sap bound to honor an agreement that you made with her years ago. Face it Pete, she needs you," he dropped the box on the floor, "I haven't known her as long as you have, but I know that she desperately needs your help even if she won't come out and beg for it."

"I'm not sure I can help," Peter picked up the box and continued cleaning up.

The tiny bell above the glass door rang and a man in desperate need of a shower and a shave stepped through the entrance. His clothes were badly wrinkled and he had the appearance of someone who hadn't slept for days. He scanned the place sensing a certain feeling a familiarity even though he had never set foot in the town before.

"Can either of you gentlemen tell me where I can find Peter Cameron?" Gallo asked, "My name's Detective Michael Sartori, it's important that I talk to him."

Peter extended his hand, "I'm Peter, can I help you?"

"I was hoping you could, Mr. Cameron. Is there someplace we can talk?"

The store was empty and Peter showed him to one of the tulip tables near the isle of book shelves. Gallo made a quick scan of the store then laid his traveler's bag on the table. He had developed the roll of film he'd thieved from the crime scene in the semi-darkness of his hotel bathroom. He pulled out a manila folder with a few of the heinous photographs clipped inside. He sat down in a chair, selected the first photo then pushed it over to Peter. The gruesome image was of a man hanging upside down and impaled on a cross with most of his bottom jaw missing. The skin was pale white and drained of all life giving fluids. Even the obscene way he was posed or the grotesque physical condition he was left in could not mask the man's true identity.

"Do you know who this man is?" Gallo studied Peter's face for the slightest reaction.

"Yes," he knew who it was immediately, "Cardinal Jeremiah Rourke, he was my friend and mentor."

"You were a priest?" Gallo was suddenly intrigued.

"Yes, but that was a long time ago."

"Did you know Cardinal Rourke was in Israel?"

"Yes, we had several conversations. He told me he was doing critical research while in the holy land."

CHAPTER X: A WHISPER IN THE DARK

Gallo opened Rourke's journal and held it up for Peter to see, "Did he ever ask you about the Desecrations, Trilogy or the Circle of Life?" He gave him the pictures of the dead girl and the photo of what little had been left of Basem. He then slid across the table photographs of the altar and the jars of human organs that had been carefully arranged around its base. Peter recoiled from the images, but quickly regained his composure.

"No, our conversations were strictly about the translation of ancient languages," Peter said, "but they are related."

"How so?"

"May I?" Peter gestured for Rourke's journal. He flipped through the pages until he came to a diagram Cardinal Rourke had drawn. "Circle of life," he held up the page for Gallo to see. The image was of a circle set inside a triangle set inside a circle. "I deciphered a dead language for Cardinal Rourke known as Thaydien. The inner circle represents life and is the first seal," he drew three dots at an equal distance from each other, "the top point represents birth, the next is your journey into adulthood and the third is what is commonly referred to as the golden years, and then of course... death." Peter drew three dots on each point of the triangle and started at the top, "These are the Desecrations, the second seal. The Thaydien people believed you could alter the inner circle by performing certain Onaric rituals such as the sacrifice of the young boy..."

"Basem," Gallo said and took notice of the unnerved effect on Peter's face.

"Basem would have been considered the Innocence Offering and the girl…"

"Fadia."

"Fadia would have represented the Virgin Offering and Cardinal Rourke the Pious Offering. The Thaydiens believed the Devil was mortally wounded in a great battle with God and his powers divided among three fallen angels. They were ceremonial sacrifices to the angels of Lucifer and once the last circle or third seal was broken it would have given those performing the sacrament his power." Peter drew more dots on the outside circle and started at the top, "The Angel Thaydien was made human and given a great book and dominion over mankind and the power of resurrection. The Angel Qeynan was given the power to destroy and turn nations to war. The last angel to rise from the Desecrations was Hector and he was given dominion over hell and the Devil himself. When all of the angels took their rightful place on the great throne of Hades, they would gain supremacy over heaven and earth and that was called the Trilogy." He leaned back and Eddie picked up the journal and examined the diagram. "But that's all part of an ancient myth and only lives within the realm of the supernatural. None of it is real of course."

"Obviously someone thinks it is real, or they wouldn't have gone to the trouble of killing three innocent people," Gallo grabbed Rourke's journal from Eddie's hand. "You said something about a great book? Is that important?"

"Yes, the libri of cado animus…"

"The book of fallen souls."

"That's right, they would have needed it to perform the Trilogy, but like I said its ancient myth. Besides you would have needed access to the original book and only a few survived over the centuries."

"Like the one locked away in the Vatican Library?"

"No, they only have a Latin version made hundreds of years later and poorly transcribed from the original Thaylic script."

"But you've read it haven't you? You had access to the original version."

"Yes, but I can assure you its kept in a very safe place and only a handful of people other than myself know where it is."

"Mr. Cameron your source was a banker named Georigo Onofri; he was murdered in Naples by members of siyah yılan. The book was stolen from him and given to a group headed by Father Alastor Martz."

"Atis..." Peter was clearly worried and his fingers tapped the table.

"Were you still in contact with Father Martz?"

"No--no," Peter shook his head, "not for years. But why…"

"Could he read the Thaydien language and decipher the script?"

"Yes he could, we used to transcribe many of the books that were sent to the Vatican Library, but I can't believe Father Martz would have..." Peter tried to calm himself, "You said he was the leader of a group?"

"Father Cameron... Mr. Cameron I know the papers reported he had died in his sleep, but he was under investigation for certain activities that may have linked him directly to the Pope's death. They were only vague allegations of course, but he committed suicide before he could be questioned. Father Martz showered petrol over his clothes then set himself on fire just moments before the guest house where he stayed was raided. We obtained information indicating that there may have been other high ranking members of the clergy that were among his group. Men who were committed to his beliefs and would do anything to carry out his plans and fulfill his vision."

"Why the hell would anyone care about a stupid book or ancient Thaydien rituals?" Eddie leaned against a bookcase, "It all sounds like bullshit to me."

"They may have wanted to humiliate the church, cause a scandal by showing that so many of them walked among the pious unnoticed for decades," offered Gallo, but Peter knew it was much more than that. "The Vatican has been understandably protective in matters concerning the church, sorry to say they haven't been of much help in the investigation either. They want the public to believe the Pope's death was of natural causes no matter how much the evidence proves that it may not have been."

"Don't tell me they don't believe a story where the Devil gave away all his power and that there are men seeking to seize it and control the world?" snickered Eddie.

"All his power except one," Peter corrected him, "he kept the power of deceit for himself and it gave him the power to lie and corrupt."

"Sorry Pete, I meant real power."

"Deceit might be the greatest power of them all, it can turn brother against brother and a lie in the right ear can bring nations to their knees."

"All the same," Eddie said in a spooky voice, "I'd rather have dominion over mankind."

Peter smirked, "They say the Angel Thaydien cursed the book so that the Devil couldn't touch it and steal his powers back less he turn to dust."

"Can you remember any of your colleagues that might have been interested or asked questions about the book?" Gallo was eager to get the conversation back on track.

"No I'm sorry I don't, but then again I left the church a decade ago."

The bell chimed and Mario entered carrying a box of glazed zeppoles. "I brought lunch for everyone," he said with a hearty laugh, "once again its Mario to the res-c-u…" His eyes settled on Peter, Eddie and the stranger, he saw the solemn look on their faces and his tone turned more somber, "Sorry, I didn't know you had company."

Gallo collected the photos, put them in his bag and slung it over his shoulder, "I'll be in town for a few more days." He gave Peter a piece of paper, "here's the number to my hotel. If you think of anything that might help, please give me a call."

"Of course," Peter stood, shook his hand and Gallo left barely acknowledging Mario as he passed.

"I hope I didn't interrupt anything important," Mario tossed a zeppole to Eddie.

"Just a brilliant dissertation on the history of ghost stories," said Eddie.

"What?"

"Never mind," Eddie took a bite out of the doughnut, "I thought guys like you didn't wake until late evening at the earliest."

"Oh I don't, but I came for Peter," Mario pulled out a chair, sat down and kicked his feet up on the tulip table, "I thought you might want to join me, I'm on my way over to Isabella's and I could sure use the company."

Gallo crossed the street and entered Nonna's Grocery Store; near the back he found a red English style phone booth. He closed the glass door behind him, deposited the correct change and dialed Cavilary's number from a piece of paper he took from his pocket. It rang three times.

"Hello."

Gallo was cautious and silent.

"Hello, who is this?"

The voice was different, completely foreign from that of his old friend. He hung up the phone, crumpled up the piece of paper and tossed it in the waste bin underneath the shelf. Had they shut Cavilary down through bureaucracy, or had it been something more permanent? Either way, his only contact at SISDE had been compromised and from here on out he was on his own. He had made deals, made sacrifices, done things he wasn't proud of and lost good friends like Hafsah and Minot along the way. He wanted to tell Peter or anyone for that matter about the beast that attacked him aboard the Oriens Astrum, but he could tell Peter was in denial about the evil that walked among men. Any description of the creature to a mildly skeptical audience would have made it seem like the ravings of a madman. All his life he had been dancing on the head of a pin, always been elusive, always keeping all options open and now it was time to make a decision whether or not he was all in. The voice inside his head was shouting forget everything, walk away, retire at a nice beach house with a beautiful woman and get out while you can. You still have a life and the shreds of what was left of your sanity. Call it a crossroad, call it a fork in the road but whatever it was he had to make a decision and it made more sense to stop and head back the way he came. Except, he knew he couldn't and it gnawed away at his guts. He'd gone too far and there were far too many questions that begged to be answered. He moved down the row of aisles and tossed a bottle of liquor, a Bagget, Camembert cheese, toothpaste, razor blades and a map of the City of Madonnella into his basket. He was deliberate, he was determined and before he left the store he returned to the phone booth and dialed a number he had written on the back of Cardinal Rourke's journal.

"Hello," a man with a deep voice answered; Gallo's hands were shaking and for a second he couldn't find the nerve to respond. "Yes, hello," the man repeated.

"It's me... I'm all in," he wiped away the sweat from his cheek with the back of his hand.

"Very good Mr. Gallo you've made the right decision," instantly the phone clicked and a dial tone resonated through the ear piece as the line went dead.

1:45 pm
Hospes of St. Cecilia

Gallo parked on the opposite side of the street from St. Cecilia and walked through the iron gate. There were hordes of children playing noisily and he playfully patted a girl on the head as he past her by. He strolled through the hall, into the atrium and up to the statue of St. Cecilia. The marble floor was scuffed and the statue's platform still retained signs of the damage inflicted by a drunken Emir Saldalha. He heard the voice of a young nun standing behind him, flashed a smile and flashed a counterfeit badge.

Sister Boyette took him up to a third floor office on the hospital side of St. Cecilia's. She knocked and opened the door to a tiny 12'x12' room, "A Detective Sartori is here to see you Father."

"Thank you Sister," Father Story paused from packing a small black bag and addressed Gallo, "Is there something I can help you with officer?"

"You had an incident here last month; a young man broke into the grounds of the Hospes. I believe he was found kneeling by the statue of St. Cecilia begging for her forgiveness."

"As I've already told your counterparts, I wasn't here on that evening."

"I know, but it's always good to follow up in case there things you might have remembered since then, something one of the nuns may have told you. The man, Emir Saldalha, do you know of any reason why he would have driven all the way from Naples to Madonnella?"

"He came to see my predecessor Cardinal Jeremiah Rourke, but he had left his position as director a few weeks earlier," Father Story zipped up the black bag, "his temporary replacement Father Joseph Principi was here and tried to console him but he wouldn't speak to him. Father Principi has since been reassigned and has been out of the country for at least a month, but he gave a full account to the police before he left." He slipped on his jacket and picked up the bag.

"Cardinal Rourke was murdered while he was in Israel," Gallo said antiseptically, "Did he have any enemies that you know of?"

"No. I can't believe anyone would have wanted to do him harm."

"Could Emir have met the Cardinal before or have had any relatives here in Madonnella, perhaps a child enrolled in the school or a patient in the hospital?"

"Our records concerning the children are strictly private and sealed Detective, I'm afraid I can't help you on that accord," Father Story escorted him out of his office and his giant loop key ring jingled as he locked the door behind him. "I'm sorry I have to go, but if you have any more questions I'm sure the Mother Superior will be able to assist you."

"Of course," Gallo faked his appreciation. "Thank you for your time Father."

He spent the next forty five minutes listening to the Mother Superior spin vagaries of the night in question. After a long tirade of insignificant details he tried to get her to focus on particular events, but the conversation inevitably returned to the mundane and unimportant pap she experienced on her nightly watch. She plodded through the mire of miracles and wonderments that had occurred within the walls of St. Cecilia and always concluded her tome with an amen or praise the Lord all mighty. In the end, he was saved by a voice crackling over the address system's loud speakers that requested her urgent assistance in one of the wards. He was about to leave when a young nun got up from behind her station desk and seized him by the arm.

"They're not telling you everything they know," Sister Marian was strikingly anxious, "Father Story and the Mother Superior, they're afraid to tell you what really happened here with the child."

"I'm sorry Sister, I don't know what you're talking about," Gallo broke her grip and pushed past her, he had wasted enough time and wasn't in the mood for petty workplace complaints or firsthand testaments to the wonders of her deep and abiding Christian beliefs.

"The child was consumed with evil... her eyes... her eyes were horrible," Sister Marian broke down, "I know it sounds incredible but that child they brought here was possessed by the Devil."

Gallo stopped in his tracks then turned around and grasped her arms tightly, "Did Emir come to see her? Do you know if he asked for her?"

"No this was much later, he never knew the girl was here."

"Can you give me her name... an address?"

"I don't know. Father Story was very strict about her confidentiality and who was allowed to see her, he was always present when the doctors examined the child," Sister Marian then related her experience the night the child fled. She showed him the patched and freshly painted wall where all four legs of a bed had once been impaled into the cement and the newly repaired window that the child had shattered when she leapt from the sixth floor. Sister Marian told him of the night of the girl's possession, the depths of evil in her eyes and the tale of the missing maintenance man that had fled after her. "Father Story told the staff that the girl was feeble minded and suffered from horrible seizures, but he knows the truth about her and what she has done," Sister Marian talked in hushed tones."That child will bring nothing but death and destruction to everything she touches."

"Has Father Story spoken to anyone else about the child's true condition, possibly the Mother Superior?"

"No."

"Has anyone stopped by his office to talk to him, a face you might recall if you concentrated? The parents of the girl, do you remember a name, a description, anything?"

"No. I'm sorry," she looked around to make sure they weren't overheard, "I'm new and you're the first person I've talked to because I didn't want to get in trouble with Father Story or the Mother Superior."

"Are there any records? Is there a log for the children that were admitted that night," Gallo saw her reluctance to offer up any more pertinent information. "Please Sister its important."

They went back to the front desk, she handed him a clipboard and flipped the pages back to October 21st. Terrified of being discovered, Sister Marian stood watch with her eyes focused on the elevators and the main hallway leading to the Children's Ward. There were nine children admitted that day during the morning and afternoon, and two later that evening. His eyes stopped on the second to last name on the list: E. Stone. He knew the name; Harkir Saldalha had demanded to see Robert Stone just before he was killed. His heart raced, an electric surge charged his body as he realized he was getting closer to finding the book. He memorized the address and slipped out of the building then headed out towards Morgenstern farm.

To me belongs vengeance, and recompense; their foot shall slide in due time: for the day of their calamity is at hand, and the things that shall come upon them make haste.

Deuteronomy
King James Bible

CHAPTER XI
THE DARKSIDE

Tuesday 2:15 pm
24, October 1978
Morgenstern (Morning Star)
Isabella Stone's Farmhouse
City of Madonnella
Bari Province, Italy

Isabella rushed downstairs as she heard the knocking from her front porch. Her mind was far away and she had wondered whether or not she'd locked Father Story out. She opened the door and was startled to see Mario's smiling face.

"Mario to the rescue, I come bearing gifts," he held up a bottle of vino, yet Isabella's face was still blank, "It didn't work for me this morning either, I must be losing my touch," he examined the bottle's label to make sure it was a good year and stepped inside. "Now before you say anything, let's stop pretending that you don't want our help."

"Our... help?" she folded her arms.

Mario turned in the doorway and grabbed Peter by the sleeve. He put his arm around him and grinned from ear to ear, "C'mon, I can almost guarantee with absolute certainty that he can do a better job than Father Story."

"Mario!" Peter walked in the doorway, "I'm sorry, I should have come by myself, but he can be very persuasive."

She closed the door behind them. "That's all right, it's just that I don't think…"

"She is my daughter too," Peter looked at the winding staircase leading up to Emily's bedroom then back at Isabella. "I told you, I want to help you any way I can."

"You want the best--you got the best and free of charge," Mario said confidently. "We'll have her up and kicking and back to her old self in no time at all."

"Enough Mario. You've made more than an ass out of yourself, she gets the point."

The sound of another car pulling up the driveway interrupted their conversation and Isabella opened the door to find Eddie and Angela standing on her front stoop. His head was down and he looked quite sheepish.

"I just thought I needed to be here… for you and Pete I mean," Eddied kissed her on her cheek.

"You're Mr. Skeptical, the number one non-believer of non-believers. I thought you didn't take seriously ghost stories and demonic possession." Mario quipped as he opened the bottle of wine.

"I don't." Eddied pulled Angela inside.

CHAPTER XI: THE DARKSIDE

"We can go up to see her, but she's been given a sedative and won't wake up for a few hours," Isabella stood at the base of the stairs then led the group up to Emily's room. "I have to warn you it'll be a shock when you first see her."

There was a noticeable change in temperature, the wood floor squeaked loudly and Eddie hugged Angela close as they marched down the hallway. It was more than the cold that was off-putting, there was a deep sense of loss and isolation seeping through the walls. Isabella pushed the door open to reveal dozens of candles spread across a darkly lit room. Emily's bedpost had marked deep grooves into the wall from floor to ceiling and the dresser and heavy furniture had been removed from the room leaving it quite sparse. The strong smell of urine on her sheets and in the shag carpet saturated the air. Angela was overcome with a sense of fear and doom, she avoided looking directly at the child as she stood in the doorway. She believed in the Devil and possession even if Eddie laughed at the mere thought of it. It was real and she could feel the oddness, the sense that something was not quite right emanating from within the child's room like an infectious disease. She had only gone to Isabella's because Eddie had wanted to and now more than ever she wished she hadn't. She shook her head, released Eddie's hand and stayed outside as he and the others moved closer to the child's bed.

"How long has she been like this?" the steam from Mario's breath hung in the air.

"A few days, it seemed to have come upon her rather quickly," she adjusted Emily's pillow.

Peter's fingers touched the scales around her face and traced across the black circles under her eyes. He picked up an empty bottle of haloperidol that lay on the floor next to the night stand. "You said Father Story has seen her and believes she's possessed? Did he tell you why he was administering this drug?"

She took the bottle from his hand, "Yes, he said it would help keep her under control until he was ready to perform the exorcism."

"The drug is for nervous tics and Tourette's syndrome; he's treating her for schizophrenia," Eddie picked up the child's wrist and was startled to find her arm emaciated and her pulse barely registering. He opened her mouth merely to discover teeth that had been broken on furniture and the metal knobs of her bedpost. With his thumb and forefinger he opened her eyelids to reveal lifeless black orbs with bloody tears that ran down the sides of her cheeks. "This is crazy, have you all gone mad? She'll die if she's not treated soon." He quickly undid her restraints and gathered her up in his arms.

"Leave the child where she is," Father Story stood at the doorway. "She is in my care now and I will decide what is best for her."

"Are you insane?" Eddie ignored his order, "Look at her, she's wasting away. Did you tell her that Emily is really mentally ill or was it easier for you to claim her daughter was haunted while you sit and do nothing except watch her die."

"Leave her," Peter touched Eddie's shoulder.

"Pete?" Eddie was stunned, "You can't be serious."

CHAPTER XI: THE DARKSIDE

"I know what you must be thinking, I know how you must feel seeing the child in the condition that she's in, but trust me I can explain everything to you. Please, wait for me downstairs and all things will be made clear to you. Please." Father Story and Isabella redid the girl's restraints while the others left the room.

3:10 pm

Gallo traveled down a long dirt road in a little red Fiat Spider rent-a-car. The engine made a worrying knocking sound and steam leaked out from beneath the hood. He was already driving on a spare tire and wondered if he'd be left stranded in the middle of nowhere on an island surrounded by waves of tall wheat stalks. The sun was blazing hot and with the air conditioning broken he had taken the rag top down. There was nothing in sight except miles and miles of corn and wheat fields. The engine overheat light had been on for a half hour and his nerves began to fray. He stopped the car, stood on the hood and scanned the bountiful terrain. Almost nine hundred feet away a farmhouse stood against the azure blue sky horizon. He saw a man on a tractor plowing the dirt near the edge of the field; success, there were signs of life after all. He drove fifty feet and made a right turn toward the direction of the farmhouse. It was old and the peeling white paint either gave it a down home natural rustic charm or the perfect feel of a horror/slasher flick. A flock of geese waddled across the road that separated the house from a wood rot barn and grain silo forty feet away. He shut off the engine, it clamored loudly for a few seconds then went silent. He stood on the porch waving his arms over his head to get the farmer's attention. The man on the tractor finally looked his way then waved his hand and headed over in his direction. The farmer slowly approached him as he headed up the grassy slope towards the driveway.

"Beautiful country you have out here," Gallo extended his hand to the heavyset man as he got closer.

"Been working it all my life," farmer Serge D'Alisa said, "We don't get many strangers around here mister. What can I do for you?"

"I was hoping I could get some water for the radiator," He glanced towards the little red car spouting steam like a billowing chimney.

"Sure thing," he put a bucket on the ground and cranked water from a rust colored cast iron hand pump.

Gallo took off the bandana from around his neck, held it under the flowing water then wiped his face and neck with it, "Do you know where I can find Isabella Stone's house?" They walked to his car and he popped the hood, took off the radiator cap then slowly poured the water in, "It appears that I am hopelessly lost."

D'Alisa squinted his eyes and gave him a good once over, "Depends, what do you want with her mister?"

"Just an old family friend."

"I've known her since she was a babe and I don't recall ever seeing you," he said sharply with all the down home hospitality gone from his voice.

"I meant I'm a friend of her husband. We went to college together back in New York."

"Oh Robert, haven't seen him in a long time. Don't think he's around much, not lately anyways."

Gallo retrieved the map from the car, "This ah… this road here take me in the right direction?" He pointed to the private road that divided the house and barn.

"Oh no, you ain't gonna find shit on those maps," D'Alisa laughed. "You come too far, you passed her place about a mile back from the main road." He placed a brown leather apron over his head and pulled out a pair of long knives from the side pockets.

"You said you haven't seen Robert for a while, he give any reason why he left?"

"You got your water mister," he slid the knives against each other making a screeching metallic sound, "unless you want to talk while I gut the pig, I got a lot of chores to do before the sun goes down." He walked away daring him to follow.

Gallo looked over at the barn where a pig hung upside down from its hooves and had its throat cut and chest cavity laid wide open, "I guess I'll be on my way then."

D'Alisa raised a knife hand and kept walking towards the barn door. He sat back in the Fiat, held his breath and turned the key to the ignition; to his surprise it started. He turned on the main road and sped off in the direction the farmer had given him. D'Alisa opened the barn door where his sweet diminutive wife hung by her feet from the ceiling's wooden cross beam. Her mouth was gagged, her hands were tied together and they dangled limply over her head. The fear within her grew as the man she had known and loved for forty years approached her with bad intent in his eyes. She was utterly defenseless; on the ground lay her dimwitted brother with his hands bound behind his back.

"You've done well Brother and you will be rewarded for your loyalty," Father Santeal stepped out of the shadows, his eyes burned red. "It is only in a moment like this that a man can prove himself to be worthy. You know what must be done."

D'Alisa nodded his head and moved towards his wife. She squirmed and a muffled scream parted her lips. He brushed her hair aside and kissed her lovingly on the cheek. He coldly slit her throat, then plunged the knife deep into the fat of her belly. She shook for mere seconds as the blood drained into the bucket he had placed beneath her. Tears burst out of her brother as he tried to get to his feet and run away. Father Santeal placed his hands on each side of the man's face and stared into his eyes. He conveyed a look of understanding and pity; the brute relaxed and stopped his futile attempt at resistance. Father Santeal put an open hand on her brother's forehead and the man closed his eyes and barely uttered a whimper. His calloused palm made contact with the skin and the intense heat emanated from the center. Her brother's skull vibrated, his jaw shook violently and his eyes rolled up into the back of his head. There was nothing left of the man who had once existed and in his place was left the submissive servant of the beast.

Cardinal Fuerst stood at an open window on the barn's second floor rafter and watched the dust cloud that trailed behind Gallo's car as he hit the main road.

"If Robert were here he would have killed him the second he got out of his car. He would have told you there was no reason to let him live," Father Santeal had suddenly materialized behind Cardinal Fuerst's back, "and I would have agreed with him."

"Patients my friend, there's always a risk in acting too hastily and without considerable planning or thinking. If he was a policeman they would surely send another in his place, and if he was sent by the Council then his death would have certainly brought more of them."

"So let them come and we will destroy them all. There is no match for the power we wield."

"You forget Thaydien, until Hector rises and the circle is complete you are still vulnerable to the hand of mortal man," Fuerst rested his hand on Santeal's shoulder, "In time the world will be ours for the taking and you can destroy all of mankind if you wish to."

3:45 pm
Isabella Stone's Farmhouse

"There are many things about heaven and hell that even the most faithful cannot fully comprehend. There are many things about my methods that I don't expect you to understand," Father Story steadied his hand as he placed a cup of coffee on the living room table. "I can assure you that I have contemplated every option in her treatment and I am doing what is best for the child."

"Can you say for certain that Emily is possessed?" Mario sat crosswise from him, "Has she communicated to you or has there been any events of a supernatural nature?"

"Listen to you," Eddie paced the room, "you sound like you've all lost your minds. Has she seen a doctor? Has she been properly diagnosed? Has she…"

"Of course she has!" Father Story slammed his hand on the table, "I didn't see her condition as an act of blind adherence to my faith. Do you really think the only conclusion I could have come to is that it was the Devil's machinations!" His voice calmed, "I run the Hospes if you have forgotten… she's seen the best doctors, the best neurosurgeons, but none of them could help her. I have seen her take the lives of two men, and if those demons inside her take hold, she will kill scores more."

The room was silent, Angela took Isabella by the hand, "Come, we'll make some more coffee."

"She is possessed. I can feel it. I can't explain it, but I know because we are connected," said Peter, "I don't know how, I don't know why, but for some time now I have felt the evil rising all around me. I can feel it now like the faint pulsating surge of electricity and it is only growing stronger."

The doorbell rang and startled the group, Isabella excused herself and opened the front door.

"Ms. Stone?"

"Yes."

"I wonder if I could ask you a few questions." Gallo hat in hand stepped thru the doorway uninvited. "Detective Sartori..." his eyes caught a glimpse of Father Story, Peter and Eddie thru the archway of the living room. "Good to see all of you again," he said a bit perplexed.

"I'm sorry but now's not a good time," she said to no effect.

"It's nothing official, I just have a few questions that I thought you and perhaps your guest could help me with," Gallo marched into the living room. "Gentlemen, I have to say this seems like a very fortunate coincidence," he wore a phony smile.

"We're friends of the family; we just stopped by to say hello," said Eddie.

He was less than convinced and turned to Isabella, "Ms. Stone can I ask you a couple of questions about your husband?"

"You can, but I haven't seen or heard from Robert in over a year."

"He hasn't tried to make contact with you at all?"

She wanted to tell him that he had in her nightmares, that his spirit hid within the shadow of the crops and plagued her land. "No, he hasn't," she stuck to the sane and reasonable.

"Is it possible he left something behind before he disappeared: notes, memoirs... a book?"

"Robert wasn't much on reading, the only thing he cared about were his ships," Isabella sat down at the end of the table, "he has a warehouse full of monuments to his work, you're welcome to look at them if you want."

"He's looking for a particular book Isabella and as I already informed him it was an extremely rare find," Peter spoke up. "It's doubtful Robert would have known of the book's existence or could have found it even if he had."

"I don't know. In my line of work I've seen that money can buy you just about anything," Gallo took stock of the large house and property, "and it looks to me like he had plenty of it."

"As I said Detective, my husband left no papers or books of value before he left."

"Very well, it was worth a shot." Gallo smirked and turned to leave, "Oh, before I forget; is it possible he left something with your daughter?"

Isabella's face turned stone cold and she tried to mask her discomfort, "No he didn't."

"It could be that he didn't tell you he gave her a special gift to hold on to," Gallo stepped closer, "a secret kept between father and daughter until he returned. Maybe I could talk to her?"

"No. My daughter is ill."

"It would only take a few minutes, I promise to be respectful," Gallo glanced at Father Story and he looked away. "After all its been a very long drive."

"I believe she has answered your questions Detective, unless you have a warrant I believe your interview is over," Father Story said in a measured tone.

"No--no warrant," Gallo spun his hat around his finger and stared at the floor, "as I said it was worth a shot." He put on his fedora and tipped the brim while Isabella walked him to the door. "You'd be surprised at some of the things I've seen Ms. Stone. Trust me I know, sometimes people get in over their heads and when they finally find the courage to ask for help it's too late."

Isabella opened the front door, "I'm sorry I couldn't have been more helpful to you Detective."

"Oh I don't know, I believe you have," Gallo turned and left.

Friday 3:00 pm
3, November 1978
Hillel Yaffe Medical Center
Hadera, Israel

The bass drum beat in his head was nonstop, he awoke to find his upper body in a full cast and tethered to hooks dangling from the ceiling. Gutman's eyes focused on the blurry image of a priest standing near the bay window, "Looks like you got the wrong room Father."

"Good you're awake," said High Commander Arens as the nurse moved from Gutman's line of sight. He was an enormously fat man dressed in all black with greased back hair and was caught with his fingers stuck in a jar of

Rugelach. He bit into a cookie and embarrassingly wiped the crumbs from his shirt. "You had us worried Mr. Gutman."

"I don't think I know you." Gutman closed his eyes while the nurse wiped his face with a damp cloth.

I know you," the High Commander's voice was deep and serious, "more importantly I know what you've been doing. Taking control over local police matters, overruling the Massad when it came to holding a suspect--your contact and now with the mess out in Haifa; let's just say you've been a very busy boy."

"And where is my contact now?" Gutman's voice was weak.

The tall man, one of Gutman's agents stood nearby, "He left Israel four days ago."

"You were very lucky," Commander Arens pointed a fat finger in his direction, "The crew of the Nemisis troller was headed out to deep water when they spotted you and Agent Gallo floating in the middle of nowhere.

"Sorry boss, Gallo made it back to the hotel and cleared out before we knew what happened," the tall agent kept his head down. "He must have made his way to Egypt and flown out from there."

"That's okay; I think I know where he's going. We'll pick up his trail soon enough," Gutman exhaled painfully.

"You broke your back," Commander Arens said flatly, "You'll be laid up for the next couple of months. Besides with Harkir Saldalha gone there is a power vacuum and a long list of terrorists waiting to fill his shoes."

"There are some things more dangerous than terrorists and wannabe kingpins," Gutman glared at the Commander, "Do what you want, I have an investigation to complete.

"You've broken just about every rule in the book during your investigation and now the alleged killers have disappeared, Emir Saldalha is dead and Agent Gallo is gone. The Massad wants your head and my superiors want you in a prison cell. You're lucky you have so many friends in high places or you would be having this conversation at the point of a gun." Commander Arens tossed a manila folder on top of Gutman's chest, "Your men have been reassigned and as for you, it's either a demotion and new assignment, or early retirement--your choice."

"If I gave you my full report maybe you'd think differently."

"The decisions already been made Mr. Gutman. You have the next three months to think about it, so there's no reason to say anything now that you might regret." Commander Arens walked to the door and just before he left offered a word of advice, "You're a bright boy, I trust you'll make the right decision."

The folder slid from Gutman's chest and a few pages fanned out across the floor; a picture of Yassir Arafat lay on top. The tall agent scooped up the loose papers and photograph and tucked them under his arm, "Sorry boss, I have to go I've been assigned checkpoint duty in Gaza. I'll leave the folder in your office." He thought about saying more, but didn't; he nodded and left.

"And what about you?" Gutman said to the priest peering out the window, "You didn't come all this way just to pray for my soul or wish me well."

"I'm sorry I got you involved," Father Joseph Principi's face was clearer as the bright sunlight haze around him had dissipated. "With Cardinal Rourke gone I'm not sure where things stand."

"So, what have you got?"

"I can't ask you…"

"Forget about what they said. What have you got?"

"I don't know for sure. A name, someone who might be connected with all of this madness; someone I should have suspected from the very beginning."

"Who?"

Father Principi sat down at the edge of the bed and rubbed his eyes; he exhaled slowly, "Father Anton Layad."

And your covenant with death shall be disannulled, and your agreement with hell shall not stand; when the overflowing scourge shall pass through, then ye shall be trodden down by it.

Isaiah
King James Bible

CHAPTER XII
THE WRETCHED AND THE DEAD

Sunday 11:08 am
5, November 1978
Morgenstern (Morning Star)
Isabella Stone's Farmhouse
City of Madonnella
Bari Province, Italy

Peter, Eddie, Mario, Angela and Father Story had stayed at Isabella's farmhouse for the last two days preparing for Emily's exorcism and in that time the child hadn't woken from her deep sleep. It appeared that the demons inside her were also girding themselves against the impending war for her soul. Peter had made several trips back to the bookstore, and in one outing retrieved a 13th century soapstone statue of a dragon that was kept in a glass display case. It was a delicate and intricately carved six inch rendering of the biblical Leviathan created by the hands of an unknown sculptor. He took a hammer and smashed the statue into pieces then carved them into the shapes of a horn, tooth and talon. He spent hours polishing the rough edges until they were smooth then fashioned each into the exact shape he desired. Father Story made frequent visits back to the Hospes to fulfill his duties, pilfer medical supplies from the basement storage room and gather holy water from the marble fountain erected near the statue of St. Cecilia. The rest stood guard over the child and took turns watching her for any indication that she might emerge from her deathly slumber. The passing hours were long and tedious and the pressure of waiting for the unknown had everyone exceedingly anxious. Peter searched Isabella's farm for the tools he could use to help protect the land from the outside forces he knew would come. He pulled back the giant sliding doors to one of Robert's warehouse storage units. It was filled with various antique vehicles, Wolfe and Stone ship engines, ship skeletons and two powder blue American made semi trucks parked side by side. He climbed on top one of the semi's cabs and unlatched a heavy 6'x8' solid oak railroad tie from the rafter. He tossed it to the ground then placed it over his shoulder and carried it to her front yard. Peter walked backwards dragging the massive beam and etched a six inch trench into the soft black dirt. Within an hour he had created a perfect circle around the farmhouse that stretched out thirty feet in circumference.

"Can I ask what you're doing?" Mario sat on the stoop of the back porch eating an apple.

"Hopefully I'm being overly cautious," he said as he hammered his second 4 foot cross into the circle's trench.

"Overly cautious about what?"

"I told you I knew something was wrong. I can sense the presence of evil around this house and it's not just the demon inside my daughter. It's Robert, he's coming for her," Peter wiped the sweat off his face, "and he's not alone."

"Is there anything I can do to help?" Mario picked up a cross from the pile and examined it closely. Carved across the face was the word Deuteronomy and there were others marked Joshua, Judges...

"Yeah, but they have to go in a certain order," Peter smiled sheepishly, "Do you know your Old Testament?"

"Sorry Peter, can't say that I do."

"That's alright, there are plenty of other things that need to be tended to."

"Like what, and keep in mind my very limited ecclesiastical knowledge; my parents were atheist after all," Mario tossed the apple core into the woods.

"I'm gonna need a goat from the pasture, you can get that for me."

"Should I even ask why?"

"Only if you're not squeamish."

"A goat."

"Right," Peter hammered the Leviticus cross into the trench, "and a very sharp knife."

Angela waded through the cornfield; she had watched Peter as he carried the beam and made the circle in the dirt. When it was complete, he effortlessly threw it somewhere among the rows of green vineyards. She had spent the last five minutes searching for it and found it twenty feet from where Peter had last stood. Angela bent down; she was fascinated and ran her hands across the top of the railroad tie.

"What are you doing?" Eddie stood behind her.

"See if you can pick this up," she tapped on the sides to make sure it was solid.

"Why?"

"Humor me."

Eddie grabbed the end of the beam and made his best effort, but it wouldn't budge, "Maybe if I had a crane…"

"I saw Peter carrying it by himself, he moved it pretty easily too."

"Peter?"

"Yes, and I saw him throw it over here--by himself," she stood and knocked into Eddie's shoulder as she passed him by and kept walking towards the house. "You still think there's nothing wrong with him?"

He bent down and tried to move it once more but it was impossible. He sat on top of the enormous beam, tired and muscles strained, he watched as his friend hammered a series of crosses into the dirt. He wondered to himself, just how much had Peter changed.

Sunday 5:00 pm
City of Madonnella

Gallo pulled up to the garage across the street from the old brick hotel in the heart of downtown Madonnella. The long drive, the blazing sun and the noncooperation from the inhabitants of this little town had drained him of all his energy. He entered the hotel oblivious to the whining call of the concierge calling his name.

"Mr. Sartori! Mr. Sartori!" she bellowed as he passed her by.

The alias finally registered with him and he turned back after reaching the elevator doors, "Yes, is there something wrong?"

"No sir; a package arrived for you."

"A package?"

"Yes sir."

"That's impossible, nobody knows..." he walked over to the check-in desk and she held out a shoe box sized package wrapped in plain brown paper. There was no return address or postage on the box. "Did you see who left this for me?"

"I...I...I'm sorry sir I..."

"Forget about it," he smiled and held it up, "Don't look a gift horse..."

Gallo returned to his room, scanned the interior and when he was convinced no one had been inside locked the door behind him. He tossed the box on the foot of the bed, took off his shirt and ran the water in the tub. After splashing water on his face, he retrieved a cigar box and matches then sat down next to the box. His mind raced with thoughts of what it might be; no one knew he was here not even Cavilary. He carefully unwrapped the brown paper with a steadied hand as though its contents held a ticking time bomb inside. He lifted the lid; no explosion. Inside was a Double Action Makarov Pistol with an attachable silencer and boxes of ammunition. A piece of white paper was neatly folded and tucked underneath the handgrip. He dumped ice from the stainless steel bucket, opened the letter and read the sender's instructions. He lit the cigar and with the burning match torched the letter and dropped it into the empty bucket. Gallo relaxed his weary body in the cold water of the tub, took a puff off the cigar and loaded a magazine into the pistol.

8:00 pm
Isabella's Farmhouse

Peter soaked his hands in ice water as he sat at Isabella's kitchen table. He had done all he could to protect the group from Robert's wrath and the all too real knowledge that he would show no mercy. He had dug the trench around her house, poured the blood of the sacrificed goat inside the track and hammered all the crosses into the hollowed earth. He had worn thick work gloves, but with every cross he touched his hands burned, blistered and bled. He decided not to inform the others of that detail. Peter knew he was slowly changing into the beast that he had envisioned in his dreams and wondered when the transformation was complete, who would save them from him?

"I saw you working outside, very impressive. Two men would struggle carrying a beam that heavy, but you handled it with ease,"

Father Story sat down across from him. "I know you well enough to know when you're keeping secrets Father Cameron."

"Everyone seems to insist on calling me Father Cameron," a slight tone of anger stirred in his voice, "you of all people should know better."

Father Story grabbed Peter by the wrists and examined the wounds on his hands, "You and your child share a direct bloodline to an apostle of evil. The Devil has infected her and he's been creeping into your soul as well. He's strong enough to resist any attempts to excise him from your daughter, but you already knew that didn't you? You plan to offer the Devil a trade, your soul for hers."

"Eddie was right," Peter broke his grip, "You were willing to watch her die while you kept her unconscious. If you're afraid Father, you can leave now and I'll take care of her myself."

A loud screech came from overhead as Emily's bed dragged across the wood floor. Isabella's stressed voice cried out and the two men ran to her aid. They stood outside Emily's bedroom; Father Story placed his hand on Peter's chest, "I know you've already made up your mind, but I'm asking you for one last chance to do things my way."

Peter nodded in accord and Father Story closed the bedroom door behind him. He could hear the wretched howl of the thing within Emily erupt in an outburst of curses and threats. He fished inside his pocket and held the three figurines he had carved from Leviathan statue then carefully unwrapped a crucifix from its silk cloth binding.

Father Story sent Isabella and Angela from the room. Eddie sat on the left side of the bed and Mario on the right struggling to hold her arms down.

"In the Name of the Father and of the Son and of the Holy Spirit, Amen," Father Story donned a long black cassock and quickly fitted himself with a white surplice, "Let God arise and let his enemies be scattered and let them that hate him flee from before his face!" He blessed a long purple stole and placed it around his neck.

Emily's eyelids fluttered and her pupils rolled down to focus on the voice in the room, "Who's there? Who has come to stand before me?" She raised her head and stared at Father Story. Her mouth opened to reveal a toothy grin; she lay her head back down on the pillow and laughed hysterically. "Vienen padre, confesar sus pecados delante de mí." (Come father, confess your sins before me.)

He knelt by her bedside as she vomited a rainbow of blood and phlegm into his face, "Let them be confounded and ashamed that seek after my soul. Let them be turned back and be confounded that devise evil against me. Let them become as dust before the wind and let the Angel of the Lord..."

"You're all going to die!" a woman's raspy voice exclaimed. Her head turned towards Mario and the bones in her neck strained and popped, "Everyone has dirty little secrets that you hide from each other. And I know what they are... all of them. You are a sinner, you the confirmed bachelor who travels across the world in the company of young men. They are your lovers and you spread your wicked disease to the bodies of the depraved," she snickered, "You have fallen so far from the grace of God... like pitiful lost sheep." She then focused her anger on Eddie, "And dear, dear Edward you haven't told anyone that you forced Angela to have an abortion have you?" Listen carefully and you will hear your son burning in hell with all of us." The cries of a wailing baby filled the room.

"Stop it!" Eddied released his grip on her and held his ears. "Stop it, please."

"Enough of your wickedness!" Father Story made the sign of the cross.

"You haven't learned, have you Father? I know your secret as well," her voice mimicked Father Rourke, "You let me die, alone. You could have saved me but you chose to save yourself and let me suffer." The voice screamed in agony, "The pain... the fire... it burns, it burns!" An invisible force looped the purple sash around his neck and pulled the ends to the ceiling. Father Story's feet were elevated off the floor and his hands clawed at the stole trying to break free from the hangman's noose. Eddied and Mario were unable to move and watched helplessly as he fought to keep his neck from snapping. "Hell is waiting for you; hell is waiting for all of you," she said in the woman's voice.

"I know what you are... the sickness-- the unclean," Peter stood in the open doorway.

"Who's there? Who speaks to me?" Emily's full attention turned to him; she released her hold over Father Story and his body crashed to the floor. "Come closer so that I may see your face."

"You are not the fallen Angel Qeynan," Peter said, "for you have no power to make war and you are weak," he threw the carved talon onto the bed and she hissed like a snake. "You are not the Angel Thaydien for you are not the great resurrector... the possessor of the book," he threw the carved tooth onto the bed.

"Stop! Stop please," she twisted and thrashed violently. "Pleeeeease I beg you."

He held up the last figurine of the ram's horn, "You are the Angel Hector, the Red King, Sado Satanus the last evil to rise and plague the corners of the earth." He tossed the statuette onto her stomach and the stench of sizzling flesh burned the air. "You are the heretic..."

She laughed and her eyes fixed on Peter's movements. "Come closer father," said a child's voice, "come closer and sit next to me your only child."

Peter stood at the foot of the bed and would move no closer, "No matter what you say or who's tongue you speak with, I will not stop until you release the child."

"She's mine now and forever," replied a rattlesnake hiss.

"Peter if you're going to do something you'd better do it now; her body's getting hotter and I can't hold on much longer," Eddie struggled to clasp onto her wrist.

Father Story rolled over onto his stomach and Peter motioned for him to stay silent. "Já vám nabízím svou duši výměnou za její." (I offer you my soul in return for hers.)

"Chceme její." (We want hers.)

"Je slabý a neschopný vykonávat znesvěcení. Jen můj obět' zajistí vzestup Hectora." (She is weak and unable to perform the desecration. Only my sacrifice will ensure the rise of Hector.)

The room grew colder; a thick green haze was made iridescent by the light of the full moon and enveloped her body. A ghostly form separated itself from the child, but kept the guise of Emily only two years older. The others in her bedroom were frozen in place as if time had wound to a halt. She placed her bare feet on the floor and her face appeared as his daughter at fourteen. Her fingers glided along the bedspread as she walked to the foot of the bed where Peter stood; he didn't move. Her hair grew longer and she physically transformed with each step. When she stopped in front of him she was a beautiful seventeen year old girl.

"Why should I believe you?" her nightgown slipped from her shoulders and she stood before him naked. Emily placed a hand on his chest and walked around him gently touching his shoulder and back. She stood behind him with her arms wrapped around his waist and her head on his shoulder. "Don't worry they can't hear us... or see us," she slipped both hands inside his pants and seized his manhood.

"You have no choice," Peter clutched her hands; his eyes glued to the child that lay like an empty shell unmoving on her bed. "Without my help she will die and you will be sent back to the depths of hell."

"Then our price is that you perform the desecrations now, so that we may witness your submission to the Lord."

"My offer is my soul for hers," Peter turned to face her. "When I decide to perform the rituals is entirely up to me."

"If you betray us, you won't be able to imagine the pain and suffering, and it will last an eternity."

"If you betray me, I will destroy all of you."

Emily smirked, the bedroom door slammed shut and the windows shook and rattled open. A stiff wind howled like a freight train as it flowed into the room. Emily's long brown hair flew around her face as Peter fought to stand in the eye of the storm. The thick green haze swirled around them and blurred out the rest of the bedroom. She put her hands on his face and pulled his head towards hers. She opened her mouth and her tongue slipped inside Peter's lips. He struggled to pry himself free but couldn't; his eyes rolled up into the back of his head. She inhaled deeply capturing the air in Peter's lungs and exhaled a hot black tar like fluid that flooded his mouth and seared his throat. His body was burning from the inside out and the weight of his head grew too heavy for his neck. He clasped her hands and she drove her thumbs through the center of his palms. Bolts of blue electricity leapt from her body and shocked him with the force of a fallen power line. He pushed the ghoul away and broke the connection. She raised her hands to her head as her skull collapsed with a wretched sound. Her body horribly deformed as her skeleton twisted and fragmented into pieces. She couldn't stop the chain reaction and screamed in vain then faded into oblivion. Peter tried to breathe only to choke down gallons more of the burning black tar. He stumbled backwards, crashed against the wall and fell to the ground unconscious. Emily arched her back, inhaled deeply then lay silent. Eddie checked her pulse and opened her eyelids; her pupils were still black but the whites of her eyes had returned. The windows flapped open and a thin watery mist sprayed the air. Father Story hurried to close them when he and the others caught sight of Peter lying on the floor.

"What the hell happened to him?" Mario tried to lift Peters head up.

"Be very careful," Father Story examined the black stains on Peter's clothes, "I had hoped it wouldn't have come to this."

"What's wrong with him?" asked Eddie.

Father Story ignored the question, "Help me get him to another room."

Isabella opened the door to an empty bedroom down the hall and the three men labored mightily as the dragged Peter's deadweight. They placed a mattress on the floor and with great effort laid him on top.

"He must weigh six hundred pounds," exhausted Eddie flopped to the ground. "I told him Emily was burning up and that's the last thing I remember," he said as Mario nodded in agreement.

Father Story retrieved a pair of rubber gloves and a stethoscope from his medical bag. He placed the chestpiece over Peter's heart and heard a faint retort. He made certain to avoid contact with the thick black liquid that pooled in Peter's eye sockets and bubbled up in his open mouth.

"What the fuck is that?" Eddie leaned in.

"It is the remnants of pure evil; the residue of death and destruction," said Father Story.

There were tears in Mario's eyes, "Is he dead?"

"Right now he's passing through the boundaries of hell. It's not his journey there that has me worried, what should concern all of us is the Peter that returns when he wakes," Father Story ushered the group out of the room and into the downstairs kitchen.

"I heard her voice in my head, I'm not even sure if it was real," Eddie offered. "She said she'd show me how I would die. I remember seeing bright colors bleeding into each other, the sky and then... emptiness. Did anyone else have that experience? Mario?"

"What?"

"Did she show you your death?"

"No. Yes, I don't know... I," he braced himself on the kitchen sink.

"Think; you have to remember."

"A mountain maybe... the sky was on fire." Mario shook his head, "I heard something... a sound. It was loud like a firecracker going off near my head. Then nothing, I woke up or the connection was broken... I don't know."

"And you?" Eddied looked at Father Story.

"She was trying to make you fear her; that's all."

"You were in the room with us, she must have shown you something." Mario was beginning to feel a rising unease in the pit of his stomach as he pieced together more of his own experience.

"Tell us what you saw Father," Eddie pleaded.

"A bright light--the clouds parted and the heavens were revealed. I assure its meaningless, just our imaginations working overtime. I insist you forget it, we have plenty of work that still needs to be done."

Angela was shaking with fear, "I knew it, we never should have come. Now we're all going to die. We have to leave... we have to leave now!"

"I can't ask you to stay if it means putting your lives at risk, but I need your help--my daughter needs your help and so does Peter. I can't do this by myself," Isabella's voice was unsteady.

"No one's going to die; you have my word," Father Story retrieved a sharp knife from the cupboard. "Whether or not you stay is your choice."

"Eddie?" Angela gently stroked the hair on the back of his head, but she already knew his answer. "And what about you Mario?"

"I'll take my chances here I guess."

"I'll take you into town tomorrow if you want?" Eddie stood and embraced her and she buried her head in the nape of his neck.

Father Story led them to the front porch. He used the knife to cut his palm in the shape of a cross and pressed the bloody hand against the outside door, "Peter constructed the barrier and consecrated the ground to keep evil from crossing the threshold of the living. It is important you know that Emily has had a connection with Peter for some time now," he squeezed his hand into a fist, "she also has a connection with Robert and in time that will bring him here. This is to make certain they can't gain access to the house."

"They?" Eddie asked.

"I believe Robert is traveling with a priest named Father Santeal and they have transformed themselves into the angels of abomination. They have the book of fallen souls and they will come for Emily, there is no longer any doubt." He looked towards the main road that led to the farmhouse and off towards the open turquoise horizon. "God help us. We must stop the rise of Hector, if we fail the world will succumb to their dominion and the earth will be turned into smoldering ash."

And there will be signs in sun and moon and stars, and on the earth distress of nations in perplexity because of the roaring of the sea and the waves, people fainting with fear and with foreboding of what is coming on the world. For the powers of the heavens will be shaken.

Luke
King James Bible

CHAPTER XIII
RISE OF THE RED KING

Monday 2:45 am
6, November 1978
Sant'Angelo Bridge
Rome, Italy

Polizia di Stato (State Police) Officer Rinaldi slowed his motorcycle to a stop as he crossed the Sant'Angelo Bridge, below in the calm green waters of the Tiber River was his friend of twenty years Alfeo Napoli. Napoli was a retired Gondolier and had frequently trekked the same route at the same odd hour while returning from visiting his ailing grandfather. Rinaldi waved a white gloved hand and Napoli nodded in return as the two men engaged in their customary early morning ritual. He tightened the chin strap of his helmet, kick-started his motorcycle and was about to cross when he saw Napoli's empty gondola emerge from underneath the bridge. He sped to the other side and ran down the stairs to river level. He walked along the shoreline with the beam from his flashlight reflecting off the surface of the murky water.

"Alfeo! Alfeo!" Rinaldi called out as he took a few more steps.

He saw something in the flow of water, knelt down and focused on a spot just feet in front of him. Napoli's blank face stared up at his while his body rose to the surface then flopped on his back. Rinaldi reached out towards him and was shocked to see the grotesque bloody stumps where his arms and legs had once been. He recoiled his hand and watched his friend sink into the depths of the river. He could see the vague outline of a giant mass traversing the bottom and causing ripples in the current. Rinaldi was seized with an intense desire to flee, but was cemented in place with an overpowering fear to move. An alabaster tentacle shot out of the deep and latched onto his ankle pulling him to the ground. A second wrapped around his right wrist and another around his chest squeezing the oxygen out of his lungs. The giant octopus like arms were covered with hundreds of sharp needle contact points that dug into his flesh. Robert Stone slowly rose from the Tiber and stood on the shoreline towering above his captured prey. His skin was completely void of color and his face closely resembled the Moai statues of Easter Island. Eight foot tentacles sprouted from his back and the three remaining arms ominously danced in the air like cobras waiting to strike. Rinaldi closed his eyes and turned away from the abomination while struggling in vain to reach for his gun. Robert slipped the forth tentacle around his throat and pulled him close. His mouth was ladened with serrated teeth and his breath reeked of rot and death. He bared a sadistic grin and gnawed away at the tender flesh around the officer's cheeks and lips. Rinaldi was able to muster a faint scream as Robert stepped backwards and dragged him under the steady current of the Tiber.

7:00 pm
Villa di Sangiamo
Naples, Italy

Gallo parked his car a block away from the gated drive of Villa di Sangiamo. Its spacious and beautiful landscape was accentuated by a long auburn brick drive with rows of Cypress trees on either side. It was magnificent, expensive and completely deserted. The guard's post had been abandoned and the coded lock on the gate was easy enough to bypass. He felt uneasy, there was an uncanny sense of déjà vu with Hafsah's desolate lighthouse. He avoided the few cameras that secured the property and slipped inside the Villa's brass and tile double doors. A 1912 Pathé phonograph sat on top the fireplace mantle and blared the symphonious, Voices of Spring by Johann Strauss II, through its twisted aluminum horn. Dozens of rare wine bottles littered the floor while the fully inebriated Chief Magistrate conducted his invisible orchestra. He picked up a bottle from an aged green wooden cart and it dangled loosely in his hand. The bullet from the Makarov Pistol shattered the glass on impact leaving only the neck of the bottle in Sangiamo's fingertips.

"Quite a pity," Sangiamo stood with his back to the intruder, "It was dedicated to Queen Elizabeth I for her ascension to the throne. I was looking forward to drinking it Mr. Gallo." He dropped the remaining bit and it cracked on the tile floor. "What?" he turned, "Aren't you curious to know how I knew it was you?"

"No, not really," Gallo used the gun to gesture him away from the fireplace, "Sit down. We need to talk."

"Of course, but should I address you as Mr. Gallo or Mr. Cecellini," Sangiamo grinned, "I would give anything to see the shock on Cavilary's face when he discovers the truth about you; it's almost too comical. You've been playing both sides for a long time haven't you? A man to all who know him is dedicated to upholding law and justice, while just beneath the surface there is someone who would cut the throat of the Prime Minister to gain control of the country. It would be very embarrassing to the government if the public found out considering your closeness with the SISDE. I guess the irony is that you'd get your wish; that type of scandal would bring Mr. Andreotti's government down, of course they'd hang you first. Tell me, did a man like Alberto Cecellini ever exist, or was he one of your many interesting aliases? My favorite theory is that you lured him to some exotic third world country while he escaped justice from the regime, killed him and assumed his identity long ago."

Gallo's expression hadn't changed, "I'm sure your old friend the late Father Martz would have been surprised at how you've decorated your house since he was last here." He glanced at the enormous mural of Jesus and Mary hanging on the wall.

"I've had the crosses blessed and hung on nearly every wall in my house to keep Father Santeal from sending his beast Qeynan to destroy me. You've seen for yourself the proof of what Robert has become. I've taken every precaution to safeguard my life; I even fired my personal bodyguard, a man I've known for twenty years. You can never be too careful, after all even Caesar was killed by those who were closest to him."

Gallo rubbed the barrel of the gun against his forehead, "And how's that working out for you?"

"You're a very callous man Mr. Gallo; I can tell you're someone who really enjoys his work."

"A man with your money and connections could afford just about anything he ever wanted. Maybe even a copy of the book of fallen souls for your own private collection. I bet if I searched this place long enough or applied just the right amount of pressure you'd be willing to tell me everything I wanted to know."

"Ahh that's right the book," Sangiamo was defiant, "How did it feel when you were cooped up in that tiny little apartment and you finally realized that you had the ultimate power in your hands and gave it all away to the priests?"

"Emir Saldalha came to see you. He stole one of your cars and nearly totaled it on his way to the City of Madonnella, yet you didn't press charges. The dearly departed Father Martz came to see you and decided to make himself into a human fireball in the walkway to your guest house. That tells me you are in some way deeply involved in what the priests were doing."

"Father Santeal and the others were once part of the Council that's true, that is until they decided we were irrelevant to the cause and wanted to keep the secrets of the book to themselves."

"The Council?"

"They're exactly what you think they are Mr.... Gallo," Sangiamo picked up a red mask with an elongated nose and black robe that rested on the coffee table and tossed it to him. He wrote on a piece of paper, "Here is the address and the password. There is a meeting in five days, you can see for yourself if you want. And as for Emir Saldalha, he may have been young and rash but the boy was very intelligent. He was able to figure out who your new employer really is. I have to say I never would have guessed it myself." He took a more somber tone, "Unfortunately, by the time he told me the noose had already tightened around my neck and it was far too late for me to save myself. He came to me because he was distraught and was desperate for a way out. We drank a lot that night, but I told him I couldn't help him, so he took my car and sought out someone who could."

"If he wanted to get away from siyah yılan or the Council why did he try to contact Cardinal Rourke?"

Sangiamo had a confused expression on his face, "He didn't tell you? The man you're working for... hahaha. Even after you tortured him he kept his secret to the grave. He really must have hated you Mr. Gallo." He grabbed a bottle of wine off the cart, "1805, to commemorate Napoleon's victory at the Battle of Austerlitz. It would be a shame to destroy this one too." He uncorked the bottle and reached in his pocket; Gallo trained his gun at Sangiamo's face. "Medicine, for my liver; it tastes awful but it's the only way I can drink my wine. To Emir," he swallowed the powder and raised his glass.

"Alright, I admit it you've peaked my interest. Tell me, what was it that Emir kept secret from me?"

"What, and spoil the surprise?" he laughed again. "You're going to kill me anyway Mr. Gallo and after all it would be a shame to betray his confidence at this late stage in the game."

"I can shoot you in the head or I can nail you to the cross. It's your choice either way." Gallo leaned across the coffee table; Sangiamo's eyes were fixed and unblinking and a trail of white foam seeped from the corner of his mouth. He knocked over the table and placed his hand on his heart. Nothing. "Shit! Shit-shit-shit!" he emptied the Markov's chamber into Sangiamo's limp body. His anger began to subside and he regained what little was left of his senses. He grabbed the bottle of wine from Sangiamo's hand, sat down and took a healthy gulp. For a while he stared in disbelief at the mask and robe then picked each up and pocketed the address that his host had written down.

Monday 11:30 pm
Isabella Stone's Farmhouse
City of Madonnella

Angela stood at the stove; Eddie wrapped his arms around her. She didn't react as he kissed her softly on the shoulder. He wondered if he had made the right decision in choosing to stay and knew the enormous strain would cause the end of the only relationship that had ever really mattered to him.

"I don't know what you want from me?" Eddie sighed.

"I don't want anything from you Eddie."

"That's bullshit, you want me to go with you and leave everything behind. You want me to say that I choose you over Peter and my friends don't you? Why don't you just come out and say it?"

"That's just it Eddie I shouldn't have to ask you to choose."

"Forgive me if I want to stay because my best friend is upstairs lying unconscious and may never wake the same person ever again. I'm here because right now Peter really needs me. I guess I'm the one who's acting like a stupid spoiled child."

Angela glared at him, but didn't say a word while Mario sat quietly at the table trying to remain as inconspicuous as possible. He sipped his coffee and had tried to avoid talking to the others ever since Emily's outburst had outed him. He knew it didn't matter to them; they were his friends but he strongly felt the need to demonstrate his loyalty to Peter by staying. Emily's demons had opened his mind to a new kind of horror and if Peter and Father Story were right, Robert would return for her with his soul burning wicked and sadistic. What was it that lay in wait for them? The fear of the unknown and the all too real possibility of death forced him to take stock of his compatriots. Eddie was young and brave, he would fight to the end there was no doubt in his mind, Father Story had the conviction of a lifelong faith to guide and comfort him, and Isabella had her daughter's soul to save. Until now the dread of his true self being exposed to his friends and to the world had been the only thing that sent chills through his psyche. He knew that if he had to he could sacrifice his own life if it meant saving the others, but what about Angela? She had been the newest addition to the group of Eddie, Peter and himself and she had always seemed quite distant. Even though the three men hadn't seen Isabella or Father Story for years, they still felt like family; she didn't.

Father Story interrupted his thoughts when he walked into the kitchen with a large pail of water and a bloody towel slung over his shoulder.

"How are they?" asked Mario.

"Her face has cleared and her breathing is normal, but she still hasn't opened her eyes. There's something residual left within her that has seized her spirit and won't let go. He may have only extended her life for a few days or weeks, it's hard to tell. As for Peter..." The sound of a van snaking its way up the main road to the farmhouse ended their conversation.

"Are you expecting someone?" Eddie rose to his feet.

"No," Father Story turned at the sound of the squealing brakes.

He and Eddie made their way to the front of the house. Outside Peter's barrier sat a powder blue Subaru van with its motor in idle and the headlights on. Eddie and Father Story crept across the living room and to the bay window. The distance and the glare of the high beams made it impossible to see the faces of the occupants. The headlights shut off and for agonizing seconds nothing happened. Simultaneously the driver and passenger doors opened and out stepped Cardinal Fuerst and Father Santeal. The van shook and the shocks protested under the stress of a great weight as something impossibly large emerged from the back. Eddie glanced at Father Story, his face was pale, his mouth dropped open and he made the sign of the cross over his chest.

"You know why we're here!" shouted Cardinal Fuerst. "Isabella, Neil, Peter, Eddie, Angela, Mario... all of you know there will be severe consequences if you decide to defy us."

"How does he know our names?" exasperated Eddie ducked beneath the window sill.

"You have a choice, give us the child and we will consider sparing your lives. There is no way out, no way you will survive unless you do as we demand." Cardinal Fuerst listened for several seconds but there was no reply, "Very well then, I can assure all of you that you have made a grave mistake."

A loud thump and the back door buckled and twisted off its hinges. Another solid kick and farmer D'Alisa stood in the open frame holding a Guerini 20 gauge shotgun in hand. Mario clutched Angela by the arm and shoved her out of the kitchen as D'Alisa took aim. He fired the shotgun through the closed door and the splintered wood clipped Mario's ear as he fell to the ground. Angela screamed, she pulled him to his feet and the pair ran into the living room. D'Alisa entered the dining room, it was dark with only slight rays of moonlight penetrating the gloom. He thought he saw movement and fired the gun twice destroying a china cabinet and the television set. He heard footsteps in another room and headed out into the hallway. He reloaded the gun and his hand searched the wall for a light switch. Eddie leapt on his back and secured his arm around his neck, but the bigger man tossed him off with ease. Eddie got to his knees and the farmer jammed the butt of the gun into his ribs. He rolled over onto his back as D'Alisa stood above him and aimed the gun.

"No!" Father Story shouted.

D'Alisa smiled, "You should've been wise enough to have taken our offer Father," he kicked Eddie in the head and stepped toward him, "I have no problem in killing all of you one by one."

Peter leapt from the top of the staircase and crashed into D'Alisa's large frame. He gripped him by the nape of the neck and effortlessly threw the two hundred and sixty pound man against the wall. D'Alisa's entire body ached, his collar bone had snapped and his humerus stuck out through the skin. He held his damaged arm and used the wall to assist him to his feet. Peter had grown nearly two feet taller and his skin glowed like the surface of the moon. His arms were wrapped in dense and powerful muscles and his hands were oversized with sharp clawed fingers. His head was larger, his skull lengthened and his brow ridge protruded significantly. His shoulders were broad and a row of sharp boney plates ran the length of his spine. D'Alisa reached for his shotgun but Peter's huge hand grabbed hold of the gauge chamber. He stared into a pair of bottomless black eyeballs and a face that resembled a beast straight from the pit of hell. An animalistic growl came from the creature and it opened its powerful jaws. A thick stream of saliva dripped onto D'Alisa's face and burned his skin like acid. Peter choked the terrified farmer and lifted him off the ground.

"Peter!" Father Story's hands grabbed at his wrists. "If you kill him inside the house the ground will no longer be sanctified and the others will cross the threshold."

The instinct of the beast was to kill but it fought it's nature and understood the gravity of Father Story's words. Peter released his hold on the farmer and slowly transformed into something closer to his human self. His skin regained a slight pasty color as once again blood began to pump through the arteries of a human heart. He held the shotgun in one hand and dragged D'Alisa to the front door and out of the house.

"I have something of yours," he tossed the farmer's body twenty feet across the yard and he landed at the feet of the three men.

"It is good to see that the progeny of Kyameron has finally found his way to the Lord," said Father Santeal. "The long bloodline proves to be strong and unbreakable in you and your daughter."

"My soul is still mine," Peter slung the rifle over his shoulder, "and as long as it is, I will never stop fighting you."

Robert stood behind Father Santeal and Cardinal Fuerst, his seven foot frame morphed instantly into a man. "Step beyond your walls of protection and you and I can settle this once and for all," his fists were tightly clenched.

"You gave away everything of yourself for revenge against me?" Peter was only feet from the crosses and could feel the preternatural hum of electrical energy dance on his skin. "I've already destroyed my life in the eyes of the church and in my own heart, there's nothing you could do to me that could harm me worse."

"Your life? Your life… always thinking of yourself aren't you Peter. Isabella and you devastated my life," Robert stepped close to the barrier and blue sparks flashed across the surface of his body. "For years I believed that child was mine while you lied and continued your affair with my wife. I was naïve to believe in the teachings of your church, and I was a fool to think you were ever my friend. I will exact a measure of pain and suffering upon you and her that this world has never seen. In the end you will lose Emily, your child will become one of us and rule hell for eternity."

He looked towards Father Santeal with a somber expression on his face, "If you promise to spare Emily's life, I'll step across and you can do with me what you want."

"You're in no position to bargain Mr. Cameron," Father Santeal said. "Unless your child finishes the desecration ritual she will die a miserable death. You really don't have a choice in the matter."

"The circle is incomplete without the resurrection of the last fallen angel and your dreams of receiving full dominion as Qeynan and Thaydien will not happen. Only the true bloodline of Kyameron can raise the Angel Hector, if she dies--you die."

"Face it Peter you lost, there are no more deals to be made," Robert reached his hand passed the hollowed barrier and inches from Peter's face. His arm was engulfed in a smoldering plume of thick gray smoke and his flesh bubbled and blistered. Circular black holes appeared and ate away at the skin up and down the length of his arm. The veins and muscle beneath the decaying tissue were exposed and from hand to shoulder his arm was set ablaze.

"That's quite enough Robert," Cardinal Fuerst pulled Robert's arm down and away from the ethereal wall.

"If any of you come near her again, I'll make sure there will be consequences for all your lives," Peter aimed the shotgun in Robert's direction.

"Go ahead Peter," Cardinal Fuerst folded his arms. "You can't kill any of us with such a crude weapon."

Peter then pointed the barrel at D'Alisa's body lying on the ground. He took aim and pulled the trigger; D'Alisa flinched fearing the white hot pain from a bullet's impact but the chambers were empty. "I guess not all of you are true believers," he said as he dropped the gun on the ground.

"The next time we meet, I swear I will kill you Peter," Robert smiled wickedly. His body ignited into a twenty foot arc of orange fire that lapped the edges of the invisible barrier. The fire rose into the air and the thin straight flame turned into a plume of smoke that cast a silhouette over the face of the moon, then disappeared behind the low rolling clouds of the night sky.

"We will meet again Peter, you have my word, and then you can decide the fate of your daughter and your friends," Father Santeal turned and headed towards the van with Cardinal Fuerst and a badly injured farmer D'Alisa following behind.

Cardinal Fuerst hit the gas and within minutes headed onto the main road leading away from Isabella's farmhouse. The van shook violently as the shocks damaged by Robert's heavy mass could no longer absorb the bumps and potholes on the unpaved road. Cardinal Fuerst and Father Santeal sat in front while D'Alisa groaned loudly as his body slid on the uncarpeted flatbed in the back of the van.

"Please help me," cried D'Alisa, "my arm is broken. You have to help me."

Father Santeal left his seat and knelt down next to him. He examined his arm by twisting and turning it, ignoring D'Alisa's grunts of agonizing pain. He violently seized the man by the throat, "All you had to do was to get them to hand over the child or at the very least kill one of them, any of them. You failed miserably and failure is unacceptable." His palm burned like molten metal.

"You can't kill me, I sacrificed my wife to prove my loyalty. She's dead because of you!"

"And now you can join her," he slammed D'Alisa's head against the exposed metal hull and snapped his neck. The back doors flung open and Father Santeal tossed his limp body out onto the road. The lifeless D'Alisa bounced twice and rolled down the side of the dense tree line embankment.

11:45 pm

Peter knew he wasn't in the right state of mind, but he wanted to see his daughter. He climbed the stairs with Father Story shouting his name in pursuit. He ignored his pleas, the feeling of loss and anger was building in him and the creature began to emerge. He headed towards Emily's room with the hope of seeing the child's face as it had been when she was human. Isabella walked out of Emily's room and met the two men in the hall.

"You can't go in there Peter," Father Story put his hand on Peter's chest, "we don't know what will happen when the both of you are together. The demons within her are greatly weakened, but they may be able to control your mind. We can't take that chance."

Peter closed his eyes, leaned against the wall and slumped to the ground. "I tried," he said as tears filled his eyes, "but I couldn't take the pain and rid her of all the evil that tormented her."

Isabella knelt and wrapped her arms around him. She kissed his ridged brow, "I know, you saved her life for now. You've done so much for us."

The black nails grew longer on his fingers and he felt his cheekbones broadening outward, "I don't know how long I can control this." His voice rose, "What happens if I lose it? No one in this house is safe as long as I'm here."

"You just feel helpless right now, you have to concentrate," Isabella sat down next to him, "You have to focus your mind on something else." She closed her eyes and thought for a second, "Tell me what your life was like before all this happened."

"What?"

"Tell me what your childhood was like; tell me anything," her fingertips glided over the bony contours of his face.

"I don't think there was a time that it wasn't a part of my life," Peter leaned his head back against the wall, "I used to think it was just visions or nightmares, but it's not. My father was one of them, a member of the Council. I had blocked it out for so long but I remember now. I remember walking into our kitchen when I was a child; I saw Father

Martz, Cardinal Fuerst and other members of the Council sitting at our table. They were plotting vengeance against the church even back then. They had searched years for the book of fallen souls and trekked across all of Israel to find the Temple of Metatron. I remember ... I remember Father Atis Martz baptizing me and my brother Simon in the Cowlitz River when we lived in America. My mother was different, she was a good woman and she feared my father, feared what I was becoming. My father and the others would have never stopped searching for her if she had fled with me and escaped the future that I was destined to lead. I was slowly being groomed as an apostle of Thaydien. She couldn't live with him, she couldn't live with the awful truth so she vanished with my brother when I was ten. I never saw either of them again." Peter's hands were normal sized and the hard ridge of his brow had receded. "It was about that time we moved to Madonnella. The Council made sure he was employed and that we lived in a nice house and never wanted for anything. He passed himself off as a small town preacher all the while he deciphered text from hundreds of books that were false leads in search for the book of fallen souls. When one was found my father and others chosen by the Council sacrificed a childhood friend of mine named Billy. My father was an only son and his bloodline and hunger for the dark powers made him a perfect spawn for the Red King, the Angel Hector. Billy's dad had no idea how evil my father was or what the Council had been scheming. He suspected my dad had killed his son, but no one believed such a fine upstanding man would have ever taken another human life. Billy's father murdered mine in a fit of rage then killed himself before they could complete the Trilogy and raise the angels from the womb of hell. Those on the Council, those who were in my father's inner circle faded from my memory and the truths of what they were, were lost in the fog of childhood trauma. From there on the Catholic church took me in and I lived and studied in Rome. I became a devoted follower of Christ and had every intention of becoming Cardinal Cameron… that is until…"

"Until you met me," Isabella held his hand, it was warm and his fingers had regained their human shape.

"I don't regret it, and I don't regret you having our daughter," his face returned to its normal size and shape, but his eyes were pitch black and his clothes had been torn to shreds.

She stood up, looked at Peter's condition and frowned, "Robert left a closet full of clothes behind, I'm sure there's something in there that will fit you. I'll run a hot bath and you can get cleaned up; you'll feel better in the morning."

He nodded and when she'd gone he took Father Story by the arm, "I need your help, you have to dig up the crosses I set and open a pathway through the barrier; I'm leaving tomorrow."

"They'll find you Peter. Wherever you go, wherever you hide, they won't stop until they hunt you down," Father Story implored as Peter walked away.

"I know, but I can sense their presence whenever they're near," long fingernails extended from his hands, "and I'll be ready and waiting for them."

I saw the Apostles Thaydien, Kyameron and Philetos standing upon the rubble of the great temple Metatron and preach the gospel to all: Rebuild our church and your cries for blood vengeance shall not go unanswered, and your hatred shall be made flesh as Sado Satanus the Anti-Christ on earth.

Phanes
libri of cado animus

CHAPTER XIV
GENESIS

Tuesday 10:10 am
7, November 1978
St. Peter's Basilica
Rome, Italy

Father Joseph Principi's shoes clicked on the colorful hard surfaced floor of the St. Peter's Basilica. He pressed his way through a crowd into the more private area of the church where Archbishop Barone was waiting for him. The two men joyfully greeted each other then moved to a private office.

"It is good to see you again my old friend," Archbishop Barone gave him a hearty slap on the back and sat him down in a chair. "It's been too long, much too long--you must tell me all about your time in France."

"Perhaps at another time," Father Principi smiled, "It's been a difficult time for all of us, I was on my way to the airport to acquire Cardinal Rourke's remains when I was told you wanted to see me. I was..."

"Oh yes, Cardinal Rourke," he clasped his hands together, "what an immense loss to the church, his absence will cause a great void that will be impossible to fill. What a pity, he was a good man... a great man."

"Yes he was."

"He was so healthy; such a vibrant man. I always told him, Jeremiah you work twice as hard and twice as long as anyone I know," he laughed. "I'm sorry, you said you were going to the airport?"

"Yes, I've made arrangements to receive his body."

"Really?" Archbishop Barone was surprised, "I was under the impression that the arrangements had already been taken care of." He searched his desk and picked up a clipboard and pad. "Yes, just as I thought, Father Layad brought his urn back earlier today."

"Urn? How is it possible that anyone in the church could have allowed his body to be cremated?"

"Occasionally Jeremiah drank too much and I warned him several times to quit entirely, but you know how stubborn he was. The police said he passed out in bed with a lit cigar in hand and the fire engulfed him rather quickly; it was a miracle the entire building didn't burn down. Unfortunately, there wasn't much left of his body and they placed his remains in the urn and sent it to us along with the rest of his possessions. A lifetime of work and goodwill stuffed inside the contents of a simple cardboard box."

"I see," Father Principi knew the truth and wanted to challenge the lie but thought better of it, "I don't mean to rush off, but I promised his sister that I would deliver him as soon as his body was returned."

"Of course," Archbishop Barone showed him the door, "If there's anything I can do for her or the family, please let me know."

"I will send her your blessings and may you have a blessed day," said Father Principi. He opened the doors to the Basilica and walked into the courtyard. It wasn't likely that the archbishop was one of them, a follower of Lucifer, but the less he knew of the truth the safer he would be. He slowed his pace when he saw Father Layad addressing a group of tourists in front of the statue of St. Paul. "Father Layad," he said as he approached, "you're just the man I wanted to see."

"Father," he was surprised, "Is there something…"

"I was informed that you assumed possession of Cardinal Rourke's remains while you were in Israel."

"Yes…"

"I'm confused, did you transfer your post?"

"No," Father Layad smiled, "Cardinal Fuerst requested that I help the organizers of the Catholic-Jewish Liaison Commission set up their next meeting in late December. I was with him when I heard the unfortunate news of Cardinal Rourke's passing. I cut my stay short and offered to bring his body back so that he could rest in peace in his adopted country."

"Did you see him while you were there?"

"No, but he wasn't involved with the Commission; it's not surprising that we never met," Father Layad squared up his shoulders. "You'll have to excuse me Father, but I'm only here for today and I'm running a little late to catch my flight."

"Ahhh yes, back to America," Father Principi kept stride with him, "Seattle isn't it?"

"Yes."

"In fact, I'm on my way to a meeting near the airport," he put his arm around Father Layad. "Would you mind if we shared a cab?"

"No. Of course not," Father Layad grinned but, despised the idea, "I'd be delighted."

1:45 pm
Hotel Blu Notte
Naples, Italy

Gallo lay in bed staring up at a chart he had pasted to the wall. A picture of Cardinal Rourke was connected by black lines to a photograph of Peter and a photo of Father Story that were taken from old newspaper clippings. Lines were then drawn from their pictures to the celebrity author Mario Pascale and to the silhouettes of two other unknowns he had seen at Isabella Stone's house. He drew a straight line from a sketch of the beast that attacked him aboard the Oriens Astrum and labeled it Robert Stone; he coupled it with Isabella and the child she refused to let him see. Next to Robert's beastly pic he wrote Father Santeal's name and left it as the only two people that had a direct link to a circle marked book of fallen souls at the center of the chart. If Father Story knew where to find another book it was going to be nearly impossible to make him confess to its location. Mario was a celebrity and probably had enough resources and influence to find such a rare copy and was marked as a possibility. The two unknowns had been too young, too steeped in the hippie culture and were excluded from the start. He didn't relish his last encounter with Robert Stone and getting the book from him and Father Santeal would always remain his last option. Peter Cameron stood out from the beginning; there was something definitely peculiar about him. As far as standard profiles go, he was slippery to pin down. He freely offered up the information that was crucial to the investigation, but he had a feeling that there was much more he hadn't divulged. Peter had helped Cardinal Rourke, knew Isabella Stone, had a relationship with Father Martz and as a former Vatican Librarian, may have had contact with Father Santeal. The Council was a new twist he hadn't thought of, but Sangiamo made it sound like an intriguing possibility of another avenue for finding the libri of cado animus. In the end, he decided that Peter was the target that would bear the most fruit. The telephone rang several times and he couldn't remember which alias he used to check into the hotel. He had been more than careful this time; no one else knew where he was, but he was beginning to expect the unexpected.

"Mr. Gallo," stated the familiar voice of his mysterious employer.

"Yes. I was beginning to wonder when you'd call."

"You've done well, so far I am very impressed. Your talents and your prudence are greatly appreciated."

"Yeah about that," he cradled the phone on his shoulder, "we need to meet face to face so we can discuss my talents."

"That was never a part of our agreement Mr. Gallo."

"Neither was being shot at or cut to pieces by a raging demon named Robert Stone."

"You knew it would be dangerous and yet you accepted the terms of our partnership. How did you say it? Oh yes... I'm all in."

"I am. I just need a few more questions answered," he desperately wanted to learn the knowledge Emir took with him to his grave. "Since you seem to have no trouble finding me, I'll be in Rome eight o'clock tomorrow night. See you then." He hung up the phone, walked to the board and with a red marker drew a circle around the newspaper article with Peter's face on it.

4:00 pm
Isabella Stone's Farmhouse
City of Madonnella

"Peter!" a disjointed voice broke through the haze. "Peter are you all right?"

The incessant humming had finally stopped and the empty blackness was replaced by the brilliant light of the afternoon sun. How long had he been lying here, seconds or minutes? He was still disoriented and unable to stand, but his faculties were slowly returning. Peter knelt with his knees tucked underneath his body and dry heaved several times before throwing up. Father Story stood behind him with the Genesis and Exodus crosses laying flat on the ground; the circle had been broken. He had crossed over the celestial wall, but the residual force was still strong and had thoroughly cooked his insides. He put his hands on the ground, braced himself and painfully got to his feet as his organs self regenerated.

"Yes... I'm alright," tears ran down Peter's face as he steadied himself.

Father Story quickly hammered the crosses back into place and closed the circle once again. They were alone for now, Mario and Eddie had dared to venture out into the fields of Isabella's farmland. They picked the corn and grapes and figs from the surrounding trees while Isabella was in the kitchen preparing for the night's meal. A car's engine howled loudly and the screeching tires of a blue Mercury Capri sent rocks and dust up into the air.

"Get in," Angela leaned over and opened the passenger door.

"What the hell are you doing?" Peter stumbled to the car.

"I could ask you the same thing," she lit a cigarette, "you wanna sit on your ass and talk, or do you wanna get in?"

"I'm going with you," Father Story pulled the front seat forward and offered Peter the back. "I need more supplies from the Hospes."

"Fine, suit yourselves," Peter poured his body into the back seat, "we can discuss this on the way."

Angela flicked the cigarette out the window and fishtailed out of the driveway and onto the main avenue. She kept the radio off and her eyes fixed on the desolate gravel road. "I'll drop you off at the end of the driveway on our way back Father, then I'm gone. And no I didn't tell Eddie, I made my decision last night and talking to him would only have changed my mind."

"I know it's been very difficult for you, and I don't expect that anything I say will ever change your mind, but if you don't mind me asking where will you go?" Father Story's voice was pensive.

"Does it matter? I can't stay here," she pressed on the gas, "I can't stay in Madonnella."

"Eddie loves you more than anything in the world," Peter curled up on the bench seat. "You might be able to lie to yourself now, but you know he'll come looking for you."

"I know how I feel and I know how he feels about me," she looked at Father Story, "and you'll have to stop him from trying Father."

"It'll be worse for him, you not telling him I mean," said Peter.

"Do you really want to talk about what it's like to keep secrets?" Angela glared at him through the rearview. "There were things happening with you Peter long before you ever decided to go to Isabella's. You've been playing your part of Robert's little game from the very beginning.

Mario was blind to it and Eddie worships you to the end and couldn't admit it, but I knew you were different. I knew you were changing."

"I wasn't trying to keep secrets from anyone, I didn't know what was happening to me."

"Look what has happened to you Peter," she gripped the steering wheel. "Can you honestly say you're nothing like them or that you'll never be anything like them?" he was silent and she concentrated on the road ahead.

Within an hour they pulled into the town center, Peter waited until the sidewalks were clear then dashed into the book store. He watched through the front window blinds as Angela made a U-turn and headed out towards the direction of the Hospes of St. Cecilia. He kept the lights off and headed toward the solace of his basement apartment. He pulled out the cross wrapped in fabric from his pants pocket and held it in his hand. The red fabric had turned black in spots where it had come into contact with his body. He gently spilled the cross from the folds of the material and it clanked on the wooden nightstand. It showed definite signs of wear, the edges were slightly melted but the Christ figure remained undamaged. He stood up, near the tiny window was a display cabinet filled with an array of Christian relics. Peter carefully reached for the purificator cloth that lay atop a silver Eucharistic chalice. He wrapped the cross in the purple cloth and slipped it back inside his pocket. He was relieved that he hadn't turned to ash when his fingers made contact with the symbols of a holy faith. The hairs on his forearms stood on end, there was a difference in the feel of the air that sent shivers down his spine. He cautiously climbed the stairs and walked onto the store's selling floor.

"What I offer you is more than you could ever imagine," Father Santeal sat in the dark, his words were precise and deliberate.

"You already know my answer Grigory; I won't help you."

"Oh, I think you will. Hector will rise and when we are complete, we will rule the world for a thousand years. Not even the greatest armies will dare stand against us. I know you feel the power within you now, but it is only a small taste of what you could be after you join us."

"Us? Aren't you forgetting the absolute hatred someone has towards me? I don't think Robert has an us in mind."

"I can take care of Robert," said Father Santeal, "once you become Hector of course."

"You know all too well what's written in the libri of cado animus; completing the circle will force the great seals to open and hasten the apocalypse and the final battle between Satan and Christ. Even with all the great power you possess, what will you do when Satan demands it back? What happens to you then?"

Father Santeal placed a long object across the length of the table. "And God said to the Israelites fashion me a sword of tempered steel from the mines of Sudea and I shall send you an angel to slay the great beast," he unwrapped the cloth and revealed the gleaming steel of a massive sword. "The sword of Sabaoth, Lord of the Armies of Israel and protector of God. Satan was once defeated by this blade and he shall be again. We will destroy him, tear him to pieces until there's nothing left to resurrect, and when we're through, we will hunt down the Christ and he will suffer the same fate as his eternal enemy."

"Your grand plan to remake the world in your image is to destroy both the Christ and Satan? You truly are insane," Peter could feel the change within him coming. "God will reap unspeakable vengeance upon you for the murder of his only son."

"You forget Peter, we are Gods too."

6:37 pm

Father Story searched the medicine cabinet in the basement storage room of St. Cecilia. Trays of yellow plastic cartons filled with patient files were stacked on shelves from floor to ceiling. Angela stood guard smoking a cigarette half way up the stairs near the bright red exit sign. She was nervous and still contemplating whether she had made the right decision to leave Eddie and start over. By tomorrow she would be in Bari and then France or England or wherever, it didn't matter as long as it was far away. Suddenly the metal door opened and Cardinal Fuerst stood in the shadows of the evening light. The glow of the streetlights traced his figure and made his appearance seem even more ominous looking. Angela was terrified, her heart raced while she gradually began to retreat down the stairwell.

"It's good to see your face my dear," Cardinal Fuerst's breath lingered in the chill of the night air, "it would be a shame if anything happened to it."

"You're not welcome here, this is a holy place," Angela said, "The grounds were sanctified by a church that stood on this plot a hundred years ago."

"Yes but the Hospes freely welcomes the poor, the rich, the good and the evil. It's impossible for them to turn anyone away. You really didn't think you could abandon your friends and walk away from their fate and be saved from our wrath?" Fuerst cupped Angela's chin in his hand. "You have been marked by the Devil's eye my sweet child; there is no way out for you--you can't escape. If I felt so inclined I could summon Robert here and he would make death seem like a welcome relief."

"Obviously Robert isn't with you so you must have something else in mind for us," Father Story stepped out from the storage room entrance.

"I do, I have an offer for you, think of it as your last chance," Furest's icy blue eyes cut deeply through Angela's core. "Give us the child of Kyameron and you have my word that we will not harm you in any way."

"Peter was right, if Emily dies the circle will be broken and your friends will decay from the inside out, their bodies will rot away and the evil will end with their demise," Father Story walked towards the stairs to confront his old friend.

"Peter is no longer the man you once knew; he is no longer entirely human. He is a student of the dark ways and a scholar of the libri of cado animus; he is a living, breathing half-demon. You have read from the text yourself, but in all your arrogance you forget the words born from the book of fallen souls," said Cardinal Fuerst. "It is written; He who walks with God shall forever see the light and feel the warmth of his grace, and he who walks with evil shall forever be cast in the Shadow of the Devil."

6:39 pm

"You have the opportunity to rule the world Peter," Father Santeal stood up. "In every way you are already one of us. Why fight the inevitable?"

"Our fates may be the same, but our paths are not. I'm not and will never be a servant of your Lord."

Peter picked up the sword and held it over his head. He tried to strike Father Santeal but Robert grabbed the tip of the blade from behind him. He spun Peter around, struck him across the face and he fell to the floor. Robert's massive frame was draped in a long brown hooded robe. His ghostly white face and glowing yellow eyes illuminated the darkness like the beams from a lighthouse. Instantly Peter changed into the demon and his scabrous claws dug into the thick muscle of Robert's chest. They were locked in immortal combat with their jaws sinking deep and shredding each other's flesh. Robert threw him across the room and into the display case on the second floor landing. The glass shattered, the case broke in half and he was buried underneath relics, wood and glass. Peter tossed the debris aside and leapt from the landing with lethal intent, but Robert caught him by the throat. His fingers squeezed around Peter's neck and he choked off his air. Robert lifted him off the ground and slammed him hard onto the white circular tulip table. Peter was dazed and for a brief moment he was unable to regain focus.

Robert kept his hand around Peter's neck and picked up the Sabaoth sword, "I told you the next time we met that I was going to kill you Peter," he gnashed his teeth; his face was contorted and seething with hatred.

He drove the long blade through Peter's sternum and through the table and its tip shattered the tile of the white ceramic floor. Only the handle of the wide sword stuck out of Peter's chest while a fountain of crimson spurted from the fatal wound. His fingers were coated in thick blood and made it impossible to grip the blade. Little by little he began changing back to his human self while Robert was transforming into something far worse. The bones in his cheeks cracked and broke as his face elongated and his jaw grew wider. Black wings sprouted from his back and his neck disappeared into a set of powerful shoulders. The air made a hollow whistling sound as it passed through dragon like nostrils. The Angel Qeynan hungered for destruction from behind the Devil's eyes. He bent over Peter's body, his mouth slowly opened and dripped with warm saliva. The double rows of sharp jagged teeth clamped around Peter's head and tore into his face. There was a sickening sound as his skull began to break and his cheekbones were crushed from Qeynan's powerful jaws. An unimaginable pain rippled throughout his nervous system with raw brutality. Peter's shaking hand reached inside his pocket and his fingers searched for the crucifix necklace. He grabbed hold of it and the agony was instant and almost unbearable. He used the last of his waning strength to press it flat against Robert's large forehead. The flesh sizzled as the mark of the cross was seared into his skull. Robert let out an ear piercing cry and fell backwards onto the floor. He thrashed violently knocking over rows of tables and chairs as he wailed like a wild animal with his hands covering his face. The large black wings smashed the bookcases while he twisted through fits of frenzied epileptic seizures. His wings spread out wide and he flew towards the fresco painted ceiling then crashed through the dome and out into the night sky.

Father Santeal stood up and stared at the open hole in the roof then back at Peter lying atop the table as he went into shock. "You are becoming what you were always meant to be. You are the Angel Hector whether you choose to accept your fate or not it is undeniable," He leaned in close; Peter's face was horribly disfigured. His skull was concaved and his cheeks were grotesquely lopsided, but his dying eyes were still focused on that of his tormentor. "For you... the end is just the beginning," Father Santeal placed his hand on Peter's mangled face and gently closed his eyelids.

And the Devil, taking him up into a high mountain, showed unto him all the kingdoms of the world in a moment of time. And the Devil said unto him, All this power will I give you, and the glory of them: for that is delivered unto me; and to whomsoever I will I give it. If you therefore will worship me, all shall be yours.

Luke
King James Bible

CHAPTER XV
BLOOD AND STONE

Wednesday 1:35 am
8, November 1978
Isabella Stone's Farmhouse
City of Madonnella
Bari Province, Italy

Angela and Father Story entered the front door of the farmhouse and were greeted by the stunned gazes of Isabella, Mario and Eddie. The group was half asleep and hadn't noticed when the car had pulled up into the driveway.

"What happened? Where were you?" Eddie jumped up from the couch, but Angela ignored him and headed for the guest room. "What the hell is going on?"

"I needed supplies from the Hospes and Angela offered to take me," Father Santeal placed the medical bag on the lip of the staircase. "I was heading out by myself and she insisted that she drive. I know it was irresponsible not to have told anyone..."

"Where's Peter?" Mario stood up.

"He's gone."

"What do you mean he's gone?" asked Isabella.

"Where is he?" Mario demanded.

"Peter was losing more and more control over what he is becoming. And he decided, rightly I may add, that he go before he put the rest of us in danger."

"You left him out there by himself?" Eddie stopped Father Story on the stairs. "That's insane, you know they're going to kill him.

"Peter had already made up his mind to leave and there was no way any of us could have stopped him," Father Story gripped the banister.

"Except there was no way he could have passed the barrier without help Father," said Mario, "You should have told us and we could have discussed it as a group."

"You have no idea of the evil we're up against. I know, I've seen it and it's unrelenting and unforgiving. The power within evil always grows stronger within someone who has been so affected as Peter is, and he knew it too." Father Story was indignant, "You want to believe keeping him here under the protection of this house would've been the right path to have chosen. What would you have done if he had turned his hatred against us? Were you prepared to kill him? Were you prepared to take the life of someone you loved and send him to the darkest part of hell?" They avoided his glare as he climbed the stairs. "We mustn't fight each other, we have to prepare ourselves and strengthen our resolve... for the hour is closer than ever to the end of days."

Unknown Time
Unknown Place

Peter was surrounded by darkness; he could feel the hard rock from above and all around press down on his body. The stone was white hot to the touch and scorched his flesh as he squeezed through the miniscule opening of the strange underworld terrain. The area around him was scarcely wide enough for his head to fit through and he constantly worried that his body would become permanently lodged somewhere in the bowels of the earth. It was hard to breathe in the acidic air and it only added to the unnerving feeling of claustrophobia. He heard nothing and saw nothing as he crawled on his belly with his ear in the dirt for mile after agonizing mile. Occasionally there were crossroads where his hands reached out and he felt the small passageways veering off to the left and to the right. He blindly guessed at which direction to take and was convinced that he would be trapped inside purgatory's never ending maze forever. He stopped abruptly as he felt the wisps of hot air cascade over his exposed skin. The walls of his tomb were narrowing and the further he descended the less he had use of his legs to propel him forward. In the weak light he saw evidence of a golf ball sized hole fifteen feet away. Every muscle burned as he painstakingly inched along the floor of the hardened bedrock. He greedily dug his fingers into the rock and dirt breaking his nails as he gradually widened the opening. He grimaced as he pushed tiny bits of the solid wall outward into the great unknown. He emerged like a newborn baby into a world unlike any he could ever imagine. The sky was blood red and absent of clouds; in the distance was a long line of rocky black mountain ranges. A river of lava flowed freely from the base of the mountain and disappeared over the horizon in the opposite direction. The lava bubbled and churned as a man's decapitated head burst to the surface. It was swept along by the strong current to the shore near where Peter stood. Bony white crab legs sprouted from the sides of the skull and it slowly crawled towards him. It stopped disturbingly close to his feet and settled on the dark soil. Soon after, an attached neck and shoulders appeared sticking out of the dirt. A full body surfaced as desperate hands shoved away piles of mud and muck.

The man stood close to Peter, his mouth slowly opened and his voice was gargled and hollow, "It is good to see your face my son." His eyes were opaque and he hugged Peter tightly, "I have waited so long for this moment of our inglorious reunion."

"I was hoping I'd never see you again," Peter said coldly. "You were always wrong about me, even when I was a child you never understood what I really was."

"You are wrong, you are the disciple of Kyameron and everything that I had hoped you would become."

"I'm not here because I believed in the lies of the God you worship, I stand here because I choose the only path I could to save my daughter's life," he broke his father's embrace. "You made your choices long ago and now your soul is damned and you are nothing more than a slave to the beast for all eternity. I will never be like you no matter how hard you tried to mold me in your pathetic image."

He laughed loudly, "You still think of yourself as a pious man? You couldn't save me then and you can't save yourself now. Whatever decisions you made and for whatever reasons you made them, there is a single truth that you cannot deny... you are here among the souls condemned and here you will stay."

"I haven't surrendered to the will of the Devil, I still have flesh and blood and I have ownership over my spirit, even in a place like this."

"The bell has tolled and you cannot unring its commanding sound," a stream of viscous liquid oozed from the holes where the legs had emerged from the elder Cameron's head. "Your life in whatever state it resides belongs to us; the keepers of the faith."

"I defy you and I deny your faith."

Loud thunder clapped startling both men and Peter's father offered a word of caution, "Beware your tongue for there are those who will take great pleasure in ripping it out of your head for the next hundred years."

"Look at you, this is the reward for being such a faithful soldier?"

I failed to bring forth the coming of the apocalypse," he began to speak somberly as he reflected on his time in the abyss, "My flesh is also real and my pain rooted out by a merciless hand. I am cursed by the demons to be torn to pieces for all eternity. But they will imagine a suffering for you far worse than mine could ever be if you choose to turn away from your destiny."

Emily spirit appeared as a haggard old woman who sat barefoot on the ground rocking back and forth. Her long gray hair draped over her deformed face and her nightgown was filthy and blighted with soot and dirt. She sobbed hysterically and her fingers pulled hard at the clumps of hair matted to her head. There was no doubt that this ungodly incarnation of her was lost to insanity. She stopped her frantic movements and cocked her head to the side as she listened intently for the sound of Peter's voice.

"Go to her Peter, your daughter seeks the warm embrace of her father."

"She is not my daughter; she is an abomination--the thing that cannot be for the world beyond this would truly perish," Peter stepped back as the old woman spread her arms out and blindly searched the ground for his presence. He took the crucifix cross from his pocket and held it up in front of his father's face, "And I say unto you as I say unto your God, I shall destroy all things in hell before the Devil's hand reaches up towards heaven."

Instantly the sky filled with tumbling ash colored clouds that spread out over the vast expanse. Peter heard thunder louder and more intense than any that had ever existed in the natural world. Lightning flashed across the sky and a strong wind blew from the east. He stared in astonishment as the mountains crumbled to the ground with a deafening roar. A heavy chain wrapped around his father's neck and the hook attached at the end tore his throat open. His arms flailed as a second chain wrapped around his stomach and cut him in two. Tartorus, a creature with the body of a man and the head of an ox stood in the middle of the fiery lake. The Ruler of hell until the Devil's return dragged his father's living parts back into the burning lava. His hand rose above his head, he cast the chain and a hook embedded into the top of Emily's skull; she begged for mercy as hot molten ore gushed from the beast's open mouth. She fell backwards and was dragged on the ground leaving behind a long blood trail as she too was pulled into the lake of fire. Peter turned and ran as the beast rose up and stepped foot onto the shore. Winged gray skinned demons darted from the sky and attacked him as he fell to the earth. Their oversized claws cut his face and scraped his chest. They hissed and gnashed their teeth as they viciously tormented him. He shoved and kicked away their razor sharp talons and jumped to his feet. He was alive, at least for the moment and he was nearly human. He kept thinking to himself that it wasn't his time to become one of them; the condemned. The ground beneath his feet began to shift; like metal scraping against metal he could hear and feel the massive wheels turn as the gates of hell closed shut. He resigned himself to the obvious fact that he had no choice; there was only one way out. He raced towards the small opening in the black rock, squeezed inside and he began the long journey back the way he had come.

2:00 pm
Olgiata suburbs
Rome, Italy

A Wolfe and Stone van pulled into the driveway to the cacophony of barking dogs. Cardinal Fuerst and Father Santeal stepped out and casually walked to the front doorstep. Cardinal Fuerst carried a metal bucket and a few other items with him as he pushed the door open. The two men entered and quickly locked it behind them. There was a large hole in the roof and the bodies of three women were near the stairway entrance. The curtains were drawn and loud disco music boomed from the speakers of a Panasonic record player. One of the women was alerted to the sound of the men's presence and crawled her way through a pool of blood towards their direction. Her eye sockets were empty and her tongue had lost its ability to form any intelligible words. She grabbed frantically at the cuffs of Father Santeal's pant leg; he placed his foot on the side of her head and effortlessly crushed her skull flat. They moved to the basement where more bodies of teenage boys and girls were scattered across the floor. A low guttural growl alerted them to where Robert had taken his solace. He chewed on the flesh of a dead boy whose face was cast in the last throes of death. His pointed claws had cleaved out the boy's guts and his mouth easily snapped the bones like pretzels. Robert had the appearance of a hideous gargoyle and sat elbows on knees huddled in the corner. His head was enormous and an arch of thick yellow fluid sprayed liberally from the center. Father Santeal placed the pail of water, towel and pumice stone on the floor next to the banister leading to the corner where he sat. Robert leaned forward, his eyes maniacal and full of hate and anger. The cross had seared into his flesh and trapped him in the body of the demon. Father Santeal sensed the hesitance to accept his help and carefully raised his hand towards Robert's head.

"You won't turn me into one of your mindless slaves," Robert's clawed hand clutched Father Santeal's wrist tightly.

"You are Qeynan, you are a God, and I have no intension of remaking you in another's image," Robert released his grip and Father Santeal flexed his freed hand, "Peter burned the mark of Christ into your head, and if I don't remove it, it will burrow through your brain and split your skull in two."

The hurting was intense and no matter how much he feasted he could not stop the awful pounding in his head. He was Qeynan, he was a God, but even a God could perish from the face of the earth. Robert reluctantly closed his eyes and Father Santeal placed his palm directly over the six inch gash of burnt flesh on his forehead. He gasped from the shock of touching the consecrated mark. A steady stream of blood ran out of Father Santeal's nose and passed the corners of his lips. He steadied himself and fought through the pain until all traces of the cross were gone. Robert exhaled and once again he was human in flesh and blood. Father Santeal collapsed to the floor; a black ash blot stained the center of his palm and he began to shiver erratically. Cardinal Fuerst rushed to pick up the pail and pumice stone. He held Father Santeal in his arms and vigorously scrubbed his hand until all layers of skin had been removed then placed the injured hand in the pail of water. He felt Father Santeal's body stabilize as his breathing steadied and his heartbeat returned to normal. He looked over towards the gore that remained from the macabre death scene; Robert was nowhere to be found.

"He's getting more powerful and more erratic," said Cardinal Fuerst, "his hatred for Peter keeps him from accepting his rightful place as the Angel Qeynan. Instead, he focuses his feelings towards one man and his obsession has made us vulnerable."

"I'm not worried about Robert," Father Santeal pulled his healed hand from the bloody water and dried it on the towel. "It's Peter who is unpredictable; we shall find out soon enough where his true loyalty lies."

5:00 pm
Village of László
Lamia, Italy

Father Principi exited a cab and stood on the corner of a nearly empty street. Most of the two story buildings lining the boulevard were identical in design and constructed with a dull gray stone. He crossed Fine Strada Street and strode into the local Village Pub. It was dimly lit and inhabited by a group of the town's less than reputable clientele. He pulled out a stool and sat at the bar; the brown wood had been badly discolored from decades of spilt beer and cigarette burns. The overall atmosphere reflected the hardhearted mood of the centuries old establishment. The men were loud, vulgar and gregarious. Their brutish voices were harmonized by an accordion player squeezing out the rhythmic tunes of old drinking songs.

"Can I help you Father?" asked the elderly bartender who's smile revealed a plethora of missing teeth.

"I'm looking for a guide, I was told there was a gentleman here who could help me," he glanced at a heavy set man seated next to him. "Mr. Malleta?" he extended his hand.

The man kept his head down, his eyes never left the bottle of Guinness cradled in his hand and he poured it into his stein then took a healthy swig.

"Can I get you something to drink Father?" said the bartender as he tapped a large brown barrel.

"I thought your friend could take me to the László Abbey," he turned to the man on the stool, "I can pay you well."

"You don't look like a tourist to me," Malleta said as he finished his beer and ordered another.

"I'm not; I was hoping to find someone, Cardinal Fuerst to be exact. I was just passing through on my way to Rome; it's been a long time since I last saw him. I was told he was here restoring the abbey…"

"To hell with Fuerst!" shouted Malleta and the music and the hearty chatter went silent.

"Watch your mouth!" the bartender snapped.

"That abbey should have been destroyed years ago; it survives only as a beacon for the damned. How much do you know about the history of are little town Father? How much do you know about the kind of horrors that went on there under the guise of righteousness?" anger and spittle came from Malleta's mouth. "Have you heard of the tales of men who were tortured there, or how the Devil appeared to young girls while they dreamed. Our daughters were violated in morbid ceremonies and made servants of the hideous and most evil and depraved men to walk the earth. The monks living in the László Abbey turned away from being men of God into the worst kinds of Satanists that ever existed. Their madness spread like an infection through our village and they raped and sacrificed our children at will."

"I'm quite aware of the abbey's horrid past, but the evil that terrifies you happened many centuries ago. I have no time for legend and superstition Mr. Malleta and I have absolutely no desire to torture anyone. Surely you don't think the Vatican would ever allow anything like that to happen now?"

"I promise you it's not superstition; that abbey is a gateway to hell and as far as I'm concerned Cardinal Fuerst serves as its wretched gatekeeper. May God summon the power to strike him dead and may he burn László Abbey down to its foundation." All heads were turned in their direction and the tension was molded to their faces. A definite sense of hostility arose within the masses.

"I think you better leave now Father," said the bartender, "you made your pitch and he gave you his answer."

"Very well," he stood and leaned close to Malleta's face intent on making his point, "Mark my word Mr. Malleta, I will find a way to the abbey with or without your help."

Father Principi stepped out into a gloomy sky filled with an abundance of low rolling clouds. The rain began to fall almost immediately. It all made a perfect picture for a depressing day. Even if he knew where the abbey was, how would he ever get there? The cabbie had been coy about discussing it and he had paid him extra for the tip on Malleta.

"I can take you to the László Abbey," said a confident voice.

Father Principi turned to see a young man standing near the entrance of the pub. "You're not afraid, like the others?"

"I am," the young man smiled, "but I'll do whatever it takes to rid us of Cardinal Fuerst."

"I'm a stranger in your village, I could be just like Cardinal Fuerst for all you know. How can you be sure that I'm not here to help him?"

He laughed, "I know," he stuck out his hand, "my names Attino." He disappeared down a narrow alley and a minute later emerged behind the wheel of an orange Daihatsu three wheel truck. He leaned his head out the driver's window, "Sorry but it's the best I can do."

They drove for a half hour passing dozens of carts pulled by horses that were the villagers' main source of transportation. They made mostly small talk with Father Principi answering many questions about the church.

"What is it about Cardinal Fuerst that seems to have engendered so much hatred amongst your friends back there in the pub?" asked Father Principi.

"As far as I can remember, ever since I was a child, he's been stationed here in László. Lately he's rarely been seen in town; Father Lentz has taken over all of his duties and runs the local church. No one knows why he took an interest in the abbey, but we've been fighting him for years to close it down. We wrote letters and even sent representatives to the Vatican and it all fell on deaf ears. Father Martz had told us that we were acting like children and were foolish for being so irrational."

"They spoke to Father Martz?"

"Yeah; nowadays most people try to pretend it doesn't really exist, but you can see the heavy toll it's taken on their faces. It's like that place is slowly draining the life out of everyone who lives here." Attino pulled over to the side of the road and stopped the tiny truck. There were two vans and six men dressed in white uniforms erecting a wrought iron gate a hundred feet from the entrance. "Well Father, I guess this is as far as I go."

"I shouldn't be more than an hour," Father Principi opened the passenger door, got out and leaned his head inside the open window, "you think you can wait that long?"

Attino felt the unease of being so close to the shadow of the monastery, he swallowed hard and replied, "Sure, I'll be here."

Father Principi hiked up the slight incline and the workers tipped their hats and greeted him as he passed. The sounds of nature had fallen silent and it merely heightened the unsettling sensation he had as he stepped ever closer to the Abbey of László. He could feel the coldness bleed through the foundation and embrace his being like a winter storm. The building had seen centuries of disrepair and the red brick fence surrounding the grounds was drained of its brilliant color. The fading and once ornate white walls of the monastery were covered with the blight of rusty water stains. A greenish patina covered the face of the entranceway and intensified the sense of foreboding. He crossed the threshold and stood inside the vestibule. The odor of mold and mildew clung in the air and most of the open spaces were strewn with fallen ceiling tile or buckled floor tiles. The windows were expansive arcade arches devoid of glass; curiously nature hadn't found its way inside the walls. If Cardinal Fuerst had called this home for the last dozen years, he had done nothing to make it feel the least bit alive. He pressed on drawn by a strong force that led him to the upper chambers. In the main prayer room the rows of wooden pews had disintegrated and what remained of their shape were barely recognizable stumps. A medieval iron cage used for torture hung from the ceiling in the far corner as an ominous testament to those who had suffered at the hands of the monks of László. He stared out from the second floor window at the sprawling grounds and the man-made lake that was hidden behind the fortress walls. A single tower with a domed roof stood out as the only modern structure that had been annexed to the ancient monastery. It all seemed so unnatural and he felt the hairs rise on his forearms. At first the quiet screeching sound seemed more mechanical than human, but as it grew in volume it was clear that is was neither. "Eh eh eh eh eh eh eh eh eh," exploded in the room like a shotgun blast emanating from somewhere deep in the bowels of the abbey.

"Your presence disturbs them. You are not welcome here," a woman's soft voice disrupted the stillness in the chamber.

Father Principi whirled around to see a nun dressed in a long light blue habit with a white coif on her head. She stood at a distance with her features hidden by the angles of sunlight and shadows that poured into the space. He hadn't seen her or heard her enter the prayer room and it made him keenly aware that he was extremely vulnerable.

"And who exactly would I be disturbing Sister?"

"You know of whom I speak," she calmly replied.

"I was always told that the spirits of the ancient priests stood guard over the Devil's pit as they have done for centuries inside this priory. How is it possible that a great evil could have ever been released into the world?"

"The greed of man, the need for power and the need to conquer all. True evil lies within the hearts of all mortal men," she clasped her hands at her waist. "The abbey has long ago destroyed everything good and pure within its walls. There is nothing but death here now."

"If you're going to warn me of grave misery yet to come, then I still have time. There must be a way to stop it, some way to keep the circle from being complete," Father Principi could feel his pulse quicken. "I need to know if Cardinal Fuerst is responsible for releasing the Devil. Is he the one who started this?"

"There are many things you do not know about Cardinal Fuerst," she silenced herself and was clearly frightened as an unholy shriek resonated off the walls. A burst of cold air rushed through the room and spun the iron cage wildly off its axis. "You must prepare yourself; they will come for you Father. Hector will rise and ascend to the throne of Hades; there are no longer any illusions. And when he has, man's time on earth will come to an end."

"Who are you?" he asked as she stepped back into the darkness, "Wait, don't go, please. I need your help." A colony of bats flew from the space where she had been standing and he dropped to his knees as they passed overhead. The wind grew stronger and the building began to rumble and shake. The awful eh eh eh eh eh eh eh eh grew more deafening. He cupped his ears as the volume rose and his eardrums nearly burst. His teeth vibrated and the blaring noise threatened to leave him unconscious. His face and body were numb and his skin had the strange sensation of burning. The walls began to bend and sway as waterfalls of thick blood flowed from the ceiling. The phantoms of the satanic monks appeared; bound together by chains for all eternity they lurched back and forth as they encircled him. Father Principi prayed on his knees as the building was engulfed by a strange malevolence that menaced to drag him down into the pit of hell.

CHAPTER XV: BLOOD AND STONE

7:45 pm
Via Cola di Rienzo Street
Rome, Italy

The streets were bathed in pools of shadows as Gallo walked towards the rear entrance of the brick apartment building. The sliding lock on the corrugated steel garage doors had been left unlatched and he pulled it halfway up. It was vacant inside; he took a deep breath then headed up the iron spiral staircase. As he closed the distance to room 333 his heart began to pound and his palms began to sweat. He pried the lock with a small metal bar and opened the door. Perfectly framed in the far window was a view of Vatican City and the dome of St. Peter's Basilica; below it in a chair sat a man whose upper torso was hidden by the dim light. A tiny lamp sat on the coffee table and its weak glow kept most of the room bathed in black. Gallo hit the light switch, but the bulbs had been removed.

"Hello again Mr. Cecellini," Marko stood at his side and held a silver Rogak pistol against his head. "You really should have introduced yourself the last time we met." Gallo took a step forward. "Unh uh," Marko put his hand on his chest, patted him down and removed the pistol and pry bar from his possession.

"You're early," Gallo quipped, "and I was under the impression our meeting was strictly private.

"Marko was just leaving," uttered the man in the chair, "weren't you Marko." He shut the door behind him and the two men were left alone.

"Getting a copy of the book turns out to be more complicated than I had originally thought," Gallo leaned against the door jamb. "I haven't found any solid new leads myself."

"You know who has the book right now don't you Mr. Gallo?"

"Yeah, well I already tempted fate once with Robert. I'm not too anxious to do it again."

"Your end of the bargain includes procuring a copy of the book. If you find yourself unable to fulfill that part of our arrangement, then you are of no further use to me."

"Why don't you get it yourself... Cardinal Fuerst." Gallo folded his arms and waited for a reply. "It would seem to me that you have greater access to it than I do. Last time we were here I foolishly relinquished all the power that was contained within the pages of that little book. I was upset to say the least and you knew you had me then. All you need do was whisper in my ear that there were others who held the text and I had a second chance at redemption. Robert could have easily drowned me and Agent Gutman in the harbor or done far worse, but you stopped him because you need me. You see, there are some things that even I am smart enough to figure out," he listened but there still was no response. "Ohhh yeah that's right, you'd rather play this silly cloak and dagger game with me. I know you lied to me about a wealthy buyer interested in the book for his own private collection; disguise your voice all you want but I know that it's you I've been speaking to over the telephone. So I'll ask you again, why don't you get it yourself?"

An orange glow appeared in the darkness as Cardinal Fuerst lit a cigarette, "My reasons are my own. What I do is of no consequence to you Mr. Gallo."

"There are others who may have a copy of the book in their possession, Peter Cameron or the Council comes to mind."

"Perhaps, but then that's your job to find out isn't it?"

Gallo clenched his fist and ground his teeth, "I made sure I wasn't followed, I've checked the cars I drive and everything I carry for tracking devices and found nothing, yet somehow you seem to know everywhere I'm going before I do…"

"And your point is?"

"I don't like being fucked with, not by you not by anyone," he paused and took a different tact. "You're hiding something big, something you'd hate for Robert and Father Santeal to discover. And, I know that there were others who knew it too. Unfortunately in my talk with Emir Saldalha he never got around to discussing you at all, and Hafsah always the philosopher, was more cryptic in his warning. Sangiamo however seemed to take great pleasure in my not knowing the truth about you Herr Fuerst. It's much more than a burning desire to obtain a copy of the book for yourself. Double-crossing your friends is pretty much standard fare with men like you and it's no surprise that you would have betrayed the Council's trust." He was overwhelmed with curiosity, "So tell me, what is the secret you're so desperate to keep hidden from the world?"

"You feel that you're at a disadvantage because you don't know who you're really dealing with. And if I told you?"

He tapped his fingers on the arm of the chair. "Come now Mr. Gallo, it obviously hasn't deterred you from showing up to our little meeting tonight, has it?"

"No more games, no more disposing of your enemies to prove my loyalty to you and no more lies about fictional businessmen; from now on I talk and meet only with you," Gallo put his hand on the doorknob and turned to leave, "One last thing, my price has just changed. After I deliver, I want an equal partnership… I want what's rightfully mine."

"Bring me the book Mr. Gallo," Cardinal Fuerst laughed loudly, "bring me the book."

And the great dragon was cast out, that old serpent, called the Devil, and Satan, which deceives the whole world: he was cast out into the earth, and his angels were cast out with him.

Revelations
King James Bible

CHAPTER XVI
THE TEMPLE OF METATRON

Saturday 2:18 pm
11, November 1978
Isabella Stone's Farmhouse
City of Madonnella
Bari Province, Italy

The tension had grown worse between Angela and Eddie. She rarely talked to him or the others and segregated herself in the sanctuary of the guest room. She ran the gambit from denial to anger to helplessness and had made the decision to divorce herself from the real world. The possibility of ever living a normal life again was fading by the second, and she knew in her heart that the door was closing all too quickly on the chance she'd ever leave the house alive. Eddie was growing ever more conflicted and depressed, he desperately tried to hang on to his fleeting sense of sanity. He passed the time by chopping wood in the backyard as a welcome distraction to the tumult that was going on in his relationship with her. It was his fight along with Peter and the others and he couldn't quite get over the guilt of dragging Angela into the heart of the dire mess they had found themselves in. Isabella spent most of her time carrying out the same repetitive daily chores as she had always done. At this time and in this moment they didn't seem as tedious and mind numbingly boring as they normally were. She sat on the back porch cleaning clothes by hand with an old washboard and tub. Her thoughts always remained with her daughter who lay still and unconscious with her condition relatively unchanged. Mario had already gone through his self reflection and began to fill his mind with new ideas. What if they survived the horrors Robert had in store for them? Even if there were those who'd view what he had witnessed with Emily and Peter as nothing more than some fantastic fairy tale, wouldn't the broader outside world want to know the truth? Didn't he have a responsibility to tell Peter's story, his story? A sense of disgust began to creep into his consciousness. He was thinking only of the profit and feared that he might be capable of trying to shape events going forward to make a better read. His agents and publicists had conditioned him well; always give the masses what sells even if it was chocked full of blood and gore and death.

He sat by himself in the living room when he heard the scratching at the front door; he steadied his nerves. He approached the door and peered through the window, but was unable to get a good angle of view. He stepped out onto the front porch and saw nothing accept the swaying stalks of wheat that seemed to cover every last inch of Isabella's property. Mario turned towards the entrance and the wooden planks squeaked loudly underfoot; he turned his head just in time to see the Rottweiler attack. He crashed to the floor with the dog on his chest and its mouth frantically snapping at his face. Instinctively he put his arm up in self-defense and the dog sank its teeth down to the bone. He screamed as it thrashed its head and split his flesh. Eddie ran to his aid and hit the dog with the side of his ax; it tumbled off then righted itself. The dog leapt on top of him and they fell to the ground with the ax sinking into the Rottweiler's massive chest. Exhausted, Eddie lay on his back and found the strength to push the dead dog off of him.

"What have you done?" Father Story shouted as he descended the staircase. "I told you that life cannot be taken inside the circle."

"It's only a dog. It was going to kill Mario," Eddie jumped to his feet. "It's not a human life…"

"You must get it out of the house, get it out now!" shouted Father Story.

The corn stalks began to rattle and Isabella stopped in place. She stood up; the heavy movement across the field made the grain appear like an advancing army on the march. It wasn't Robert, she was sure of that, but whatever it was it was headed towards the house. The army of the dead appeared from the field by the hundreds. The rotted and pewter fleshed corpses walked, crawled and dragged their failing humanity forward for an unholy purpose. Mounds of earth shifted aside as fingers pushed up through the dense black soil. Isabella ran inside the house, locked the door behind her and yelled for the others. Eddie peered out the front bay window; they had overrun Peter's barrier and trampled the crosses beneath their feet.

"Help me move the cabinet in front of the window!" Eddie shouted to Mario and Father Story.

They struggled but eventually moved the heavy furniture in place as the thumping of bloody palm prints banged on the glass. The house was too large and way too vulnerable to defend against forced entry. They would have to find a suitable place to make a stand or the end would come like a giant tidal wave crashing over them. The sound of shattered glass hitting the floor resonated throughout the house as the appalling throng gained access into the kitchen and back dining room. A giant with only patches of decaying flesh clinging to his bones stumbled into the living room with obvious lethal intent. Mario picked up an iron fireplace poker and slammed it across his face. The iron hook dislodged the man's jaw and knocked out several of his teeth. The dead man fell to his knees and Mario drove the poker downward through his skull. The living room and the stairway to the second floor were soon flooded with hordes of the depraved and undead. Blank stares were plastered across the faces of the formerly living and dearly departed as they cut a path of destruction throughout the house. Mario, Father Story, Isabella and Eddie thrashed, beat and stomped their way through the mob and yet they kept coming in at an unending and unyielding flow of devastation. Their mouths wide and biting, fingernails broken and yellowed dug into the flesh of the home's living residents. Long knotted hair, diseased eyes and macabre expressions brought into stark reality an impending sense of final days. Isabella twisted away from the hold of an old woman and hid in a small bathroom off the hallway. The panic within her rose as she could hear sounds of battle rage just outside the door. She searched the cabinet and the mirrored shelf for a weapon, but there was nothing. A large brute splintered the bathroom door and was inside within seconds. She broke the mirror with her fist and as he dove towards her, she jammed the broken shard into his neck. He continued to paw and snarl at her while black liquid leaked profusely from the diagonal gash across his throat. Eddie pulled him off and struck him across the forehead with a hefty table leg. The dead man clutched at the rose pedal shower curtain and pulled it down over himself as he fell into a freestanding tub. His neck was broken and his head was bent at an odd angle; he lay motionless. They grouped together, unable to reach the second floor they retreated to the safety of the basement with the army of the dead in quick pursuit. Heavy fist pounded on the thin walls that separated the cellar from the upstairs quarters. They were vile and they were angry and their venom was taken out on the door as it shook fiercely off its hinges.

"The door isn't going to hold them out for very long," Mario pressed his full weight against it. "We need something to fight them off, we need weapons."

"Robert never kept his guns inside the house," Isabella tried not to sound unhinged.

"Find something, anything," Eddie said as he added his weight against the door.

Isabella and Father Story ran down the wooden stairs and searched through rows of metal shelving units. Their luck held out and they retrieved a hammer, garden shears, spade shovel and a pickax. A strange scratching sound came from the center of the basement. A middle aged woman had dug her way up through the cement floor and her torso jutted out of the rubble. Isabella screamed, her hands shook and she dropped the hammer and shears. The woman's green eyes burned with all the rage and hatred of an aborted humanity seeking vengeance from beyond the netherworld. Father Story pushed Isabella aside, with a healthy swing of the spade shovel he decapitated her misshapen head and it thumped against the wall with great force.

"Is there an exit door or some other way out?" Eddie asked as he hurried down the steps.

"No," Isabella thought for a second, "there's a dumbwaiter we haven't used in years, it goes all the way up to the second floor."

"Show me," Eddie grabbed her arm.

Tucked in the corner behind a metal shelf and a pile of cardboard storage boxes was a cobweb encrusted square frame that slightly protruded from the wall. Eddie quickly tossed the debris aside and wiped away the years of dust and spider webs from its face. He hastily pulled up the door to the dumbwaiter then tested the walnut plank bottom and the hemp ropes attached to an upstairs pulley.

"Get in," he said as he shoved her inside.

The pulley wheels squeaked loudly from a decade of neglect and unuse. After a minute he felt the dumbwaiter stop and her weight exit the box. Isabella ran through the master bedroom and quickly locked the door. She pressed her ear against the frame and could hear the movement of scores of feet pattering up and down the hallway. Eddie helped Father Story into the dumbwaiter and quickly hoisted him up.

"Mario!" Eddie shouted across the cellar, "Get over here now!"

Mario let up on the basement door and could see it give from the weight pressing on the other side. He ran in the direction of Eddie's voice and without his having to explain, got inside the box. Eddie gave him the hammer and shears.

"How are you going to get out?" Mario asked as Eddie shut the cage door.

"Don't worry about me, I'll find a way."

Eddie could see mounds of earth forming on the floor as more mud covered fingers broke through the cement. He heard the door give way and a crowd of footsteps running down the stairs. He felt the click as the dumbwaiter finally stopped at the top and Mario's weight was gone. He quickly lowered the box and leapt inside as the horrific sight of eight men with leathery skin hurried towards him. He pulled the gate shut and listen to the unnerving beating of fists on the outside door. He maneuvered himself on his back and kicked the lid of the dumbwaiter out of place then pried it off with his fingers. He stood up in the shaft, the hemp rope was frayed and in far worse shape than he had hoped. With both ends of the rope in his hands, he hoisted himself up. The rope began to snap from the heavy strain and the fibers quickly unwound. Eddie had only climbed ten feet when he was sent crashing back down into the cellar. He hit the back of his head on the tip of the box and lay temporarily dazed. The small door was forced open and dozens of hands reached and clawed at his legs and waist. He gripped the frame of the box but was pulled out of the shaft and back onto the basement floor. Eddie cringed and gnashed his teeth as several mouths bit into the muscle on his thighs and the bone of his ankle. He kicked his legs madly into the maggot and worm infested bodies of his assailants until he was able to free himself. He jumped back inside the safety of the shaft as more of the dead flooded into the cellar. He slammed the dumbwaiter's gate shut, braced his back against the wall and pressed his feet against the door holding it closed. His body strained and his legs burned while he kept the horrifying monsters at bay.

Angela hid in Emily's room, the door was locked and she had placed a chair against it. She knelt on the floor and the tears flooded her eyes; she knew there was only seconds before the mob broke in. She moved to Emily's bedside and knelt down next to the girl's frail body and prayed for her soul. The wood door began to crack and splinter and she could clearly see the awful faces of her harassers. She scooped Emily up in her arms just as the door broke apart and dozens of foul smelling cadavers stormed into the bedroom. Their eyes were cloudy, their skin and clothes in tatters, they stopped just inches from where she knelt. The hatred on what was left of their decomposing faces changed to awe and worship as they saw Emily in her arms. Angela took a deep breath and slowly got to her feet. She knew that they had come for the girl and held her body aloft as though it were a tribute for their masters. She nervously took short and measured steps as she waded into the crowd. The dead closed in their ranks and surrounded her. Their lifeless hands eagerly reached out and gently touched Emily's face. Their bony fleshless fingers sent chills down Angela's body as they brushed against her bare arms. The sea of nonhumanity parted in the bedroom and she moved through the multitudes gathered in the hallway. They congregated by the dozens on the staircase, living room and front yard and all stood aside as she passed. She was careful not to look back in their direction for fear of drawing their ire. Angela had gently placed Emily's lifeless body in the back of the Mercury Capri when she felt an arm wrap around her neck and squeeze tightly; she let out a silent scream.

"Do as I say and I won't kill you," Marko spun her around and grinned happily. "Keys please or would you rather I let them tear you apart."

The thunder of fist hammering against the door faded, then suddenly stopped; Eddie listened intently. His legs were drained of energy; he relaxed his feet and eased off the pressure on the dumbwaiter's gate. He was exhausted and strained to hear movement over the sound of his own breathing; nothing. Surely they were still out there, waiting for him to drop his guard, waiting to make him a quick and easy meal. His hand quivered as he reached out towards the metal door. His reason told him to stop, but he had to know; he hesitated as his fingers made contact with the gate.

"Eddie!"

Eddie's heart jumped, he quickly pulled his hand away and recoiled into the safety of the shaft, "Yeah!" he said as the fear began to subside.

"They're gone," Mario leaned over the shaft's opening. "Are you all right?"

"Yeah, how's Angela and Emily?" he tilted his head up, there was a sick feeling rising in the pit of his stomach as he waited for a reply. "Mario!"

"They're gone!" shouted Isabella as she collapsed on the bedroom floor, "They took them."

6:00 pm
Manna Book Store

The room was eerily silent and dark; too dark. Peter inhaled deeply as his lungs took in air for the first time in hours. He coughed uncontrollably and rolled off the tulip table onto the floor. The room was still spinning and he fought hard to get his equilibrium. He staggered to his basement apartment, turned on the light and stared into the tiny bathroom mirror. Dried blood was matted in his hair and his face and clothes were covered with the splotches of ugly charcoal stains. He ran the sink then splashed his face with cold water; a black liquid swirled around the basin and down into the drain. He was deathly pale and thick purple veins were noticeably visible on his face. His mind began to piece together what had happened at the hands of Robert and Father Santeal earlier in the evening. He tore off his shredded shirt and tossed it on the floor. There were little physical signs of the battle he had with Robert or evidence of the wound where the sword had impaled him. He opened the refrigerator, the temperature of his skin and throat was a raging inferno. Peter quickly downed a full gallon of orange juice, a gallon of milk and a half gallon of grape juice. He tore open a packet of raw steak and sank his teeth into the bright pink flesh. The uncooked meat and blood slightly eased the throbbing in his head and the aching in his bones. He squeezed the blood from the Styrofoam tray and licked the plastic wrap clean. His hunger for blood was growing and he knew it. Father Santeal/Thaydien, had resurrected him from the dead and in doing so drew him closer to the monster he had feared he would become. The image of his father and knowledge of what awaited him in the afterworld shook him deeply. He sat on the cold basement floor, leaned against the open refrigerator and let the cool air wash over his body.

6:05 pm

"We have to do something. We have to go after them," Eddie paced in the living room.

"Where? We don't even know where they went?" Mario sat on the couch nursing his wounds.

"They're probably moving through the corn fields as we speak," Eddie said, "If we leave now we can cut them off at the main road."

"I don't think so," Isabella stared out the front window, "I don't think they took them after all. Your car is gone. Angela must have Emily with her."

Mario sat puzzled, "Why would she… she must have thought she was saving our lives."

"She's going to deliver the child to Father Santeal," Father Story handed Eddie and Mario gauze for their open cuts.

"I'm not going to argue with you, I need your keys," Eddie turned to Father Story, "I'm going after them."

"Wait a minute, we need to think this through," Mario implored.

"Give me the keys now or I'll hot wire your car and take it myself," Eddie glared at Father Story, his face was stone cold.

6:20 pm

"Keep your head and everything will be all right," said Marko, the Mercury Capri slowed down twenty feet from a police road block. He showed Angela the gun and took the keys from the ignition, "We're just a husband and wife taking our very sick daughter to the hospital. Don't do anything foolish and they won't get hurt."

The police strode at an easy pace towards the car, "Evening," a cop stood alongside the passenger window and another took his place by the driver's. "You folks live around here?"

"No just passing through," Marko smiled warmly.

"Where you headed?"

"Does it really matter?"

"It might. You see we've had some real troublemakers in this area," he rested his arm on the roof and looked in the back seat. "It's awful risky being out here on these long desolate roads."

"We'll keep that in mind officer."

"You have identification?"

Marko knew even if he could shoot the first cop, his partner was in the perfect position to blow his brains out, "No. I... I think..."

"Could you exit the car sir?" the officer said as he put his hand on the rolled down window.

"Something wrong?"

"Out of the car sir," he opened the door and pulled Marko out of his seat.

"We haven't done anything wrong," Marko protested as the officer spun him around.

"Nice gun," the cop slammed his nightstick into Marko's ribs and he buckled over. "Tell Father Santeal he should have never have been so stupid as to cross the Council. He will atone for his betrayal."

The officer swung again and clipped the back of Marko's head; he slumped to his knees then fell back and lay unconscious against the car. The second cop grabbed Angela by the wrist, tossed her to the ground and grabbed Emily from the back seat. He carried her to the open rear doors of the police van and the two quickly removed the roadblocks and sped away with lights flashing. Stunned, Angela jumped back into the car and reached for the key to start the ignition. They were gone; Marko had them. She eased herself out of the front seat and calmly walked around to the passenger side. Marko's eyes were closed and blood ran down his ear and neck. She knelt over him; her shaking hands carefully opened his jacket and reached inside his pocket. He grabbed her wrist and she attempted to pull away. His eyes slowly opened as he pointed the gun at her face.

6:30 pm

Eddie spun the tires of Father Story's station wagon and accelerated down the main roadway. The green tree line was left a blur as his foot pressed the pedal hard to the floor. The sun was low but still lit the way for miles. Eddie jammed on the brakes, he was caught off guard by a seven foot man standing in the middle of the road. He swerved to avoid a head on collision and clipped one of Robert's massive legs. His face slammed into the steering wheel and the car flipped twice and careened down the side of the embankment. The hood was crushed and hot steam and fluids burst out of the engine bay. The bridge of his nose was flattened, his jaw ached and he spat out two of his molars. The horn blared nonstop as he pushed away from the crumpled dashboard. His legs were badly injured; he opened the smashed door and fell to the ground. The blood leaking from his head poured out freely onto the fallen brown leaves. His cheek lay flat against the cool earth as he spotted a blurred figure in the distance approaching at a deliberate pace. His eyelids shut, then trembled open and focused on the menacing figure of Father Santeal standing over him. Terrified, Eddie scooted back in the dirt until he was pressed against the car's wheel well. Father Santeal's eyes burned bright red, he stretched his fingers out and placed his hand over Eddie's forehead. He felt Father Santeal's palm grow from warm to blazing hot and his skull began to vibrate. The bright orange of the setting sun and blue sky bled into each other in a swirling pool of color. He wanted to cry out but couldn't. He knew it was the vision Emily had shown him and he knew it meant his death. His eyes rolled into the back of his head, then... emptiness.

7:45 pm

Gallo felt a slight sense of unease as he drove down the gravel road that separated the old barn from farmer

D'Alisa's house.   The lights were off and the home was silent. A mile later he crossed a covered bridge and headed down the dirt road. He was in the middle of nowhere and the isolation made his stomach do back flips. He looked at the folded map and at the address Sangiamo had given him. He knew he was on the right course even if the road indicated on the map had ended miles back. Then he saw it in the distance. It stood out over the tree line and it blended into the landscape like a small hill. Morgenstern, Robert Stones replica of the Temple of Metatron, loomed like a giant gravestone against the black bark of the tree line. He cut the headlights, veered off the road and parked the car on the opposite incline of a small green hill.   He took Sangiamo's mask and hooded robe then ventured into the woods in front of the temple. The dirt parking lot was filled with cars and several others lined the road with their headlights flashing across the barren landscape. He donned the costume and kept low as he weaved through the parking lot.   Two armed men stood guard by the entrance and stopped and frisked a man before allowing him passage. Gallo stood up from behind a gold Mercedes and reluctantly tossed his gun underneath the front bumper. He never liked entering into dodgy situations without being armed to the teeth, but he had no choice. He had walked to the front line of cars just as a police van pulled up and parked in front of the entryway. An officer opened the double doors at the back of the van and another exited with a small lifeless child in his arms. They hurried pass the guards and into the temple. His nerves began to fail him, the mask was suffocating on his face and it affected his stilted breathing. He had convinced himself that if Peter didn't have the book then surely someone on the Council did. He tensed and thought, what if Sangiamo had given him a false password? Would it mean an immediate shot to the back of the head or worse? And what if he did gain entrance, where would he begin to look for the book without being detected?

"Vita incerta, mors certissima," (Life is uncertain, death is most certain,) Gallo waited endless seconds for the guard's response. Beads of sweat poured down the inside of his mask.

They opened the doors and he walked down a flight of stairs that led to a circular balcony. He passed several men wearing ornate masks that hid the faces of celebrities, judges and politicians. Thirty feet below, the floor was painted with a circle inside a triangle inside a circle and on the Thaydien symbol was a white stone altar. Gallo watched as the policemen gently placed the young girl's body on top the stone. The temple was spherical from top to bottom with a balcony walkway that spiraled its entire length. Nearly twenty feet above his head was a domed ceiling painted with blue and green demons, black clouds, frescos of the fallen angels and the Devil himself. At the center enclosed in a wood beam trellis was a gigantic bronze tower bell. As Gallo ascended two men in purple flowing robes passed by without barely a notice. The bell rang and the groups of men headed toward the bottom pit. Gallo quickened his pace and kept moving upward. He stayed away from the railing and peered into the many rooms that lined the temple's floors. Most were small uniform bedrooms with sparse interiors that closely resembled prison cells. At the very top of Morgenstern temple, Gallo broke into a room with a locked door. Inside was a giant master bedroom with a beautiful white marble floor. He was amazed at the elegance, but what captured his attention the most was the wall-to-wall-floor-to-ceiling bookcase. Thousands of leather bound books lined the sixty shelves and ranged from very old volumes to yellowed ancient parchment. He feverishly scanned the shelves looking for a book the size and color of the book of fallen souls. The tower bell boomed as it rang again and it forced him to cover his ears. He listened closely as an authoritative voice filled the voluminous chamber.

"We are gathered here to celebrate in the ancient Onaric Festival of Thorns," the voice echoed off the fortified walls. "Through his deeds and through our prayers, good fortune has brought us the child of Kyameron." Gallo crawled to the railing; lay flat on his stomach and peered down into the chasm. A man wearing a ram's head with enormous horns stood on a pedestal and conducted the proceedings. "It is now our time. We are the chosen and we will control the Angels of Destruction." The others began to chant in a low rhythmic tone.

Three women stood at the base of the pedestal and by command they dropped their white robes revealing decoratively painted nude bodies. They danced and swayed around Emily and tied her wrists and feet to the altar. Clear glass jars were placed in a circle around the sacrificial stone and three figures were pushed inside the room. Sacks were placed over the heads of the unwilling participants and when removed revealed terrified faces to their captors. A priest, a young girl and an adolescent boy quivered as they were forced to kneel at the blade of a knife. The man with the ram's head costume held his arms above his head, and that's when Gallo saw it. In his right hand was a book that had the Thaydien crest embossed on its cover. Two men stood behind the priest and simultaneously removed their masks. Gallo recognized one as a judge from Rome and the other as an up and coming young politician. The priest took off the heavy ram's head and one of the naked girls took it from him. His face was lightly painted with orange streaks under his eyes, but he could still identify him as General Salvatore Rapetti.

"We are on the doorstep of greatness," Rapetti said as his audience bowed in supplication. "We and we alone dictate the destiny of the entire world." All but one man fell to their knees and knelt on the floor as an act of submission. It startled Rapetti and his gaze focused on the arrogant blasphemer. "Only a fool would come into my house and disrespect my law. On your knees or I will have your legs cut off and your body put to the spike."

"That won't be necessary," Father Santeal removed his mask. "I've come for the girl... and you will give her to me."

"How pitiful, a stray sheep that has lost his way wishes to return to the flock," Rapetti sat down on a chair atop the pedestal. "You forget I have the book and it gives me great knowledge and great power over all walks of man, kings and presidents. You were wrong to leave the Council Grigory, you were disloyal to our trust and you are no longer surrounded by your friends. On your knees and beg me for my forgiveness so that I may decide just how you shall die."

"You're right in one narrow aspect," Father Santeal pushed his way through the men and to the altar where Emily lay. "You do have a book... but you're wrong in so many other ways, I have all the power. I have already committed myself through the trial of desecrations. You couldn't really appreciate the kind of power that I possess; I am greater than you could ever wish to be. I am closer than ever to fulfilling my destiny of becoming God, and as for you... there will be no forgiveness."

There was a commotion and loud screaming from the front and the entire congregation turned their heads in that direction. Robert bent his enormous frame through the archway; in his claws he held the severed heads of the two entranceway guards. One of the women cried out and ran for the exit, but all avenues of escape were sealed shut by Father Santeal's will. Robert leapt on the altar and his clawed feet seized Emily's body. His wings spread out wide; in a blur he flew straight up and smashed through the arc of the ceiling. The trellis broke apart and the large bell dropped earthward with incredible speed. It crushed the altar and spun wildly killing four men cowering nearby. Large chunks of the dome crumbled and showered the crowd below.

"Why have you done this?" a bloodied Rapetti clutched at the bone in his broken leg. "We were to be the rulers of the world."

Father Santeal climbed the steps of the pedestal, "Because there can only be one true master of heaven, hell, and earth." He touched Rapetti's foot and his body was instantly engulfed in flames.

The faithful flock began pounding on the doors and trampled each other without compassion. They were desperate to find a way out as the temple was set alight. Father Santeal closed his eyes and the flames grew higher and higher and the fire burned with horrific ferocity. Morgenstern, Robert's contribution to his faith and a place of worship for the demonic soul was instantly turned into a smoldering crematorium. The thick gray smoke wafted from the pit below and covered the spiral walkway with the heat of orange flames and the wailing of dying men. Gallo ran back into the large bedroom, wet a towel from the bathroom sink and covered his nose and mouth. The outside door was hot, but he summoned the courage and opened it. The choking smoke and burning ash made visibility nearly impossible. The fire roared on while the pleas of the dying fell silent. Through the plumes of smoke he spotted the broken trellis that held the tower bell. He checked the sturdiness of the railing then balanced himself on it. He leapt as high as he could and grabbed hold of a piece of splintered wooden beam. The entire structure jarred from the impact of his body and he quickly climbed the center of the framework. He reached out for the gaping hole in the ceiling left by the demon's exodus and could feel the trellis weaken beneath his feet. His eyes stung and he frenziedly coughed as his nostrils and lungs filled with black soot. His fingers clasped the crumbling stone and he pulled his weight up through the gap. A twisting hot gray cloud rose through the hole and emptied into the dark navy sky. The roof was blistering to the touch; he righted himself as the building began to pitch. Gallo weighed his options carefully, the curve of the roof was set at a steep and worrying angle. He slid down the side as large sections of the temple began to disintegrate behind him. Gallo hit the ground at full force dislocating his shoulder and fracturing his rib cage. His face was badly bruised and all of his fingers were numb. He crawled to the safety of the parking lot as his lungs greedily took in the fresh air. He ignored the pain that enveloped his body and headed into the woods with the intensity of the fire lighting the night sky and guiding his way.

The disciples prayed in the valley of Sudea and sayith;

O' Lord how shall we know the time of your coming and the commencement of your glory? And the Lord sayith unto them, three seals shall be broken and my covenant revealed, three angels shall rise and three nations shall fall; for three is my number. Three is the number of the beast.

Serafeim
libri of cado animus

CHAPTER XVII
THE HUNGER

Sunday 3:10 am
12, November 1978
City of Madonnella
Bari Province, Italy

The sprawling green hills decorated the tranquil countryside a short distance from the heart of town. Comisana sheep grazed on a hillside and trailed in a long line down to the fertile pasture below. Their ears perked and a few heads turned sensing the looming danger. A nine hundred pound saber tooth hulk tore through the flock scooping up a thinly muscled animal in its jaws. The beast cut down two more from the pack then dragged its kill to the steep side of a grassy knoll. The teeth ripped at the flesh, gutted the carcass and its long cat like tongue lapped up the pooling blood. The powerful paws morphed into human hands and the wide brim nose and feline features returned to its natural human form. Peter finished feeding on the animal then disemboweled the other two. He drained as much of the blood as he could into two empty stomach pouches then carried them away. The throbbing in his head had abated, but the desire for human flesh and blood hadn't. The change was coming quickly and there was no way to stop the hunger growing inside. He noticed a light was on inside a log cabin nestled in the heart of the valley. He stopped on the stony hillside trail and listened for movement. Two large Cumberland sheepdogs barked loudly as they ran towards his direction in hot pursuit.

"Stop right where you are!" the old shepherd cocked his shotgun as he climbed the hill. "In all my life I've never had anyone senselessly kill my animals. Looking at the mess you left back there, you must really be sick in the head mister. Or maybe you're just a fool who wants to stalk my land and destroy my livelihood." A flashlight illuminated Peter's back. "Whatever it is you'd better give me a good reason not to shoot you where you stand."

Peter carefully placed the sheep stomachs on the ground next to his feet. His jawbone dislodged and his claws extended; he could feel the change coming. He felt the insatiable burning in his soul, he knew the awful horror of what was going to happen to the old shepherd and he welcomed it.

5:00 am

The Mercury Capri lumbered up the drive to the László Abbey. The headlights shut off and the engine turned silent. Marko dragged Angela from the car and shoved her into the cold dank entrance hall. She stumbled and fell to the floor. Marko still felt the nauseating symptoms of his concussion and almost blacked out while training his eyes on the girl.

"Have you a desire to contribute a blood offering?" a voice ricocheted through the shadowy abbey. "Or have you decided to offer yourself as a sacrifice for the glory of the Lord? It seems your fate is now in my hands."

Marko spun around and tried to gauge the direction of the speaker. "Where are you? Come out so I can see you," he pleaded. "She had the child and I... I was going to bring her to you."

Father Santeal walked towards him, "Interesting, I never asked you for your help."

"I knew you needed the child."

"And yet you do not have her, do you?" Father Santeal slowly circled him and quoted Matthew from the bible, "Therefore if thou bring thy gift to the altar, and there rememberest that thy brother hath ought against thee. Leave there thy gift before the altar... and go thy way."

"She was taken from me I swear," his throat tightened and his voice cracked. "I'm on your side. I haven't conspired against you I swear. The Council..."

"I know all about the Council and I've taken care of them myself... I have the child now. You haven't answered my question, why were you following the girl without my orders?" he pressed him flat against the wall. "The problem is that you bear no gift, and you haven't gone away."

"I was... I was..."

"Your head... you're injured," he raised his hand to Marko's forehead, "Don't worry, I can heal you."

"Enough! I'm responsible. I told him to watch the house," Cardinal Fuerst descended the steps of a dilapidated white staircase. "I thought it best that we had someone at the house at all times." He pushed Father Santeal's arm away from Marko's head, "I can assure you he would have brought the child to us... and now we have the girl too."

Robert's presence interrupted the group. He held Emily in his arms and her body dangled limply. He was human, but his face showed no trace of sympathy or love for the child he had once called his own.

"You said you wouldn't harm us if we gave you the girl," Angela got to her feet. "You have her, now please let me go."

"And where would you go my dear? Back to your old life in Madonnella. Back to the farmhouse? Maybe you would like to tell Peter that we have his daughter and that she is a prisoner of the abbey," Cardinal Fuerst lovingly put his arm around her shoulder. "Very well; if you wish you may leave, but Eddie is here and he'll want to see you before you go."

"Eddie?" she cried, the fear rose in the pit of her stomach. "Where is he? Please tell me."

"Come, I'll take you to him," Cardinal Fuerst escorted her to the second floor and unlocked the door; Eddie sat on the ground with his back to them.

"Eddie!" Angela ran and threw her arms around him.

There was a deep purple bruise on Eddie's forehead and his thick brown hair was singed and falling out. His eyeballs were cloudy and his lips were fixed in a permanent bestial grin that barely covered the double rows of teeth. He pulled away and growled like a wilding animal when Angela touched him. The heart and soul had been violently ripped from a man who had once been warm, caring and human.

"What did you do to him? You changed him!" Angela crawled away and as Eddie lunged toward her she kicked him in the chest. "Keep him away from me, please!" she cried. "You said you wouldn't hurt me. You promised."

"I won't hurt you," Cardinal Fuerst scoffed, "but he will."

Eddie dug his fingertips into her wrists and pinned her to the ground. Angela's frightened stare was only met by a set of callous and unsympathetic eyes. His mouth slowly opened and a dreadful growl vibrated from within the center of his diaphragm. He sank his teeth into her shoulder blade and bit-off a thick slice of skin and muscle then tilted his head back and fervently gulped down the fresh meat. Angela was surprised she hadn't yelled louder than she did. She closed her eyes and prayed it would soon be over; it wasn't. Eddie's fangs dug deeply into her lower lip and burst her pupil as it exited through her eyeball. His tongue eagerly lapped up the nascent river of crimson and with a wicked grin, he began to consume her piece by screaming piece.

Cardinal Fuerst closed the door behind him as Angela's gurgled cries were drowned out by the ferocious blood soaked sonancy of Eddie's manic feasting.

CHAPTER XVII: THE HUNGER

9:00 am

Gallo pulled up to Isabella's house, the pain from his arm was excruciating and he had stuffed a rag in his mouth to stop it from bleeding. He was an awful mess, but time was running out and he couldn't afford to lose more ground. It was the second time he had failed to secure the book and the anger within began to boil over. It was also the second time he had nearly died at the hands of Robert and Father Santeal, and the thought of revenge ebbed and flowed within the span of mere seconds. He slowed the car, the front lawn was strewn with broken crosses and scattered piles of upturned earth. The spindles on the porch fence were splintered and the windows smashed. As he approached the door he held his elbow and a sick clicking came from his dislocated shoulder. The door jamb was busted and the lights inside were off. He drew his gun and kicked the damaged door off its hinges. The room inside was in no better shape than the land outside. He thought the house might have been abandoned until he heard a faint shuffling in the kitchen and headed in that direction. There was a black doctor's bag on the table and Isabella sat crosswise from Mario as she bandaged his injured arm.

"Where is he?" Gallo holstered his gun.

"I can't really answer that question, it depends on who you're looking for," Mario slyly grinned.

"Peter, I need to talk to him."

"Oh, then you're shit out of luck, he's gone."

"Do I have to ask fifty stupid questions or can you tell me where he is?"

"Don't know, he didn't say where he was headed," Mario winced as Isabella tightened the bandage.

"Was Robert here, did he do this?" Gallo sat down next to him.

"No," he tested the flexibility of his hurt arm. "I guess in a way we were lucky he didn't; if I told you what happened you wouldn't believe me."

"You mean like Robert's long ceased being a part of the human race and he's transformed himself into a ten foot monster with black wings?"

"You've seen Robert?" Isabella's hand began to tremble.

"Up close, too close actually. If you want to stop him you have to help me find Peter."

"Father Story dropped him off at the Manna Book Store two days ago. I don't know if he's still there," she replied.

"Thank you."

"Wait, I'll go with you," Mario stood up.

"I don't think so, it's too risky and I don't want to be responsible for babysitting a civilian," protested Gallo.

"That's crazy, we're not going to wait here for Robert to show up," Isabella said, surprising both men, "besides, you look like you could use all the help you can get." She noted the skepticism on their faces and before they could respond she stated firmly, "Robert has my daughter and if either one of you think I'm going to stand aside and let you attempt her rescue without me, you're dead wrong. I'll find them by myself if I have to."

Mario looked at Gallo's defeated expression and said, "I guess that's settled then; we all go together."

"Greaaat," Gallo said sarcastically. He rubbed his aching shoulder, "Before we go, do you have any ice for a wounded warrior?"

"Sit down," Isabella guided him to a chair.

She set Gallo's arm in a sling and cleaned up the cuts and bruises on his face. The bone had broken through the skin of his ankle; he had been filled with a cocktail of fear and adrenaline that he hadn't even noticed it. She knelt in front of him and expertly set and wrapped his injured foot.

Gallo looked in her eyes, she was insanely determined and a lot tougher than he had originally thought, "Robert has a lot of hatred in him and it's not just for Peter, he also seems to harbor an enormous amount of it for you."

She stopped and returned his gaze, "I've been dealing with Robert all by my little ol'e self for weeks now, I think I'll be okay."

"Oh I absolutely believe you can handle yourself," he said not wishing to offend her any further, "it's your friends I'm worried about, he might just take his rage out on them."

"My friends know the risk they're taking to help me, they stayed with me and my daughter..." her voice steadied as she thought about her missing child, "I have no doubt they'll fight till the end if they have to."

"That's why he took her, Emily? He wants to hurt you."

"My daughter is gone Detective and he has her. It doesn't matter why, I just need to get her back."

"You know the last time I was here I remember two other people in this house, other than yourselves, Father Story and Peter. Something happen to them too, or are they still in hiding?"

Maybe it was a selfish reflex, a mother's single minded conviction, but she hadn't even thought about Eddie or Angela's safety. Her mind, her entire being was fixated only on Emily.

Mario broke the silence, "We're wasting valuable time, we need to leave now if we have any hope of catching up to Peter and Father Story."

"I'll bring the car around," she wiped her eyes and exited the kitchen.

Isabella hesitated as she crossed the driveway on the way to the garage. She convinced herself there was nothing there, nothing ready to pounce out of the fields or from behind the tool sheds that were rooted near the house. She rolled opened the warehouse garage door and headed towards a Lincoln Town car that was first in a row of thirty exotic vehicles. She stopped, crimson droplets splattered on her head and she stared up at the rafters. The Spanish maid Rosa was plastered to the ceiling with her fractured legs and arms spread wide apart. Her skin was pasty and her stomach was distended and had been grotesquely honeycombed. A swarm of bees flew around the bloated fleshy hive and crawled out of her mouth and nostrils. A thick green gel seeped from her eyes and dripped onto Isabella's cheek. She covered her mouth and muted her scream as she ran to the car. Her fingers fumbled nervously to unlock the door and she slammed it shut once inside. She turned the ignition and in one quick motion put the car in drive and sped recklessly out of the garage and away from the horror.

9:45 am

Father Story searched the Manna bookstore not knowing exactly what it was he was looking for. A holy book, scrolls of a lost language used to fight an unholy war, a divine weapon or Peter himself. He found nothing but the cold emptiness of a lifeless building. Isabella, Mario and the detective entered the store wearing the scars of battle. They collapsed on the chairs and queried him about Peter, but he could offer no answers. A dull thud came from Eddie's upstairs apartment and seconds later heavy footsteps reverberated on the staircase. Peter held two of the sheep stomachs in his hands; they looked like balloons filled with water hanging at his side. Gallo was tempted to withdraw his gun as he eyed the dead white face staring back at him. Peter stopped and stood at the edge of the broken balcony.

"Angela and Emily are gone," Mario's voice was shaky, "and Eddie went after them. They've already unleashed a graveyard full of the walking dead to attack us, God knows what else they're capable of doing next. We don't know where they are, and we need your help to find them Pete."

"I know exactly where Emily is, the demons inside of us are one and the same, we share an unbreakable bond.

Father Santeal wants me to find her; I can feel the deep pull of his thoughts scream out to me like a clarion call."

"She's unconscious, useless to him now. She can't perform the desecration and won't be able to give him what he wants. He knows that you'll come after her and he'll force you to become one of them," said Father Story.

"Looks like you're already one of them," Gallo walked closer, "I've seen Robert or Qeynan or whatever the fuck you want to call him. I've watched him eviscerate men-- tear them apart close up, and I know all the sick horrors Father Santeal can inflict. I can help you Peter, if you let me."

"And how could you help me?" an electric green spark flickered in Peter's eyes as he shot Gallo a cold stare. "You're only human, all of you are... there's no way any of you can stand up to them."

"You're forgetting about the Trilogy, if we can take the book from them, we can bring this whole nightmare to an end. Without you the circle is incomplete and their full power can't be restored." Gallo stood next to Peter, "Believe me I know full well of the danger, and if I can't stop them; I'll stop you."

Peter grinned, "You really think you can? I'm prepared to die, are you? I'm going alone. Stay here and I'll bring them back to you, I give you my word." He turned his back to them, the lights flickered and in an instant he was gone.

Gallo was physically and mentally exasperated, "You know what will happen if he joins them; they'll enslave the entire world. And when mankind has served out its purpose we'll be destroyed in a blink of an eye. I don't know about you, but I don't feel like sitting here waiting for the world to end."

"We're out of options, Peter was our only way of finding them and we don't know where he's going," Isabella slumped in her chair.

"I think I know exactly where he's going," Mario's eyes fixed on the painting he'd given Peter that hung over the entrance to his apartment, "The Devil of László." The centuries old Abbey of László glowed in the background like a beacon in the dark as the giant leviathan devoured souls and came alive through the aged canvas.

They piled in the Lincoln and Isabella gunned the vehicle down the City of Madonnella's only road leading out of town. The traffic was sparse, only a few busses and lorries dotted the double lanes. It hadn't escaped any of them that they were heading straight on into the mouth of hell without a plan.

"What do we do once we get there? I mean, we all know what we're facing, right?" Mario fidgeted nervously.

Gallo examined the Makarov pistol's clip and handed a Berretta to him, "You know how to use one of these? Just point and squeeze."

"Against monsters from hell, will that even work?" he passed on the offer.

"Suit yourself."

"You said you had fought Robert," Isabella glanced at Gallo in the rearview.

"Not exactly, I said I've seen them kill before... I never said I confronted them."

"You told Peter you could help him. If you don't know how to fight them, how were you planning to stop Robert and Father Santeal?"

Gallo leaned back and yawned loudly, "I don't know but it's a long drive to Lamia, maybe I'll think of something by the time we get there."

Father Story rubbed a cross and chain between his fingers, "There is a deeper evil within László; one that is more obscene than Father Santeal or Robert, one that is the living breathing soul of the abbey. He is a relic of evil and responsible for bringing its horrid past into existence. We must seek the guidance of the Lord. If it is God's will we shall be protected and we will win this holy war."

"See... problem solved," Gallo stretched his legs out, closed his eyes and went to sleep.

Then I saw an angel coming down from heaven, holding in his hand the key to the bottomless pit and a great chain. And he seized the dragon, that ancient serpent, who is the Devil and Satan, and bound him for a thousand years, and threw him into the pit, and shut it and sealed it over him, so that he might not deceive the nations any longer, until the thousand years were ended.

Revelation
King James Bible

CHAPTER XVIII
THE DEVIL OF LÁSZLÓ

Sunday 1:45 pm
12, November 1978
Abbey of László
Lamia, Italy

A metallic gray painted the breadth of the heavens and was covered in cumulus clouds. Lethal streaks of lightening discharged throughout the landscape while a heavy rain fell to earth. Father Story guided the group through the village proper and up the hilly dirt road to the gates of the László Abbey. Thirty feet away, Isabella placed the car in park and shut off the headlights. The newly erected iron gates had been ripped from their hinges and were bent at an awkward angle.

"Looks like Peter beat us here. Any suggestions on what we do now?" asked Mario.

"Yeah," Gallo opened the door, "we get out and ring the damn doorbell if we have to." He got out of the car and was somewhat intimidated by the size of the building. "Let's go!" he tapped on the roof, "it's not going to get any easier from here on out."

They squeezed underneath the heavy wrought iron bars and saw Eddie's Mercury Capri sitting abandoned on the monastery's lawn. The thunder boomed while they made their way to the entrance under the steady downpour. Mario pushed against the rotted door and it squealed open. A dull light infiltrated the foyer while rain from the storm battered the outside brick. The hall was lined with torches lit and unlit; a confirmation that someone else was here.

"Must be over a hundred rooms. We'll be here a week before we find anyone," Mario unhooked a torch from a steel sconce and shown the light in multiple directions. "Where do we start first?"

"It'll be easier if we separate, if you find Peter first he'll take you to where they're holding your daughter. If you find Robert first ... well I guess the rest of us will hear you screaming," said Gallo as a roaring thunder brought with it a rush of air that made the fires flicker. "Here, take it," he held out the Berretta and insisted, "just point and squeeze." This time Mario accepted. "I'll check out the third floor, you, Isabella and ... where's Father Story?"

"I don't know? I didn't see him leave," Isabella said.

"Great," Gallo shook his head, "you two take the second floor, I'll take the third and if neither of us find anything, we'll head to the basement." He took a torch from the wall and disappeared down the long hallway.

Mario and Isabella headed in the opposite direction. They peered through the Gothic archways of a mess hall and spotted a staircase along the far wall. A disturbing fresco of the Devil holding the severed heads of St. Peter and John the Baptist was visible behind the centuries of black mold. Marino's *Devil and the Righteous* had once been painted with bright blue, red and yellow colors that were now cracked and faded and it made Isabella feel more unnerved. They climbed the staircase, beams of natural light trickled through the open pass-throughs and cast long shadows into the interior. Halfway down the hall they came to their first room with a locked door. Mario struggled as he unhooked the latch and slowly opened it. A row of tiny transoms ran the length of the exterior wall and bathed the room in gloomy lightlessness. They moved to the center where they found a shattered skull and a pile of bones stripped clean and gleaming white on the floor.

Isabella examined a piece of torn gray cloth embroidered with tiny purple flowers. Tears began to flow from her eyes, "It's a part Angela's dress she had it on today."

"Are you sure? We don't know how old these are, they could have been here weeks or months…"

"Of course I am. They killed her and tossed her away like garbage."

He knew she was right, there was no use in pretending otherwise. He put his hand on her shoulder, "Look will search a few more rooms then find the Detective. Okay?"

He heard the resonance of a tortured inhaling and exhaling from somewhere in the room and signaled for Isabella to be quiet. His eyes locked with hers as he slowly raised the gun; whatever it was--it was getting closer. He spun around and pointed the torch in the direction of the labored breathing. Eddie's glazed eyes and maniacal grin froze Mario in place. His mind let precious seconds slip away as he failed to accept the sight of the abomination. His old friend stood before him with all his humanity stripped away. Isabella screamed; Eddie leapt on top of him before he could react. Mario's arms flailed from the force of the sudden impact as he was sent tumbling backwards. He dropped the gun and the torch flew from his hand and rolled across the floor before it was extinguished.

Father Story crossed the span of a huge subterranean vault where a large crater lay near the center. The corpse of the twelve mummified priests that had once been amassed around the entrance to hell were uprooted and scattered across the floor. Their skulls were crushed into powder, their bodies had been horribly desecrated and showed the aftermath of being burned. A lone warrior Sabaoth, Lord of the Armies of Israel, sat atop a stone pedestal on a golden throne cloaked in dust and cobwebs. His face was void of color and his long curly black locks had turned gray and stringy long after his death. A golden crown sat firmly upon his head as homage to the destroyer of the Red King, last ruler of Sudea and Tallse and the Kingdome of Thaydien and Kashar. His mighty sword had been taken from him and in its stead his hands clasped around a wooden replica that he held between his knees. Father Story knelt down at the feet of the king and began to pray.

"Bravo Brother Story you finally found the world's last savior of a lost cause; kneel before the mighty King Sabaoth," the heels of Cardinal Fuerst shoes clicked off the stone floor, "He is the last guardian that remains from the bloodiest days of the great war. We spared him the fate of the priests so that he may be resurrected and given the punishment he's earned throughout the centuries. Only this time the great king will battle with a weapon more fitting of his status," he pointed to the wooden sword. "He will be severely judged and made to suffer many times over for his trespasses against the one and only true God. I will fuse his precious crown to his head while he screams towards the heavens and begs for his God's mercy." He stood only feet from Father Story, "Pray to him all you want, Sabaoth can't save you no; no one can."

"My God will save my soul… and destroy yours. You're more than a blasphemer, you are the blackest of spirits that only pretends to be a man. You were birthed in the cradle of filth and crawled out from the depths of mankind's sins. You are nothing more than a vile and worthless creature."

"It's a pity Neil, ten years ago Father Martz offered you a place at his side and you refused; you made the wrong choice. The others you brought here will die a miserable death far worse than your mind can comprehend. However, I am prepared to offer you one last chance to save your life if you join us."

"Your beliefs come from a sacrilegious book," Father Story kept his head down and eyes closed. "Only a fool believes he can harness the power of the Devil without consequence."

"Only a fool would enter the Temple of Metatron armed with just his faith."

"I know what you are," Father Story raised his head, "you do not frighten me and I do not fear Robert or Father Santeal."

Cardinal Fuerst laughed, "You should. For I am the abomination; I am the creator and the destroyer, the light and the dark. I have no mercy Brother... you have chosen death and I am your willing and eager executioner."

Peter watched Father Santeal and a very human Robert as they stood at opposite ends of the altar. Emily was wrapped in heavy chains and strapped to the stone block with the sword of Sabaoth dangling above her head. There were candles on the floor assembled along the edge of a white chalk line that formed a perfect circle. Three jars containing brains, three jars of hearts and three jars of intestines and genitals were carefully placed around the circle's circumference. Father Santeal read from the book of fallen souls and began chanting an ancient Thaydien incantation to raise the Angel Hector.

"My daughter will never surrender her will to Hector," Peter entered the room, "but then again that's not what you want, is it."

Robert's eyes opened, the calm expression on his face changed as he realized Father Santeal's betrayal, "I ended Peter's worthless life and you brought him back... that was a mistake."

"The child was never strong enough to accept the spirit of Hector," reasoned Father Santeal, "He is the only way forward; only the blood of a true descendent of Kyameron can raise him from the netherworld."

"You were in my head all this time. You resurrected his soul from the afterlife and kept him hidden from me." Robert's anger steadily grew in passion.

"Peter has come to us willingly to trade his soul for his daughter's. In a few moments you will have the full power bestowed upon a God and you will have the ability to rule as one as well."

"He's lying Robert, you're much too feeble minded and what little remains of your life is quickly fading away," Peter stepped to the edge of the circle a few feet from where Robert stood. "Admit it, you can feel the sickness growing inside your soul. Qeynan is dying because you kept the human part of yourself alive so long seeking out ways you could satisfy your hatred for me. Your foolish desire for vengeance has made you disgustingly weak, so pitiful and unworthy of the gift. We will take great pleasure in killing you. You were never meant to be one of us, you were never meant to be a God."

"And what about you? You haven't committed the desecration Peter, I'm so much stronger than you could ever dream of being. If I chose, I could tear you to shreds and there's nothing you could do to stop me. And this time I promise you, I won't leave anything left for him to bring back," Robert's hands let go of the six inch iron posts that jutted up from the head of the stone.

"I can guarantee you Robert, this time things will be different," Peter opened his mouth revealing the long set of sabered teeth.

"Don't be a fool Robert, with him the circle is complete. He is the only chance for both of us to survive," Father Santeal pleaded to no avail, "The strength you have now is nothing compared to the great power we will receive once the Trilogy has been consecrated. You will rule the entire world once dominion is given to the Angel Qeynan."

CHAPTER XVIII: THE DEVIL OF LÁSZLÓ

Eddie sunk his teeth into Mario's injured arm and blood spurted from the gash. Mario repeatedly pummeled him with his fists to no effect. A desperate Isabella scratched Eddie's face and tried to wrestle him off but was effortlessly shoved away.

"Stop it Eddie... stop it!" she searched the floor for a weapon.

Mario kicked Eddie off but he immediately pounced on top of him and bit hard into the nape of his neck. A flood of intense pain coursed through Mario's body and his legs kicked wildly with uncontrolled spasms. He choked down the vomit rising in his throat, Eddie's breath was tainted with decay and his skin stank heavily of fire and brimstone. Mario's body was pumping with an overload of epinephrine in his veins and it kept him from surrendering to his fate. He battled through the fear threatening his conscious mind and focused on the beast attacking him. He knew if he passed out Isabella would suffer the same fate as Angela and it made him fight on with an enhanced determination. He jammed his fingers into Eddie's eyes then shoved the palm of his hand into his face and forced his head back. A loud bang and a dark red circle appeared on Eddie's chest; the room was still. Isabella stepped closer and Eddie jumped to his feet and raced towards her. She fired the Berretta again, the bullet struck his leg, his patella exploded and he fell to his knees. He raised his head and the last bullet in the chamber shattered the bridge of his nose as it exited through the back of his skull. Even in the dim light she could see Eddie's eyes were wide open and his body convulsing. His dying heart barely pumped oxygen into his lungs as his shallow breathing gradually ceased. She knelt down and pressed her hand against the open wound on Mario's neck to stop the rapid flow of blood. Isabella cradled him gently in her arms and felt his body shake and the temperature of his skin grow colder.

"Help me up; we need to find Peter," Mario's voice was weak and he grunted his words through clenched teeth.

Father Story sturdied himself against the grimy cold wall. His cheek was bruised and a stream of blood ran down his chin. He held his aching ribs as he tried to stand but his legs gave out.

"You were always too stubborn for your own good," Cardinal Fuerst rubbed his sore knuckles and flexed his fingers. "You would rather die for your faith then live forever under mine." He studied Father Story's face; his lips were moving and his hands were in prayer. "God can't save you now," he laughed, "I will shepherd you from purgatory to a damnation that your God hasn't prepared you for. Your last vivid memory will be of me devouring your flesh until nothing holy remains."

Father Story willed himself to his feet, "You believe in a twisted lie that you call faith, but in the end you will find it meaningless, an empty void where darkness only leads to more darkness. You won't discover any truths or enlightenment only that you've wasted your life worshiping a wretched God. You can bow down and worship at his feet, but in the end those who do mean nothing to him."

Cardinal Fuerst struck him again and he collapsed to the floor. He grabbed him by his hair and forced him to look at his face, "Dear-dear Brother Story, you want to believe your will is stronger, that you are morally superior to us and that makes you feel righteous. You told me that you knew what I was; maybe it's time I actually showed you."

A dull wet thud echoed off the walls and Cardinal Fuerst's muscles locked from the intense pain. The wooden sword stuck out of his chest after being driven through his back with tremendous force. He was stunned; his hands grasped the tip of the weapon as he tilted his head upward to see the face of his attacker. The dead King Sabaoth towered over him with a vacant leathered face and a stare that borne lifeless eyes. His arm wrapped around Cardinal Fuerst's throat and he pulled him close as he drove the weapon in deeper. Sabaoth's stiff legs moved backwards with Cardinal Furest's heels scraping against the stone tile. His fingers desperately tried to pry loose from the hold of the Lazarus king, but it was to no avail. He twisted and turned to shake loose and it only intensified his pain. Father Story followed as his old friend struggled for his life knowing full well of the dead king's true intentions. Sabaoth's lumbering walk came to a halt with his heels at the edge of the Devil's pit.

Blood seeped down the corners of Cardinal Fuerst's mouth; he smiled, "I must confess Neil… you sur… prised… me… I never th--thought…" his head slumped and his breathing slowed. Father Story was only inches away; he sensed his presence and slowly opened his eyes.

Father Story gripped Cardinal Fuerst by the chin and turned his head to the side, then whispered in his ear, "This is the end Rudolph, to hell with you."

Cardinal Fuerst seethed with hatred as Sabaoth tightened his grasp around him. The dead king leaned the full weight of his body back and they fell into the blackness of the great abyss.

Gallo peered through the archway and watched Peter engaged with Robert and Father Santeal. Boney plates appeared down Peter's spine as his demon form began to show. He wasn't quite the dreaded Angel Hector, but he was far from human. He leaned back against the wall with his gun drawn, just how was he going to stop them anyway? He breathed deeply and ran through a series of implausible scenarios.

"What's it gonna be Robert? One last time--just you and me," Peter braced himself anticipating an imminent attack.

"Stay inside the circle," begged Father Santeal, "or you will endanger everything we've done to come this far."

"Master or slave, which one are you?" Peter inched closer.

Robert leapt through the air and transformed into a screeching winged half-demon. He crashed into Peter and their teeth ferociously cut into each other like wild dogs. The two Goliaths slammed into the entrance wall and dislodged the mortared brick sending dust and pebbles cascading down onto Gallo's head. Peter's claws slashed away at Robert's belly and he bit deeply into muscle and tissue. Robert temporarily disengaged and held his wounded stomach; his eyes shown only hatred. He fully extended the thin bat like wings and sliced into Peter's chest with a harsh downward thrust. Peter fell to the floor with blood covering his chest and face.

"That's enough!" Father Santeal shouted, "I can't let you kill him Robert."

"You can't stop me," Robert jumped on top of Peter and his talons dug into his neck.

Peter's face contorted as Robert's enormous hands little by little crushed his thickly muscled neck. With a loud swoosh the blade cut the air and the steel tip clanged off the stone floor. The sword of Sabaoth had cleanly severed Robert's arm and he immediately clutched at the throbbing stump. A stream of black sulfuric acid gushed liberally from the amputated limb and spilled on the ground. As the blood pooled, a white noxious vapor rose from the floor and corroded the tiles. His eyes were wide with disbelief as he struggled to comprehend what had happened. Father Santeal stood at his side with the offending blade in his hands. His confusion turned to anger; he struck Father Santeal solidly with the back of his wing and hurled him to the opposite side of the room. It was an unwelcome and unfortunate distraction that caused him to lose focus on his kill. Peter bore his weight into Robert and rammed him into the side of the altar stone. He bit down hard and his saber teeth effortlessly punctured Robert's jugular.

"You want the power of a God," Peter lifted Robert off the ground by his throat, "then you can have all of mine."

Electric blue streaks of high energy emanated from Peter's body and hit Robert like a sledgehammer. The alabaster tentacles sprouted from his spine and wrapped around Peter's chest and neck. Robert squeezed tightly and prevented his captured prey from inhaling another breath. The pain was incredible as Hector's essence was transferred to him. The tentacles constricted even more and he could feel Peter struggling to maintain his hold. Suddenly, he felt Emily's tiny hand touch his leg. Her eyes opened and tears ran down her face. She felt the pull of the demons being drawn from her and channeled into the only man she had ever called father. She wanted to make Peter stop. She chose to see Robert as he was, as the kind and caring man she would always remember. But Emily knew it was too late, she had no control and as her soul was cleansed, she imagined her father's image where Qeynan now stood. She closed her eyes and regrettably relinquished the full charge of the demons' force into Qeynan soul. Robert's muscles physically stiffened, his organs fully cooked and his skin smoked as he fried from the inside out.

Father Santeal slouched against the wall suffering the after effects of Robert's attack. The cloudiness in his mind was gradually clearing, but he was still disoriented. He lowered his chin and placed his hand on the back of his bloodied head. His first conscious thought was that he had to stop them both before they destroyed each other and ended any hope of completing the ancient rights of the Trilogy. He sat up straight and his eyes slowly focused on the distorted image of the man standing above him.

"And Thaydien was made mortal," Gallo drove the heavy Sabaoth sword downward into Father Santeal's chest. His eyes bulged and the air rushed from his lungs as the lethal blow was wheeled. He gripped the blade; despite his unearthly power he was keenly aware of the dire consequence of being struck by the sword. Gallo placed the heel of his shoe on the handle's cross-guard and coldly drove the blade in deeper until he severed Father Santeal's spine.

"Peter!" Father Story shouted; Isabella stood behind him with Mario's arm around her shoulder assisting him to walk.

Robert's eyeballs burst into a gusher of liquid green sludge and his pale skin was turned raw and red. He struggled to keep his form as his molecules disintegrated and the strands of his DNA were ripped apart. There was a loud popping from his bones as they were pulverized under the pressure of an unrelenting ethereal force. The tentacles released their grip and Robert's body fell limp and lifeless. Peter removed Robert's necklace with the Devil's talon attached and tossed his carcass aside. He then stepped pass Gallo and retrieved Father Santeal's necklace that was fastened to the Devil's jagged tooth. He knelt down and searched inside his jacket for the book of fallen souls. Father Santeal's eyes opened, but his arms and legs were useless. He watched haplessly, unable to stop him from pilfering the sacred book. Peter placed both necklaces over his head and with the book in hand hurried back to the altar. Gallo eyed the sword sticking out of Father Santeal's chest; he wondered if it was worth the risk to confront Peter to get his hands on the libri of cado animus. Peter gently opened Emily's eyelids; the orbs were still black. He raised her head up, slipped the necklace with the tip of the Devil's horn over her head and secured it around his neck.

"You should leave," Peter told the others, "she's still harbors demons inside her; I have to remove them before she's lost forever."

"If you take full dominion of all three evils you will become Sado Satanus, the Antichrist on earth. You cannot risk destroying the entire world for the life of one girl," Father Story desperately tried to persuade him.

CHAPTER XVIII: THE DEVIL OF LÁSZLÓ

"If I don't stop them now, their spirits will find others to inhabit," Peter opened the book but his mind found it difficult to focus, "Robert and Father Santeal will be resurrected as wraiths seeking vengeance on all of us."

"Look at you Peter. You can barely stand."

"I'll be alright. Please, you have to leave now."

"If your words aren't precise, if you can't finish the invocation the Devil will rob you of your soul and the world will be burnt to a cinder," Father Story took the libri of cado animus from him. "If it must be done then I will read from the scripture."

"I can't ask you to do that Father; once you step inside the circle…"

"I know the outcome of my choice," Father Story took his place at the foot of the altar and opened the book.

Peter placed his hands over the two six inch spikes that protruded from the head of the altar. They were ancient and the points were worn dull, but he kept the flat of his palms steady. He slammed both hands downward impaling them until he reached the base. He slowly disengaged his hands from the device and with a sharply clawed finger deeply engraved an inverted cross from his chest to his abdomen. He gripped the spikes to keep balance as Father Story read from the pages of the ancient text. A strong wind flooded into the abbey and knocked Gallo, Isabella and Mario to the ground. The candles, the jars of human organs and everything inside the circle remained unaffected. Peter could hear the awful cries of the tortured and the damned as he was burdened with their suffering.

The final remnants of Hector were drawn out from Emily and Robert's bodies and were united with his brothers Qeynan and Thaydien inside Peter's dying soul. He was afflicted with a fit of convulsions changing from the more humanlike Thaydien, to the winged beast Qeynan, to the Red King Hector fashioned with black ram horns and blood red skin. He couldn't control the timing or speed of the transformation and he morphed rapidly between the personas of the three fallen angels. The howling wind increased in velocity and pressed down on Gallo and the others and its strength wouldn't allow them to move. They squinted their eyes and looked towards the altar, but Peter and Father Story were concealed behind a tornado of green fog and a wall of gray dust. Peter's muscles strained and he leaned backward; his body writhed from the trauma. An electromagnetic pulse burst from his chest with immeasurable energy and a bright blue flash ended with a shock wave of red and orange flames. The abbey rumbled as the walls threatened to collapse in on its foundation. The air slowly cleared; Gallo rose to his feet and raced to Peter side. He lay still with his back against the wall. His body was illuminated internally and his skin glowed bright red as if it were powered by a nuclear explosion.

Isabella took a position next to the altar; Emily's eyes were a sharp blue and she joyfully smiled when she saw her mother's face.

"Mommy," Emily's frail voice cried out.

Isabella was seized with emotion and unable to respond with words. She embraced her daughter tightly and kissed her several times on the forehead. She felt an overwhelming sense of relief as she lifted her daughter from the stone block and held her in her arms.

"Are you ok?" Gallo fingers burned as he touched Peter's shoulder. Three inch rays of yellow light beamed from the emptiness of his eyes and mouth. "Can you hear me? Can you stand?"

Peter shook his head, "Forget about me," his voice was raspy and weak, he tore the Devil's chains from around his neck. "Destroy these… and… destroy… the book."

Gallo nodded, Peter dropped the necklaces into his hand and the metal was surprisingly cool to the touch. A few feet away Father Story lay slumped against the wall behind the altar. His entire right side was a heap of blackened charcoal and parts of his body began to crumble away. His left side showed little signs of the devastating physical damage; he was aware and alert and his eyes followed Gallo's every movement. There was a discomfiting exchange of stares, almost as if he knew of Gallo's true intent. Gallo kept his gaze locked on Father Story's face as he pried the libri of cado animus from his good hand. The ceiling cracked and the archways collapsed to the sound of a volcanic eruption as the Abbey of László entered into its final death throes. Gallo put his shoulder underneath Mario's arm for support and joined Isabella as she carried Emily from the disintegrating monastery.

Peter pushed his back against the wall and rose to his feet. He staggered over to Father Santeal and removed the sword from his chest. He placed his palm on Father Santeal's forehead and it blistered under the searing heat. His eyes opened as life was breathed back into him. He felt the loathing in Peter's heart while the ever morphing demon picked his crippled body off the ground. Peter dug his fingers through the skin and muscle on Father Santeal's back until his hand clutched his spinal cord. Father Santeal winced as the dead nerves were reanimated. He carried him to the altar like a living-breathing human puppet as large chunks of the ceiling above gave way. The rumbling soon stopped and the sky above opened up to reveal a wide beam of warm and brilliant light. They found themselves standing inside the center of a surreal courtyard. The dimensions of a stone building encircled them and stretched far into the heavens like the ancient Tower of Babel. Hundreds of thousands of men, women and children dressed in white robes swarmed to the arched balconies with their voices jumbled in waves of indecipherable speech.

"And I saw the holy city, a new Jerusalem coming down from God out of heaven," Peter's appearance embodied the Angel Hector, but the face was his own, "Look upon the almighty glory for you are being duly judged." His voice was clear and the internal yellow light had ceased its burning.

"I see nothing," Father Santeal kept his head bowed, "nothing at all."

With his free hand he reached across his body and pulled Father Santeal's hair back until his head angled upward, "Look again. See the faces of God's children of every creed, color and race; those who are blessed and those who have received his word. There before you is the resolve of the saints who kept the covenant of God and faith." His eyes found Basem laughing and chasing after other children his age while under the gaze of his loving mother. He saw the stoic face of the teenage girl who had been sacrificed in the name of the unholy Trilogy, along with his old friend Cardinal Rourke standing by her side. "Look upon the faces of those you have murdered; those whose lives you took in pursuit of an immoral purpose."

A ghostly apparition of Father Story's body separated from its earth bound form. His head, arms and legs dangled as he was carried by an invisible hand and rose up through the middle of the tower. The angels pointed and whispered to each other while he passed the many floors and ascended towards the center of the shining white light.

"You are an abomination, a blasphemer who has been discredited for your lies and condemned in the eyes of the Lord," Peter was fully human and draped in the liturgical vestments of a priest's pristine white robe. "From now until the end of time the gates of heaven are forever closed to you."

"You forget Peter; you too have committed the desecrations; even if it was to save the life of your child, your soul is polluted with the Devil's seed. You are as wicked as I am and heaven has no place for you." The weight of the angels' glares began to affect him and he shouted out, "'Tis the wearied traveler who knows his fate, I stood alone and cursed at heaven's gate. Look upon the face that you will one day fear, for I will break down your gates and the ruin of heaven shall be at hand."

Peter's eyes searched for the visage of the Christ and when he found him, his lips moved in silent prayer. His feelings of apprehension and his fear of what lay ahead faded instantly. He knew Father Santeal was right, his time on earth was almost over and it didn't end within the confines of the holy kingdom. He had crossed over into the underworld and traveled so far down the path to perdition that there was no chance for his soul's redemption. Yet possessing that knowledge only made him more determined to see the task complete. Father Story neared the end of his long journey and his spirit's shape dissolved into the radiance of the blinding omnificent light. Christ turned and disappeared from the balcony and the masses little by little slowly began to wane. The vision of heaven faded like a mirage, the miracle was gone, and the reality of the abbey's crumbling ceiling took its place.

"Behold, for the hour of our soul's recompense is at hand, the full measure of our sins will be weighed and the full sum taken," Peter pointed to the floor and it began to cave in.

The stone altar tilted off center, the ground gave way beneath it and it fell through the floor. A circular hole formed at their feet and they stood at the edge of a steep precipice. The room went black as the hole grew wider and the earth gave way until a canyon formed under their feet. It stretched out into infinity and the only light came from the enormous waterfall of lava and the red-orange lake of fire miles below. A foul smelling steam rose up and its heat burned the tender skin on Father Santeal's face. Imbedded in the canyon walls were the once living, breathing, human beings stacked too high and too deep to count their multitudes. Writhing heads, arms and legs were wedged in the black dirt and stood as a full testament to the souls of the condemned. Terror marked the faces of the corrupted that could see outward as they looked into the gorge below and saw what was to be their fortune. Winged gargoyles plucked the fated from their lodging only to have their vacant positions cliffside replaced by others buried from deeper within the dirt. The demon's talons scratched and clawed at the eyes and skin then disposed of their human cargo into the rolling lava. "Eh eh eh eh eh eh eh," came the cry of tens of thousands of voices meshed together screaming out in agony. It was the beginning of their journey into suffering and eternal damnation, and it was their misery twisted and mangled into the horrific sound of death.

"Our souls have been condemned by God and Satan alike, and now this is our fate for all eternity," once more Peter went through the different incarnations of Hector-Qeynan-Thaydien.

Sitting on an enormous throne was Tartorus, the mammoth guardian that ruled hell until the Devil regained his dominion. The enormous ox head exhaled smoke from its fiery nostrils as it reveled in punishing those who were forced to stand in judgment. Its pointed teeth sank into warm flesh and its clawed hands held Robert Stone's frail body. Robert's legs had been chewed and consumed and his left arm was caught in-between Tartarus's vicious gnawing mouth. He saw Father Santeal standing above him and reached out for his friend. The unrelenting pain was chiseled on his face and his pleas to Father Santeal were drowned out by a tidal wave of shrieking voices. A cloaked figure rose from the stream of liquid fire and stood unaffected by the macabre scene that surrounded him. He removed his hood to reveal a repugnant and cruel face. His features were foreign to Father Santeal, but his cold blue eyes made him unmistakably recognizable.

"Don't be a fool," there was panic rising in Father Santeal's voice, "there is still time to find another Qeynan, we can rule the world together you and I."

Peter also recognized the hooded monster and he knew the depths of brutality that lay in waiting. He had stopped the rise of the fallen Angel Hector and his father and every creature in hell were eager to exact their revenge, "This has all been preordained Grigory; our lives have been an illusion to a future that could not be, where mankind is forevermore a slave of the Devil. And now... we accept our destiny together." He said one last prayer then closed his eyes and stepped off the ledge.

Isabella pushed the Lincoln to its limits as they fish tailed down the hilly road. They could see the streaks of lightening bombarding the abbey and heard the deafening roar that came from within. The abbey walls caved inward and the heights of the mighty tower collapsed upon itself. A powerful shock wave lifted the car off the road and sent it careening down the hillside. The earth opened wide as it seized the Devil's tribute and the Abbey of László was sent tumbling down the gateway to hell. The end came with a flash of radiant blue light and a mushroom cloud that reached into the sky.

And I will show wonders in heaven above, and signs in the earth beneath; blood, and fire, and vapor of smoke: The sun shall be turned into darkness, and the moon into blood, before that great and notable day of the Lord comes...

Acts
King James Bible

CHAPTER XIX
REVELATIONS

Saturday 8:15 pm
May 17, 1980
Gable Book Store
Portland, Oregon, United States

The Gable Book Store was relatively small, charming and a standard in the indie movement. The shelves were lined mainly with foreign writers or new authors from around the Portland area. Tonight there were fifteen people inside and only ten of them were fans who came to see the latest writer to grace the tiny shop. Mario sat behind a short metal desk; a small banner over the door read Book Signing, Mario Pascale's The Devil Within, The Peter Cameron Story. He was still shaken and deeply troubled by the ghosts of his past. He sported a full beard and grew his hair shoulder length in a mild effort to change the simplest things in his life. It had been a long and arduous journey and the demons always haunted him in his dreams. He had been sued by family members of Angela, cousins of Eddie's and distant relatives of them both. The truly grief stricken and those only interested in monetary gain had more than their fare share of his and Isabella's fortunes. At first the public treated them like victims and consoled them for their losses, but when no bodies of their former friends were found the view rapidly changed to innuendo and suspicion. Mario's life was put under a microscope and turned upside down and inside out. All the sorted details of his personal life hit the covers of every major tabloid magazine across Europe. He was inundated with threats on a daily basis, called abnormal and personally blamed for reviving the debauchery and degradation of the Abbey of László's ancient past. In a vain attempt to find possible links to murder, prosecutors tried to show Emily's true lineage as evidence Isabella had motive to commit the heinous crimes. Peter was cast as a delusional priest that demanded human sacrifice to raise an army of loyal followers and revive the teachings of a medieval sect. As the pressure grew, the Vatican stepped in and ended all avenues that led to Peter as Emily's father and any connection to the bizarre claims of the occult. After a three week circus trial and a short botched trial two months later, he and Isabella were cleared by the courts of any involvement in their friend's disappearance. The Vatican gave public praise and grand televised funerals to Father Neil Story and Father Peter Cameron in absentia, while the names of Father Santeal and Cardinal Rudolph Fuerst were quietly excommunicated and expunged from church records. Isabella and Emily left the City of Madonnella and quickly vanished after the court's final gavel fell, and it marked the last time Mario had laid eyes on either of them. His publishing company and his agent had dissolved their relationship with him after he insisted that his latest novel be distributed strictly as a work of non-fiction. It was a flop in Europe and he was currently on a six month tour of the U.S. financed by the last of his dwindling funds. The crowds were always smaller, the venues were less than he'd been accustomed to, and the universal adulation he'd once received had faded from memory years ago.

The bell over the bookstore entrance rang and two men approached him, "I was hoping we could have a word with you Mr. Pascale," the younger man held out his hand, "my name's Elon Gutman and this is Michael Cavilary."

"If you want to schedule an interview with me, I can have my publicist take down your number."

"I'm sorry Mr. Pascale but it is imperative we speak now," Gutman reached inside his jacket pocket for his credentials.

"Print or television?" asked Mario.

"What? No, we have an interest in an old acquaintance of yours; Mr. Cameron," he held out his I.D. badge from the IFA, the agency he had resigned from nearly two years ago.

"Peter Cameron?" Mario's interest peaked.

"Is there someplace more private we can talk?" asked Gutman.

The store was clearing out and there was little prospect of new customers walking through the front door. He wasn't obligated to stay more than a few hours and it looked like the night was turning into a colossal waste of time. They headed off and strolled to Gutman's rent-a-car; Mario sat on the hood.

"How well did you know Peter?" asked Gutman.

"He was my best friend; I knew Emily was his daughter if that's what you're getting at."

"Were you aware he had a brother?" Cavilary eagerly waited for a response.

"Yes, he told me once, but he never showed up at the trial or Peter's funeral. I even wanted to use him in my book as corroboration of Peter's childhood background. But, regrettably I was never able to locate him for an interview."

"We have," Cavilary remarked, "Simon took his mother's maiden name Rossellini and shortened it to Ross. His place is about a two hour drive from here."

"Really? As remarkable as that is, what does he have to do with Peter?"

"I enlisted the help of one of my best agents Vincent Gallo, to find a man who had disappeared named Jeremiah Rourke on a strictly off the records investigation," explained Cavilary. "Cardinal Rourke had traced Robert Stone and Father Grigory Santeal to members of a deadly cult."

"I met him in Israel," Gutman opened the driver's door, "by that time Cardinal Rourke's missing persons case had turned into a homicide investigation, but it seems Mr. Gallo was more eager in finding a rare book than he was in solving the crime."

"It was Agent Gallo who contacted you, he may have used one of his many aliases," Cavilary opened the passenger door. "Please, we can talk on the way."

Mario slid into the back seat, "There was a detective that talked to Peter; he came to his bookstore and to Isabella's farmhouse. He offered to help us find Isabella's daughter and fight Robert and Father Santeal."

CHAPTER XIX: REVELATIONS

Gutman turned in his seat, "In your book I believe you wrote you last saw Father Santeal lying on the floor of the abbey, dying with the libri of cado animus in his hands right before the Abbey of László collapsed."

"Collapsed? That's right the papers said it was devoured by a sink hole and the earth swallowed her up. Only thing is they never found a trace of the building or any of the bodies inside no matter how deep they excavated. They said it was ground to dust, pulverized by an avalanche of rock and earth. In the end it was as though the abbey and my friends never existed. The police said I was mad--that Isabella was mad and that it was preposterous to believe anything supernatural had occurred inside those walls. They said we fabricated our story and accused us of being masochist who inflicted the wounds on each other. There's no denying there was an evil presence there and it grew and got stronger and stronger over the centuries. Those people had reason to hate that place, it was a disease and everyone wanted to avoid being infected. None of the villagers would admit to hearing the deafening explosions or seeing the mushroom cloud rise into the heavens, but I know the truth. For centuries the people of László were terrified of that abbey and what it truly was. And now that it's gone, they don't dare speak of it. Deep inside they believe what I believe, the Abbey of László is lying in hell where it belongs," Mario felt relieved to finally unload his burden amongst others of like mind and relaxed against the cloth seats.

"And the book is it in hell too?" Gutman asked.

Mario thought for a second, "I don't know. To be honest, I don't remember."

"Agent Gallo was a difficult man to track," Cavilary explained, "I lost touch with him before he left Israel and arrived in Madonnella and met you and your friends. The more I searched for him the more disturbing things I discovered about who he really was. After the László incident I contacted Agent Gutman and it soon became obvious to the both of us as to what he had been doing all along. As of today we believe he has Father Santeal's copy of the book in his possession. About seven months ago we were able to trace him to London where he made contact with someone with an expert interest in the fallen angels."

"That's a fascinating story, but I still don't know how I can help you gentlemen," Mario looked confused.

Gutman gazed in the rearview, "Like I said we read your book; either you have incredible insight into ancient Thaydien rituals or Peter left a copy of the book with you."

"I have been doing a lot of basic research for a second book," Mario confessed, "Peter left behind some notes and copies of his correspondence with Father Rourke, but not a copy of the libri of cado animus. He had a unique gift; he could memorize everything--even the book word for word. Any secrets it had died with him two years ago."

"I've personally witnessed what someone like Robert can do with the power of the damned and I know you've seen it for yourself. Gallo's here in the United States; we have to make sure he never finds Peter's brother, and we need to know how to stop him if he's already begun his transformation," Gutman was desperate and it showed through in his voice.

"Gallo used a sword blessed by God and cursed by the Devil that was given to Sabaoth, Lord of the Armies of Israel to kill Father Santeal, but it's gone forever along with the abbey."

They drove from Oregon and entered Washington across the mighty Bridge of the Gods that extended over the Columbia River. Father Principi had been a key asset to their investigation and was waiting for them with Peter's brother Simon. Gutman related the details of the priest's story and what he experienced while he had dared venture inside the Abbey of László. The ghostly nun, the strange feeling of absolute evil unrestrained and a warning of death on a scale not yet seen before. He had barely escaped the abbey with his life, but it made him more resolute and more determined to stop anyone from possessing the book of fallen souls and gaining power from the Trilogy. He told Mario of Father Principi's suspicion of Father Layad's all too fervent interest in the book and it seemed more than mere coincidence that he was serving as pastor of a church in the Seattle area. Soon after Gutman left the hospital, he had made the decision to leave behind his old life in Israel. The former Israeli secret agent and the stubborn priest were single minded on finishing what Father Rourke had started. Gutman used his sources, back channels and well paid snitches to hunt Gallo down. He had closed many of his accounts at home, sold his belongings and had gone underground. Through his contacts Gutman was sent a tape of Gallo and Marko caught on camera at a Barclays Bank in London. They stayed one night at the Corian Hotel in Croydon and were joined soon after by a third man, then boarded an early morning flight at Heathrow. The black and white tapes from the airport security cameras were grainy and of lesser quality than the bank's. The images of the men seem to faze and shift out of focus as they passed by the camera's lens. Father Principi spent hours studying the tape and was convinced that the third man was Cardinal Fuerst.

At 10:25 pm they pulled into Skamania County and drove east on Yacolt Road until they arrived at the doorstep of Simon Ross's home. They knocked on the door several times, but the lights were off and the house left vacant. They waited an hour then left a note under the door with the name of the nearby motel where they were lodged. On the way back they spotted the pink neon lights of Nickey Bean, a silver 1950's styled dining car restaurant that was open 24/7 and stopped in.

"You look like something's bothering you," Gutman squeezed into the red leather bench seat next to Cavilary.

"Father Story once told us that he had to face down the true evil of the Abbey of László, and I'm absolutely convinced he did, and killed him. After surviving our ordeal, I went to the town's library and searched the village records for the abbey's legal owner, there was only one name listed, Cardinal Rudolph Fuerst."

Cavilary looked at Gutman, "Maybe there's someone else who was the true evil of László or maybe Father Story was wrong; he might have badly injured him and only thought he had killed Cardinal Fuerst."

"Father Story ran the Hospes of St. Cecilia, I think he knew a dead man when he saw one," Mario used his fork to pick at the plate of hash browns, "besides, other than the long dead and buried Father Martz, I couldn't find anyone else associated with the abbey's recent ownership. I've gone over it a dozen times in my head and there's no doubt in my mind he was talking about Cardinal Fuerst."

Gutman sighed and looked up from his food hardly impressed, "Looks like one way or the other we're going to find out who really is the true evil of László."

Sunday 6:25 am
May 18, 1980
Coldwater Motel

A knock on the door awakened the men inside room 323. Gutman fought to shake the sleep from his head and eased out of bed. He flexed his toes on the shag carpet then got up and opened the door.

"Mr. Gutman," Deputy Sheriff Simon Ross was dressed in full police regalia, "I'm sorry to wake you, but I have to change our plans for later this afternoon."

"Of course, is there something wrong?"

"No. The volcano is acting up a little and we're taking precautionary measures and escorting some of the townspeople to safer ground. If you want you can ride with me; I have a few rounds I need to make then I can take you to the cabin where Father Principi and my family are staying."

"Give us ten minutes?"

"Sure," Simon smirked, "I'll be waiting outside, my trucks the one with all the fancy lights on top."

They took turns at the bathroom faucet and splashed water on their faces then quickly dressed. The three men crossed the small lot bathed in the dim orange haze of the motel's lamp posts and jumped inside Simon's Ford Bronco. Mario was immediately struck by how similar Simon was to Peter. He looked younger and was taller, but there were only a few modest differences in the facial features that separated the two men.

"Father Principi's been trying to get me to read your book," Simon talked over his shoulder, "I have to confess, I am a little skeptical of mysticism and exorcism. I guess in this job my mind can only focus on what happens in the real world."

"Unfortunately, I can assure you every word is true," Mario leaned forward from the back seat, "I hope I'm not being too personal, but you didn't come to your brother's funeral, can I ask why?"

"My brother and I were never close; once my mother left my father, I didn't have any contact with him. It would have felt strange to show up and grieve for someone whose life I knew nothing about."

"You are a descendent of Kyameron and a disciple of the Angel Hector," Mario placed his hand on the shoulder of the driver's seat, "even if you don't believe there are others that do and they will come looking for you. They won't stop until they find you."

They drove for 45 minutes passing several police check points where Simon flashed his badge and was granted access to the long hill roads. They entered the lush greenery of Gifford Pinchot National Forest at 8:15 am. Mario leaned forward and gazed out the windshield, rising in the distance like Olympus from the heavens were the beautiful white caps of Mount Saint Helens. Simon stopped the truck near elevation at the marked 177 Observation Point and the men got out.

"There's a couple of geologist too stubborn to get off the side of the mountain for their own good. They have their base camp about ten minutes from here; we're just gonna give 'em one last stern warning then will be on our way." Simon took down a hunting rifle strapped inside a compartment on the roof of the truck, "These woods are filled with black bears, never can be too careful."

They walked along a gravel footpath and every few feet Mario took a glance over his shoulder. There was an audible rumbling emanating from the mountain but it still felt all too quiet. The melodic sounds of the birds chirping far in the distance and the crushed pebbles beneath their feet made for an unnerving sense of isolation. Maybe it was the lack of sleep, but he couldn't shake the feeling that something was wrong.

"You all right there partner?" Simon smiled dryly.

"Yeah Mario, you're making me nervous too," added Gutman as he laughed.

A large dark mass soared overhead and cast a distorted shadow on the trail; the men instinctively ducked for fear of being struck by a low flying plane or a long extinct prehistoric bird.

"Oh shit!" Cavilary reached for the gun tucked inside his jacket. A bullet struck him in his stomach and propelled him backward and on to the ground. He grabbed at his bleeding belly and instantly began to go into shock. He desperately tried to raise his weapon and return fire but a second shot struck his right eye and obliterated the socket. His head snapped back and he lay motionless with his mouth agape. Two men almost twenty feet ahead on the trail walked closer into view. Marko's Winchester shotgun was still pointed in their direction and at his side was a seven foot man draped in a dark brown hooded robe. His pale skin and yellow eyes were all too sickeningly familiar with the half-demon Robert had once been. Whatever humanity was left etched in Gallo's being had been worn away when his soul surrendered to the wicked force of the darker side.

"It seems to me Father Layad was right, everyone has a purpose," Simon cocked the rifle and shoved Mario and Gutman forward, "and I've known all my life what mine has been."

They moved to a clearing where several of the geologist bodies had been strewn across the roadside and cut to ribbons. A low lying grassy ridge overlooked the log cabin that had been erected and served as Base 7. A wooden placard over the window declared it as Camp Mobius, and hanging next to it was the lifeless body of Father Joseph Principi. He was crucified upside down with iron spikes driven through his palms and shattered ankles. His eyes and tongue were missing and the inside of his mouth had been charred black. Isabella was also among the dead, she sat strapped to Sabaoth's golden throne near the edge of the long green grass. Her features were horribly mangled, her white blouse was stained with blood and her neck slit ear to ear. Her gaze was frozen in time and fell upon her daughter's body lying still in the weeds. Emily had suffered a worse fate, her empty shell had been gutted and her organs removed then placed in three jars aligned in a circle around a stone altar.

"What man wouldn't give his only child for something much greater than he," Simon stopped the men then stood next to Cardinal Fuerst. He whispered in Simon's ear and he headed down the ridge to join Gallo and Father Layad in the valley.

Simon's dead wife lay on her stomach, with her last breath she had crawled to the altar and to where her teenage daughter lay. A circle was drawn in the dirt and set around the altar were jars of brains, hearts and intestines and genitals that lined the perimeter. Three empty jars were waiting to be filled after the sacrifice of Simon's daughter. Father Layad donned a plumb colored robe trimmed with gold leaf; on his head was a Triregnum and in the center was the image of a beast with seven heads and ten crowns. His eyes burned red and were the mark of the fallen Angel Thaydien. He stood at the foot of the stone block with the book of fallen souls cradled in his hands. Gallo took his place opposite him and held the sword of Sabaoth over the young girl's head. Simon's daughter screamed as she struggled underneath the weight of heavy chains. Tears began to fill her eyes and she begged her father for mercy.

"We are truly blessed with an abundance of offerings to the Lord," Cardinal Fuerst instructed Marko to bind Mario and Gutman's hands and ankles then forced them to their knees. He then sent him down the hillside to join Simon and the others. He held Marko's silver Rogak pistol in his hand.

"You were there the day the Abbey of László was destroyed," Mario spoke in a quiet tone, "I know you were. Father Santeal and Robert Stone died there. And you died too, didn't you. I know Father Story sent you to hell."

"You should choose your next words very carefully for they will be your last," He stood on a boulder overlooking his minions and stared out at the magnificence of Mount Saint Helens.

"I know what you are; I know the truth about you Cardinal Fuerst. I know the secret you're keeping from your friends and have hidden from the rest of the world," Mario stated firmly.

"And when I came into the nations of man, I asked, whom do men say that I am? And they sayeth, some say that thou art the Accuser some, the Persecutor and others, the Oppressor. And I sayeth unto you, But whom say ye that I am?" Cardinal Fuerst outstretched his arms, his hair grew long and his face was covered with a black beard in an overt mockery of Christ.

"You are the Deceiver of man, you are the Angel cast out of heaven," Mario inhaled, his head was down and he knew there were no other possibilities left to Cardinal Fuerst true identity, "you are Satan the Lord of the underworld."

Gutman stared at Mario not wanting to believe, "No you're wrong, that's impossible..."

Cardinal Fuerst stepped from the rock and as the heel of his sandal touched the earth he took the form of Peter Cameron. The earth shook and the screams of Simon's daughter came to an abrupt end. "I find flesh and blood to be a crude form of existence, but I have no other choice for deception is my only power. Men like Father Santeal would never have relinquished the highest dominion which he had attained, and in time, Father Layad will fight to keep his. If it helps, you may take solace that Father Santeal and Robert are suffering without end in hell... along with Peter of course." He pulled the collar of his purple robe down and revealed the raised scar from Sabaoth's wooden sword on his chest. With his fingers he opened the wound and brought forth from inside the cavity the conjoined heads of Robert and Father Santeal. Their outer skin had melted and what was left had been burnt and stripped away to expose the raw dermis and muscle underneath. Their mouths moved frantically, but their voices were long rendered silent; only their eyes could convey the depths of their unimaginable torment and sorrow.

"The book is cursed to you, that's why you needed the assistance of Father Santeal and Father Layad. You couldn't touch it yourself or your human form would be turned to dust and you would be sent back to the world beneath hell," Mario watched the heads of the ghouls retreat into the black of the Devil's chest, "So you let them posess your power, take it for their own, and then you plotted to take it from them."

The Devil looked towards his few compatriots gathered in the valley below, "I am as you say I am, and I will have all of what belongs to me, for flesh and blood hath not revealed my purpose unto them."

Another strong tremor and the north side of Mount Saint Helens collapsed causing a violent earthquake. A mud flow of ice and snow tumbled down her north flank. The superheated gas and rock burst from her belly as the pressure ripped the mountain apart. A thunderous eruption sent a plume of ash cloud ten miles wide and fifteen miles high into the sky. The Devil briefly changed into his true form, blood red skin and large black ram horns stood out against the scene of a cloudy gray apocalypse. Gutman's eyes were shut tight and his lips moved as he prayed.

The Devil was intrigued and walked towards him as Cardinal Rourke, "You still wish to pray to another in the presence of your Lord?"

"You are not my Lord, you are nothing but an abomination," Gutman refused to look at him. "I spit on the ground you walk."

The Devil spat in Gutman's face and a thin trail of magma dripped down his cheek. Gutman refused to scream out; his lips trembled as he held back the pain. With Marko's gun in hand, the Devil fired a shot into Gutman's head at close range. The sound was deafening like a firecracker going off nearby. The back of Gutman's skull exploded and he lay flat on the ground with his eyes wide open. The Devil turned and casually raised the gun and shot Mario in the stomach. The bullet tore through his abdomen and he lurched forward and fell to the earth. The Devil bent over him as Peter, his fiery hot breath singed Mario's ears, "And I say also unto thee, That I am Satan and upon this rock I will build my church and the gates of hell shall forever be open. Whatsoever thou shalt loose on earth shall be loosed in heaven." He fired the gun again.

Mario could feel the numbness in his head where the bullet had lodged. His lungs instinctively made desperate attempts to pull in air but grew ever weaker by the second. A tidal wave of burning ash and smoke poured over the valley and up the ridge where he lay. Simon had transformed himself into the Angel Hector; with long black wings he flew towards the volcanic plume and down into the gaping hole of the mountain. The angels Qeynan and Thaydien appeared on the ridge next to Marko and Cardinal Fuerst. They watched as Hector took his rightful dominion in hell, then their images vanished behind a blanket of thick ash cloud. A high wall of molten rock moved towards him at incredible speed decimating everything in its path. His eyes burned from the noxious sulfur and his lungs choked from the blood that filled it. He filled his conscious mind with the mundane and desperately tried to block out the thought of being roasted alive at a thousand degrees. He would be judged and his soul measured and he welcomed that. He no longer feared public humiliation, his agent's impossible deadlines, the everyday what ifs that would have taken his life in a very different direction. Gone from him was the madness of an unforgiving humanity, the burden of his past and a lifetime of guilt. All his friends were dead: Peter, Eddie, Isabella, Emily, Father Story and even Angela. There was nothing and no one left that he truly cared about or who cared about him. He regretted not being able to say goodbye to all those he had called his family; he regretted not being able to write and entertain the few loyal fans that still remained. He would miss the beauty of early morning sunrises and late afternoon sunsets, and mercifully, he would miss the coming apocalypse and the thousand years of pain and suffering from the cruel hands of the Devil. Mario closed his eyes and braced himself as the lava rushed over his body and incinerated flesh and bone. In those last few precious seconds he prayed for himself and for the lives of the world he left behind.

EPILOGUE

And I looked, and behold a pale horse: and his name that sat on him was Death, and Hell followed with him. And power was given unto them over the fourth part of the earth, to kill with sword, and with hunger, and with death, and with the beasts of the earth.

Revelations
King James Bible

From the fiery mouth of Vesuvius came the Angel Qeynan in the form of a thick black cloud piercing the heavens; free to spread a merciless death upon all of mankind. Free was Thaydien to judge and condemn, and send all to Hades who defied the great beast. Brother slain brother, and nations set war against nations. Day was made as night... and we feared the coming of Hector.

Heironymos
Book of Heironymos

And it shall come to pass in the last days that my spirit will be seared on the souls of all flesh; your sons and your daughters shall have visions and they shall prophesy. I shall show them all the great horrors of hell. And the Angels and Fallen Angels shall proclaim these truths; He who walks with God shall forever see the light and feel the warmth of his grace, and he who walks with evil shall forever be cast in the Shadow of the Devil.

Serafeim
libri of cado animus

Author:
Dean Julian Davis

THE END

www.ingramcontent.com/pod-product-compliance
Lightning Source LLC
Chambersburg PA
CBHW031546240626
47153CB00002B/398